For L.H., co-conspirator

A DEADLY BLUFF

A DANA MADISON MYSTERY

KATHLEEN
CONCANNON

This is a work of fiction. Names, characters, places, and incidents are products of the author's imagination or are used fictitiously and are not to be construed as real. Any resemblances to actual events, locales, organizations, or persons, living or dead, is entirely coincidental.

ISBN-13: 978-1539036913
ISBN-10: 153903691X

A DEADLY BLUFF

There are no words that can tell the hidden spirit of the wilderness, that can reveal its mystery, its melancholy and its charm.

—Theodore Roosevelt

CHAPTER 1

Yosemite National Park

October 2010

PARK RANGER DANA Madison loved autumn in Yosemite. With the stampede of summer tourists over, she could roam the trails without interruption and hear the granite cliffs giving up their fight against gravity, like shedding dead skin.

It had taken five years, but Yosemite had finally allowed Madison to cast off her old wounds.

She was lucky. Her desk was a half mile from The Ahwahnee Hotel, the grand lodge bearing Yosemite Valley's native name. Its towering granite entrance blended into the natural rock walls behind it. In the 1920s, European craftsmen had built huge stone fireplaces and hand-carved the exposed old-growth sugar pine beams. The valley's stunning beauty, her chance to continue Teddy Roosevelt's preservation movement, seemed a perfect fit after Denver Homicide.

Madison drank the cold remains of her third cup of coffee and opened a window. She watched the wind rip dried leaves off the oaks. The cool air smelled of wood smoke, and the hint of snow on the way.

Park Superintendent Henderson's office door opened. "Madison! Get in here."

Madison slid into a chair next to Henderson's desk. He wasn't smiling. "Why do I get the feeling I should have called in sick today?" she asked.

"Don't start, not after the call I've had from HQ." Henderson moved aside a stack of papers with yellow *Sign Here* flags on their edges and found his pen. He tapped on the empty space he'd created. "I could do with some help here."

Madison grinned. "Ah, you admit you need me."

Henderson grunted and grabbed his reading glasses. He looked good for a 60-year old career man. With his climber's wiry body, he could still run the trails to the upper falls.

"Listen," he said. "Those damn DC risk management folks called today. Two bean counters who've never been outside the Beltway, let alone out West, said the number of people who decided to die in national parks spiked last year."

Henderson peered over his glasses. "I didn't express astonishment, so they thought I didn't understand. They started explaining their computer modeling and 'scatter diagrams' and 'sensitivity analyses'. My god I wanted to shoot myself." He leaned back in his chair. "I told them I'm statistically-challenged."

"That should've shut them up."

"Oh no," Henderson said. "The poor bastards only stopped when I asked them for a scat diagram for bears shitting in the woods." Henderson shook his head. "I felt so sorry for them I suggested they visit us next spring and promised you'd give them a personal tour. They might be your type."

Madison held up her hands. "Thanks for reminding me of my pathetic social life."

Henderson winked. "Just trying to help."

He took a breath and lost his smile. "HQ wants us to check our records and make sure they're correct. Car accidents, falls, everything. And they want this by *tomorrow*. Probably for some Congressman. God knows Congress ought to be more interested in funding our friggin' trail maintenance budget, but then nobody asked me about that."

Madison had planned to check some willow plantings along the Merced River to see if they survived the summer. "The Park Police can't do this?"

Henderson rolled his eyes. "Off at Homeland Security training *again*. Get HQ what they want and then maybe *you* can convince the bean counters we need maintenance funds while there's still some wilderness left."

Back at her desk, Madison opened a file on her computer. Since she quit being a cop in Denver, she'd investigated only one death. And she'd stopped herself from looking beyond the simple facts. There it was on the spreadsheet, "Mel Tibbetts, deceased, June 15, 2010, accidental fall in personal RV."

⁂

Mel Tibbetts was dead.

Madison had climbed the short metal stairs into the Tibbetts' Winnebago parked in Yosemite's Big Falls

Campground. The bedroom door was open. A crocheted throw rested on the unmade bed. Another draped a chair. The pressed curtains dripped a fringe of yarn.

Mel Tibbetts lay on the waxed kitchen floor. His wife Ivy had covered him with an unfinished afghan. One lifeless finger protruded through the loose weave as if Mr. Tibbetts were trying to escape the tangle.

About the only thing unencumbered by yarn was the big flat screen in the corner of the living area. Like everything else in the room, no dust had been allowed to settle on it. The lone disorder was a jumble of extension cords running along the floor. And the blood on the edge of the kitchen counter.

Madison took off her ranger's hat and set it between matching pillows on the seat at the dining table. She pulled latex gloves out of her back pocket and snapped them on.

She squatted next to Tibbetts and lifted the afghan off his face. A few strands of graying brown hair had slipped across his unmoving blue eyes. She brushed his hair gently aside as she said a silent prayer. Madison wasn't religious anymore, but she respected this man's life.

She put the side of her hand against his cool, pale cheek. He'd been dead a few hours. Swollen skin surrounded an open wound on his forehead where he'd hit the countertop. Blood had congealed underneath his head on the floor. A faint red indentation crossed his throat above his Adam's apple.

When Madison was on the Denver police force, she and her partner Stan hated being called out in the middle of the night to confirm the obvious: someone had done something stupid and accidently killed himself. Another visit to "Mr. Dumb Fuck American," Stan would say. He would have added the tripping Tibbetts to his list.

The morning's wind carried cold from the high country as Madison stepped outside the RV. Ivy Tibbetts sat at a nearby picnic table, her hands folded in her lap. Her oversized *Friends of Yosemite* shirt with Bridal Veil Falls on the front fell loose over her shoulders.

Madison took in a long breath. She'd thought she'd left this kind of sorrow behind.

Madison put her hand on Mrs. Tibbett's trembling arm. "I'm so sorry, but I need to ask you some questions." Madison knew the county coroner would rule this death an accident, but as a former cop, she found it hard to not investigate.

Madison sat next to her. "Let's start with what you and your husband did yesterday."

Mrs. Tibbetts looked up, her damp eyes wide. "Mel promised me," she said. "He promised to hike to the high ridge. I wanted to see the top of the falls, where the water rushes over the edge…"

Madison let her talk on and on about the view, the golden monkey flowers, the glints of mica in the boulders, all the beauty anyone with a soul and love of nature would notice, and the pieces of yesterday she was holding onto instead of thinking about her dead husband.

"We were barely halfway up," Mrs. Tibbetts explained. "I didn't want to come back, but his Lakers' playoff game was on." She stared into Madison's eyes.

Madison nodded. Mel wasn't the only camper who had the game on last night.

"Nothing unusual happened?" Madison didn't expect an answer.

"No, nothing, except for the trees," Mrs. Tibbetts said.

"Trees?" Madison said.

"It was the wind, the way it comes up the ridge." She looked up toward the cliffs. "I know that's what it was, but I thought I saw something moving high in the pine branches… Mel thought it was a bear, isn't that silly?"

Madison shook her head.

"I mean, a bear moving between trees. He could be so…" She looked away. "But we hurried back down the trail just in case."

Madison kept her face blank. "After the game was over, you went to bed?"

"Mel was so happy his Lakers won," Mrs. Tibbett's hands opened and closed as if she couldn't get the blood flowing. "He only had one beer. I'm such a sound sleeper… and now he's…" Her voice faltered.

Madison patted her back.

Part of Madison wanted to dissect the scene, examine and replay the last few moments of Mel Tibbetts' life. And that mark on his neck… But she wasn't a detective anymore. She'd just make a note in the file and let the coroner decide.

Sunlight poured over the valley's eastern ridge. Above the campground a man cupped his hands next to his lips. He blew into his hands and a low warble bounced off the cliffs like light off the crystalline rocks. He watched the ranger glance up and raise her hand to shield her eyes, then turn away.

CHAPTER 2

THE DAY BEFORE, Madison had finished reviewing her spreadsheet and was wondering how Mrs. Tibbetts had fared in the five months since her husband's fall when Henderson blasted out of his office. He didn't say much, just that HQ demanded she jump on a plane with the information they wanted, and attend an important meeting about it the next morning. Henderson had no choice but to send her.

She'd only had time to grab a few things and rush to make the red eye flight from San Francisco. Five hours later, the jet banked to follow the Potomac River into Reagan National Airport. The sunrise illuminated the subtle start of Virginia's autumn colors, then the long stretch of the National Mall from the marble columns of the Lincoln Memorial to Capitol Hill. This scene, even if she was fresh from Yosemite's majesty, could still move her.

A spit-and-polish Marine approached Madison as she left the plane. "Welcome to DC, Ma'am."

The "Ma'am" stung. When did everyone get so young?

"Please come with me," he said. He took her bag and put his other hand behind her, but didn't touch her.

Madison admired his pressed uniform. She'd barely made the plane and had no time to change.

"So, why the special treatment?" she asked.

"I'm not at liberty to tell you, Ma'am." He kept his eyes forward.

The Park Service budget never included a private driver, let alone a military escort. She checked her cell phone to see if Henderson had called with an update. No messages.

The Marine escorted her directly to a staff car parked next to the terminal. No military flags flew from its windows, a concession to the nation's heightened security level since September 11th. The driver was another Marine, who looked like a teenager to Madison. The glass between the front and back seats was so clean she could see the precise shaved line around his ears. The first Marine sat with her in the back.

They drove along George Washington Parkway, then around the U.S. Marine Corps War Memorial with its rough granite base and weathered bronze figures of Marines raising the flag on Iwo Jima. A horn sounded and startled Madison. The traffic hadn't improved since she was last in DC. Her driver quickly got on I-95 and headed into Virginia.

She shifted toward the Marine sitting next to her. "Listen, my boss said to get to Park Service headquarters as soon as possible. Unless they've moved from the Interior building, I'd say we're going the wrong way."

"I'm sorry, Ma'am, our orders were to deliver you to another government building outside the city." The Marine didn't smile, but lowered his chin a bit. "Perhaps the venue changed during your flight."

Madison knew that was logical. Didn't explain the

escort, but it appeared pointless to ask. If Henderson knew and didn't give her a heads up, she'd get him back later.

They took an exit and followed surface streets east, past fast food and big box stores, with old brick and timber buildings torn down to make way for strip malls and golden arches. She could have been anywhere in America. Only the occasional magnolia tree or local restaurant peddling "southern" cooking distinguished the locale. Here and there an isolated 200-year-old house resisted demolition and remained in the middle of the new suburbia, protected by tall oaks. The Park Service had been trying for years to save land where many Civil War skirmishes had been fought, but was losing the fight. Rolling hills and remnants of battlements were traded for a taco chain.

The driver turned off the interstate onto a two-lane rural road. Development was more spread out and changed to gated communities broken up by farms. Finally, the houses disappeared and the road was outlined by tall deciduous trees with yellowed leaves bright against the graying sky.

They came to a side road without a sign and turned and stopped at a 1960s-style office building, dust its only ornamentation. Men who looked like undercover security milled around the front, one speaking into his sleeve.

The first Marine opened the door for Madison. "They're expecting you."

Madison thought they were expecting someone obviously more threatening. She got out of the car and entered through the building's double glass front door. Whatever the building was, it didn't have the usual welcoming trappings of the Park Service. She'd never been surrounded by this much security, even when she was on the police force. Maybe they'd picked the wrong ranger exiting the plane.

Security officers sat behind the front desk's high counter, eyes glued to video monitors. Madison stepped in front of the lone guard next to the metal detector and held out her Park Service badge.

The guard touched the photo on her badge, then scrutinized her face.

Big brown eyes, but all business. His shoulders the definition of "broad." Madison bet nobody ever told him he had a baby face on top of those shoulders. He either just missed getting drafted for the National Football League or was wearing a thick Kevlar vest. Or both.

"Please wait next to the elevators," he said. He waved her through.

A man and a woman stood by the elevator bank. Madison smiled. The woman was tall and her fit-for-an-interview red suit set off her dark skin and perfectly applied auburn blush and tan eye shadow. Straightened black hair, turned up at her shoulder, shaped her face. She nodded to Madison without any upward turn of her lips, then lifted an invisible hair from behind her ear with a manicured blunt cut nail the same red as her suit.

Madison took off her ranger's hat and pushed down the ragged cuticle on her left thumb.

The man next to Ms. Red Suit shifted his weight and smiled at Madison. He was as tall as the security guard, but half as broad. His gray suit wasn't tailored like the woman's and made him colorless next to her. He cinched up his tie, then ran his finger inside his collar as if he hadn't worn a suit in a while.

He, at least, looked approachable and Madison

was about to speak to him when another man appeared. Nothing casual about the military cap folded and tucked under his arm, and the mirror shine on his shoes.

"Ms. Mobley, Mr. Greaves, Ranger Madison, my name is Lieutenant Soto, please step this way." Without waiting for them to respond, he unlocked one elevator with a card key and held the door open for them. He hit "B6" and the doors closed behind them.

Greaves turned toward Madison and shrugged. He didn't appear to know anything either. Mobley raised an eyebrow, but said nothing.

The elevator doors opened onto a long hallway. The yellow concrete walls lacked decoration. Only gray metal doors broke up the expanse of yellow. The concrete floor was bare. Lt. Soto started down the corridor and didn't stop until the last door, where he swiped his card key.

The door opened to a large conference room. The contrast to the hallway was striking: a spotlight on a full-color satellite map of the United States on the paneled far wall, deep blue carpet under the polished walnut conference table, filled water glasses and notepads on the table next to each upholstered chair. Not typical government issue, not this room.

What had she walked into?

The woman standing behind the opposite side of the table acknowledged her with a nod and a smile. Madison recognized her, Secretary of the Interior, Gail Edenshaw. Since when did Madison get to meet with her?

Edenshaw towered over the man next to her. Madison didn't recognize him when he turned his full attention to her. He coughed into a handkerchief as he stepped away to write in a black notebook.

Behind Edenshaw, in a dim corner of the room, another security guard stood at attention.

Madison bit her dry lip and looked to her companions for any sign they knew what they were doing there. A small twitch by Mobley's left eye was the only change in her cool expression. Greaves squinted and rubbed imaginary stubble on his chin.

Madison was about to reach for one of the water glasses when a door opened at the back of the room. A familiar thick head of blond hair around a ruddy face, and trademark khaki pants and polo shirt were flanked by more security. The well-tanned Secretary of State, Alfred Meyers, formerly the Governor of Colorado. Madison no longer was the news junkie she was in Denver, but she thought he'd just returned from another attempt to calm the Middle East.

"Good morning, Al," Edenshaw said.

"How's everything, Gail?" Without waiting for an answer, Meyers moved to the head of the table.

Madison's cheeks flushed. The security now made sense. What didn't make sense was why the hell she was in the same room with him.

"Sit, please sit," Meyers said to everyone.

Meyers opened a black leather portfolio with the Presidential seal centered on the front. "Thank you for coming so quickly. The Secretary and I don't have much time, and staff will brief you on details, so let's get right to it."

Madison realized that everyone was looking at the three of them. Her uniform felt beyond rumpled.

"Ranger Madison, I'm sure you're wondering why we've plucked you from Yosemite?" Meyers said.

"Yes, sir," Madison said.

He smiled, but his shoulders tensed. "The President needs you, all three of you, to work on a special assignment."

Madison put her hands around her water glass and wished it had been filled with something stronger.

His blue eyes locked on hers. "If I told you that innocent people had been killed in many national parks, for political gain, would that shock you?"

Madison didn't want to move, but she nodded her head. "Yes, sir."

"What if I told you we believe these murders were committed by Native-American activists?" He didn't give her a chance to answer. "Including at your park."

Murders? All Madison had found were accidents and heart attacks. And the park had a good working relationship with area Tribes. It didn't make sense. And why was Meyers speaking to her before the others?

"Skeptical?" Meyers asked. "President Eliot had the same reaction, but Roy convinced him."

The slightest smile moved across the face of the short man next to Edenshaw. Roy nodded to Madison. Who was this guy?

Meyers closed his right hand into a fist. "Let me quote the President ... 'We can't let someone scatter a poor father's brain in front of his kids at Old Faithful.'"

Greaves started to ask something, then closed his mouth.

Meyers folded his hands on the table. "Whoever is responsible disguises the murders as accidents. Seems our past attempts at finding these people haven't worked so well." He glanced toward Roy, then back to Madison. "The President determined that we need a special team to take this on. Outside the usual channels. And none of this has been made public. You can understand why. So far, the killers have made no concrete demands."

Madison squinted at the overhead lights reflected on the polished wood. She sipped water from her glass and tried to steady her hands. What was Meyers saying? Native-American killers? The whole thing was surreal. What did it have to do with her? If she had not been in this room, and someone told her she'd be asked to do something for the President, she'd think Henderson had used some chits to get her one good. But he didn't operate this high up and she was a bureaucrat biologist way down the food chain. She'd never worked outside channels on anything. When did someone on her level ever rate an assignment from the President?

Meyers leaned on the table. "Ranger Madison, we handpicked your team. Ms. Mobley has used her own Native-American heritage to become the Department of Justice's best legal mind for tribal affairs."

Mobley's eye twitched as she stared at Meyers.

"And Mr. Greaves…," Meyers said. "At the Commerce Department they say he's outsmarted the best smugglers in the business. He'll help flush out these bastards."

Greaves nodded so fast Madison thought his head would fall off. "Thank you, sir, a privilege," he mumbled.

Meyers nodded to Roy, then straight at Madison. "Until further notice this is your priority. Roy is your direct line to the President. You'll have all the resources of the government at your disposal. Find out once and for all who's behind this."

He stared at them one by one. "This remains classified. Understood?" He left without an answer.

CHAPTER 3

Theodore Roosevelt's Elkhorn Ranch

Dakota Territory July 1885

THEODORE ROOSEVELT SADDLED his horse Manitou and crossed the darkening plains. Wrinkles lined his face, but not all from the sun. How he wished his late wife Alice could have seen his ranch. Nothing had prepared him to become a widower at 26, and lose his mother the same day. It was more than he could bear. The splendor of the Badlands' cliffs in the fading sunlight helped him endure his empty evenings.

He tethered Manitou next to the Little Missouri River, built a fire, and sat on an old log. Upstream, light poured through the windows of his house. A few of the ranch hands would still be rocking in chairs on the veranda, staring across the sand bars and shallows to his fire, until the cold forced them inside.

Summer stars drifted through the clear sky. He had once hoped to teach a brood of his children about the constellations. But he had had only Little Alice, now living with her aunt, away from the wilds of the West. Maybe when she was older he could share his curiosity about the natural world, show her the prairie coneflower, teach her the flycatcher's birdsong.

Manitou pulled on his rope as he reached for grass under a cottonwood. Earlier in the day Roosevelt had ridden beyond his ranch looking for bison. With the overgrazing he'd seen, it was little wonder the vast herds he'd read about as a boy no longer roamed the plains.

Manitou whinnied. Roosevelt stood and patted his shoulder. "Steady, now." A figure moved beyond the firelight. "Who's there?"

"A traveler, sir." A copper-skinned man emerged from the shadows. "May I share your fire?"

"You're welcome to," Roosevelt offered his hand. "I'm Roosevelt."

"They call me Sky Capture." He shook Roosevelt's hand.

Roosevelt nodded to the Indian. The man was not much older than he, wearing buckskins with signs of wear from real work that Roosevelt envied for his own.

They sat cross-legged in the sand near the fire. The man held his hands up to the flames. "The chill is early this night."

As a breeze brushed the burning wood, sparks rose above their heads. Roosevelt took a deep breath. The man had no horse, had crossed the prairie at night on foot. Roosevelt admired that. For a quick moment his thoughts drifted from the grief within him. This man could confirm what Roosevelt had seen himself, the earth depleted, sterile. "Have you traveled far across the plains? Tell me what you've seen."

"Far enough to know things are not as they were." The man leaned closer to Roosevelt. "The tall grasses used to glow, swaying with the summer wind across the prairie." He paused. "Now, the ranchers and hunters come and the grasses and buffalo disappear. The lands change and we mourn our loss."

Roosevelt knew the very landscape that gave him solace was threatened. He waved his hand in front of his chest. "My neighbors do not understand they will lose forever what cannot be replaced." His voice trailed to a whisper. He looked away, then back into the blaze. He could not bring Alice back, but he could do something in her memory, protect his land from the misuse he saw around him.

Roosevelt hit his thigh with his fist. "I won't let that happen on my ranch."

A strong breeze rustled through the trees. Sky Capture listened to Roosevelt explain how he would manage his ranch without destroying it.

Sky Capture's eyes drifted from the face of Roosevelt to the sky and back again. "I can see you value the land of my people because it has also touched your heart. Rare, sir, among the men I meet."

An owl's call interrupted him.

"I know that bird's song," Roosevelt pushed his glasses up on his nose. "Not from here, but from my home in the East. Perhaps it is lost here."

"Perhaps we can somehow help it find home," Sky Capture said. "Thank you for sharing your fire. May our talk keep the light around you for a time."

Roosevelt stood. "And to you. Safe journeys."

Sky Capture whistled a bird call as he disappeared into the dark.

From a distance, a different bird song echoed through the night air.

Then Roosevelt heard nothing more but the whirring wind and the Little Missouri coursing slowly over ancient river gravel.

CHAPTER 4

AFTER MEYERS AND Edenshaw left the conference room, Madison was alone with Roy and her new "team." Her upper lip was wet, her Nixon Sweat she called it, a rarity after years of hard-core interviews and slamming punks against walls. Life could still surprise her. She feared Roy was going to tell her how much.

Whoever Roy was.

Close up he was older than she had thought, beyond retirement age. A slight draft from the ventilation system moved the last bits of hair on either side of his head. His suit jacket lay slack on his shoulders as if it needed to be taken in.

Roy handed each of them a leather-bound notebook. "This briefing book contains all the information you will need to get started. If you have any doubts about this assignment, this is the time to speak. As you know, because of your federal status, the President can assign you to any mission he deems important." He pushed black-rimmed glasses up the bridge of his nose.

Greaves' eyes bugged out as he leaned forward. "No doubts for me. I'm definitely in," he said.

A weak smile creased Roy's face.

Madison wished she was as certain as Greaves. She didn't like Roy's implied threat. She didn't realize when she took her oath as a federal employee that her life was no longer her own.

"I have a question," Mobley said. Her expression remained the same except for a slight squint.

Madison sensed again Mobley was a cool one, someone Madison would want on her team, not an opponent's.

Mobley picked a pen off the table and rotated it between her fingers and her thumb. "What role would I have in the overall assignment?"

"Your extensive experience in tribal relations will be invaluable," Roy said.

Mobley sat even straighter in her chair. "And who would have the lead?"

"Ranger Madison," Roy said without hesitation. "I thought Secretary Meyers made the President's wishes clear."

"Interesting," Mobley said. She smiled at Madison, but there was no warmth behind it. She leaned back slightly in her chair, crossed her legs and adjusted her skirt.

Greaves sunk a little on his chair and looked as if he would rather pass a kidney stone than be in the room with her.

Madison had dealt with women like Mobley before. Brilliant minds, control freaks. She'd be a challenge.

"Other questions?" Roy asked.

Madison had many. Like why was she was in a room filled with talk of murder and high-priority government affairs. And why did she have to keep it all secret.

Her five peaceful years at Yosemite had suddenly disappeared. She forced her old game face to stall. "It's hard to formulate questions without more information."

Roy picked up his book. "Let's get to your materials then."

Madison rubbed her hand over the smooth leather and opened her book. The title page said "Chapter Seven, Operation Leon. White House, October 2010." The next page was the table of contents: summary, team members, map in the back.

"This is just an overview," Roy said. "There are case files in that box next to the wall."

Madison scanned a few pages. They were hardly typical of police files she had seen. Pages clean, not smudged with traces of lunch. Words spelled correctly. Slick, expensive paper formatted to be read quickly, with bullets and boxes and color. Nothing like the hand-written reports she used to read.

Madison turned to the section about the team she was supposed to lead. Her own tanned face grinned back from a photo behind the first tab. Not too bad for 44. She didn't have the body she had in her 20s, but she could still run an 8-minute mile on a flat trail. And her uniform didn't have that telltale middle-age spread in the butt yet.

A local news photographer had taken the photo last summer when she and two other rangers had received awards for pulling 10-year old Billy from the Merced River and reviving him. Everyone in the photo smiled wide. She had her arm around Billy, long recovered and wearing her ranger's hat. Henderson was in the background, hands in his pockets, posing like a new grandpa. That was a good day.

Behind the photo was the story of Madison's life in two

pages. Vital statistics, police work, Masters in Biology after leaving the Denver Police force, all the facts that make up a lifetime vetted by the FBI. Except the psychological profile.

She turned a page and couldn't help but stare at the photograph of a grinning Mobley. Her vitals spelled over-achiever. Smith College Valedictorian. Harvard Law. Clerk for Supreme Court Justice Barlow. Recruited by a long list of the biggest New York law firms, international firms and the Justice Department. Madison knew the Justice Department couldn't match the money the law firms offered, but DOJ paid off her student loans, and gave her a retention bonus. No wonder she was smiling.

In his photo Greaves resembled a less-than-handsome Indiana Jones kneeling over a shipment of partially unwrapped stone sculptures, his Commerce Department cap askew, a Coast Guard officer behind him. He had intercepted more than one large illegal shipment, with resulting convictions.

Roy pulled a folded color map of the United States from the pocket attached to the inside back cover. He opened the map and spread it across the conference table. "**DO NOT RELEASE UNDER THE FREEDOM OF INFORMATION ACT"** was printed in blue across the top. Small red circles dotted the landscape of national parks across the country.

"If you look at the map," Roy said, "you can see how extensive the problem has been. National parks aren't immune to crime, but we believe these incidents were in fact committed by one or more extremist groups. The letters we have received claiming responsibility threaten more killings unless some vague demands about sacred sites are met."

Madison had a few questions now. "But what is the threat? Is it specific?"

"Killing any innocent Americans is a serious threat," Roy said. "As to specifics, it's as specific as they choose to be," Roy said. "But there are no dates, times, or places."

"So, you expect the three of us to make sense of this?" Madison said. "Surely you have the FBI involved."

"We do," Roy said. "But in a limited way." He glanced around the room as if Madison should understand what he meant or not ask about the details.

"This sounds ludicrous," Mobley said.

"I agree," Madison said. "If someone came to me and said the three of us could do better than the FBI, I'd tell them they were crazy."

"I wouldn't call the President crazy," Roy said. "To him it's personal."

Personal in the political sense or in the family member dead sense, Madison wanted to know. Surely if a friend or family member of the President's had been killed, it would have made the news. Or maybe not.

Greaves leaned toward Madison. "The President picked us. That's enough for me. Last week I was in the filthy hold of a Liberian ship opening containers that could have exploded in my face. I'd rather work on this for as long as it takes with two attractive women. No contest." Greaves folded his arms across his chest. "As I said, I'm in."

Greaves smiled at Madison, but she didn't return the favor. The assignment would be a disaster. Instead of seeing Henderson this morning bursting into the office crusty but respectful, she was stuck with Greaves. This guy was down-right obnoxious. But she didn't know of a way out.

Madison waited for Mobley, the brilliant lawyer, to come up with an escape. Mobley didn't offer any.

"Other questions, Ranger Madison?" Roy asked again.

Madison felt cornered. Ludicrous or not, she had to take this on.

"Logistics?" Madison asked.

"Time is of the essence." Roy said. "Lt. Soto has been fully briefed. He will collect your signed non-disclosure agreements and handle all materials and arrangements. How you approach this is entirely up to you. I'll be available to you at any time."

Roy started toward the door, then looked back. "And please don't misplace your briefing books, or, as they say, we'll have to kill you." He chuckled and left.

CHAPTER 5

ROY'S SICK ATTEMPT at a joke didn't win him any points with Madison. Mobley and Greaves stared at her with two distinct expressions: disgust and excitement. She sighed. She'd start with the excitement. She asked Greaves to bring the box of case files to the table.

"I thought there'd be more than one box," Greaves said. He handed Mobley the first manila folder.

"It hardly seems worth the three of us," Mobley said. She opened the file on the table. "Wind Caves National Park, never heard of it." She flipped through the first few pages.

"Wind Caves is in the Black Hills," Madison said.

"Evidently the bison aren't too friendly," Mobley said. "A tourist got too close and was gored. Not much of a mystery there." She put the folder aside.

"Well, I wouldn't recommend the great Northwest either," Greaves said. He held up a picture of a body bag on a sled being guided down a snow-covered slope by the ski patrol. "A very nasty avalanche on Mt. Rainier. Never knew what hit 'em...hell of a last run though."

Madison was lifting a file out of the box when her eyes drifted over a note at the bottom of the map Roy had spread out on the table. "*For a complete list of incidents since 1900, see Chapter Seven.*" The words made Madison shudder.

"Did you see this?" she said.

Greaves ran his finger under the note on the map. "Holy crap…do you suppose this has been happening for a hundred years? Is that why I'm here? I'm an expert in antiquities." He cocked his head.

Mobley leaned on the table. "One hundred years is nothing if you are talking about Indian and U.S. government conflict. Most Indian wars and signed treaties predate that by a long time."

Greaves winced. "That's right, I forgot, *you're* that tribal expert."

Mobley's face remained blank.

Greaves lowered his head, turned his hands palm up. "I bow to your authority, forgive me." He lifted one eyebrow. "Am I growing on you yet?"

Mobley shook her head in disgust.

Madison closed her eyes. Henderson would call Greaves another 'live one.'

"Okay, we can't refight the Indian wars here." Madison flipped through the briefing book. There was nothing in it about 100 years of murders. The special assignment the President laid on her was getting more special every minute. Her head hurt. "I need coffee, daylight and food. Greaves, can you suggest someplace to eat?"

"There's Pete's Café in Georgetown. Great scrambles, breakfast all day."

"Local vegetables?" Madison asked.

Mobley's hands tightened around her water glass. "We

have bigger problems than where your vegetables come from. We need to get organized."

Madison laid her hands on the map, palms down.

"Mobley," Madison said, "Have you ever headed a murder investigation, interviewed suspects, fired a gun?"

"What does that…," she said.

"Thought not," Madison cut her off. "Greaves, how about you?'

Greaves put his pen down. "Years ago I had some training through the Commerce Department. And I used to hunt with my Dad. I can still shoot a rifle. That's how I got interested in artifacts, out in the woods with Dad, finding arrowheads…." His hands moved in the air.

"Fine," Madison interrupted the beginnings of his life story. "But now?"

"With some practice," he said. "I could hit the side of a barn again."

"Good," Madison said.

Mobley's eyebrows knit together. She put her hands on the polished table, pushed herself up and shifted her weight on her chair.

Madison looked directly at her. "That leaves you, Mobley. I would guess your life hasn't allowed time to learn to shoot. Probably never wanted to get near a gun. Wrong side of the tracks sort of thing. I understand, really I do. Am I correct?"

Mobley didn't move.

"Check my résumé. I'm the ex-detective. You want to get organized, I'm getting organized. While I'm 'wasting' time talking with Greaves about my next meal, I'm thinking about what my, our, next step is. If these alleged murders have been happening since 1900, then taking time to eat won't hurt."

Mobley didn't respond.

Madison leaned back in her chair. "This map has a red mark in Yosemite. I've been there for five years, and other than a fight in a campground when a drunk got beaned with an axe, any deaths were accidents. I don't believe this theory yet."

"We never went to the moon either, you know." Greaves crossed his arms. His eyes widened, he tilted his head and smirked. "All a conspiracy. Filmed the whole thing on a sound stage in Hollywood."

"Please." Mobley shook her head.

"It's true," Greaves said. "Would I lie to you?" He tried an innocent grin, but Mobley wasn't responding to it.

"Let's stick to one conspiracy at a time," Madison said. "If we're supposed to piece this one together, we'll need a strategy, including being able to protect ourselves. With lethal force if necessary. You see, Mobley, I've already thought a lot about organizing."

Madison scanned the park names on the rest of the folders. Cases spread from Washington State to the Everglades. They could end up running around like the Three Stooges all across America if they investigated them all. The tripping Mr. Tibbetts in the Winnebago had a file too. What could tribes want at Yosemite? It was protected, as much as the Park Service could. Sure there were too many people, but they tried to keep the numbers and impacts down. If the local tribes were unhappy, surely Henderson would work with them. He never said anything about receiving an odd letter from the tribes. And she knew Tibbetts' death was an accident. Looked like she'd miss Christmas dinner at The

Ahwahnee, and the spring waterfall thaw if she couldn't prove it.

Madison found the most recent deadly so-called accident. "Here's the latest case. A guy named Keller slips and falls from a cliff at Grizzly National Park just after Labor Day. Seems simple enough. Let's tackle that one first. Okay with you Mobley?"

"I hear fall fly fishing in the Rockies is great." Mobley nodded without a smile.

Madison wouldn't have taken her for an angler, but if it would get her there… "Greaves, maybe you can get Lt. Soto to arrange for you to fire a few rounds, just as a refresher before we leave."

"I'll do that," Greaves said.

"Great." Madison grabbed her briefing book and hat. "I'm starving. Let's get out of here."

Lt. Soto directed them to a new SUV with civilian plates parked at the curb. "Your bag is at your hotel, Ranger Madison."

"Thanks," Madison said. She told him they wanted to get to Grizzly National Park as soon as possible.

Mobley and Greaves waited next to the vehicle.

"Greaves, you ride in front with Lt. Soto. We'll take the back," Madison said. She didn't want Mobley and Greaves sitting next to each other the long way back to DC. It could end up like having kids screaming about who's touching who on a family road trip.

Soto drove through the landscape as it transitioned again from rural to urban, a timeline of America's history.

Greaves asked him for a trip to the shooting range,

his arms and hands taking over the whole front seat, then rambled on and on about some big discovery he had made on a ship headed for New Orleans last year. Mobley was quiet, adjusting her suit jacket, trying to make sure the seatbelt didn't wrinkle it. Madison wasn't sure if Mobley was going to let her take charge without more of a fight or if she was just plotting her takeover strategy. Madison figured the latter.

Madison looked out the window as traffic stalled. On the off ramp to D.C. a homeless man and his German shepherd sat on a weathered Oriental rug. A used galvanized bucket rested in front of him. He held up a sign *"Will beg for cash. Need a Jack Daniels."* Madison grinned. She could use one too.

Madison pulled her phone out of her coat pocket and dialed Henderson's number. "It's Dana."

"What the hell? I've had a couple of calls from HQ telling me how important you and those numbers are already this morning and it isn't even 8 a.m. here yet."

"You know, government overreaction. Some congressman wants those numbers checked. You've seen this kind of thing before."

"Not in the Park Service, unless it's a natural disaster that has everyone running in prayer circles. That's when they send in the Marines," he laughed.

"Just the runaround this time." If Henderson only knew how close he was. She hated keeping him in the dark, he'd been so good to her.

"Damn, this leaves me in a bind. Thank God it isn't summer season. I depend on you," he said.

"Then maybe you should tell HQ I need a raise. Do

me a favor? Looks as if I should've brought more clothes and my running gear."

"We'll overnight what you need. But you'll owe me."

That Henderson, she missed him already.

Commuters crowded the sidewalks leading to the Metro Station. She opened the window and a warm breeze blew her hair into her eyes. Damn it. What was she doing here? She brushed strands of hair away from her face and smelled an exhausted city.

CHAPTER 6

LT. SOTO DROPPED Madison off at the Sovereign Hotel. She'd never seen so much marble in a lobby. She was used to less glamorous hotels in D.C. Roy must have gotten a special White House rate. Her room was all floral good taste, as if someone had made a grab from a castle in the French countryside. And the basket of muffins and fruit on the small table next to the window was a nice touch. She'd have food at last.

The wheeled luggage she brought from home was on the bed, with a pile of clothes and a note. "Additional personal effects will be delivered from California tomorrow at your next destination. For your convenience, running clothes and shoes have been provided. Other essentials are in the bathroom." The note wasn't signed.

Madison wasn't fond of the words "personal effects" in the note. When she was a cop, personal effects meant someone was dead and the victim's family would soon be handed a plastic bag filled with grief.

Sure enough, the neatly folded pile of fresh running clothes was next to a new pair of the only kind of running shoes that fit her pronating feet. Everything the right size, even the underwear. Madison grabbed a cranberry muffin and pulled back the lace curtain from the window. The sky had cleared and the Washington Monument blinked two red eyes at her. She was tempted to call Henderson back, remind him about something else to pack, but that would be an excuse. She couldn't tell him what she wanted to, that she was leading some mystery road trip across the country to solve a crime the Feds couldn't. It didn't make a whole hell of a lot of sense. And what could he tell her? Keep a lid on it, play it out a few days, wait for a bureaucratic screw-up to cancel the whole thing. As if that would happen.

She grabbed a banana and slumped down in the armchair upholstered in the same pink and peach-colored rose print as the bedspread. If she put her feet up there would be no stopping sleep. Maybe she would wake up and be back at Yosemite, watching the first trace of snow send most of the tourists home, leaving the park to recover a little before the winter crunch. She rubbed the top of her stomach in the spot that always hurt before she went to a crime scene. The pain behind her eyes would be next. She needed endorphins.

She finished off the banana and pushed herself up from the chair. The worse part of any run is always the first two miles. Better get it over with.

She grabbed the running clothes and entered the cavernous bathroom. Resting on the granite counter, between two identical sinks was shampoo, lavender soap and a matte-black 9mm Beretta, with a box of rounds, two empty clips, and a shoulder holster.

Madison's tan drained from her face in the wall-to-wall mirror. She picked up the gun and felt its familiar weight in her hand. "They even know I prefer you to a Glock. Jesus, what don't they know?"

CHAPTER 7

SHE NEEDED TO think, to figure out what she really should do next as opposed to what they might think she would do. She hadn't really thought she needed a gun. If Mobley hadn't played the hard ass card first, she'd never have taken that tone with her. And she'd sent Greaves off with Soto mainly to get rid of him and have time to herself. Jesus, what a pair. She put the gun, the incident files and her briefing book into the private safe, entered her old badge number as the pin number and closed the door.

Outside, the weather was clear, about 60 degrees, perfect for a run. Madison jogged the few blocks from the hotel past Rock Creek and the remnants of the old water gate used to move boats from the Potomac River to the Chesapeake & Ohio Canal. Tourist shops, lift locks and mooring for boats lined the first blocks of the red-bricked path. A park ranger fitted a barge with new ropes, preparing it for winter. The mules that pulled the barges were gone and the rangers wouldn't have to wear period dress until next spring. She nodded to the ranger, and stepped onto the gravel and clay towpath. A million bicyclists and runners had packed it down. She settled into her 8-minute mile pace. The humidity was just high enough to make her face feel as if someone's hand was pushing against it.

The towpath was wide enough for the few people using it to pass without contact. She ran up to a young couple oblivious to their surroundings, holding hands and talking low to each other, the woman leaning into the man with the softest pressure so that she was only slightly off balance. Madison passed them on the left, and the woman's laugh followed her for a few steps. A turtle swam through the murky water of the canal to a low cottonwood branch, the turtle's wake drifting into a swirl at the end of the branch.

Madison breathed in the ordinariness of the scene. Life at this moment was so simple. But not for her. Why had they picked her and pulled her into a homicide investigation? Of course they knew the official story about what happened in Denver, that she was a wash-out at 39. And they knew she rushed from Denver to the wilderness gold of the Sierra Nevada. She couldn't do that this time. Madison wiped sweat from her forehead. They knew too much about her; that made her more anxious. And though they had sent her a gun, no one said this could be dangerous. Her team was inexperienced. Even if they could figure out what was going on in a few days, then what? What could she expect afterwards? A big bonus after she did what the President wanted? Unlikely. What she wanted they couldn't give her. A one-way ticket back to the kind of a family she had found in Yosemite.

Damn them all. She had to keep her head up and keep going.

Madison checked her watch. She'd been running a half hour. A homeless man sat on the edge of the canal, one pant leg ripped at the knee. His nose was red, but no blood vessels were broken. That was unusual. All the alcoholics she'd ever rousted off the streets of Denver had the disease written in the capillaries of their faces.

The man started to stand, seemed to struggle more when Madison looked at him directly. The pockets of his overcoat bulged and thumped against his thighs. He turned away and stumbled the opposite direction from where she was going.

Madison looked back once. The man was gone. For someone hobbling, he got to where he was going faster than she would have expected. She picked up her pace.

The scarlet and orange leaves of the sweetgums and sycamores lining the bank of the canal framed brief views of the Potomac River. She stopped to let a ranger and a small group of people pass. The tourists listened to the ranger talking about the history and nature of the canal. She loved the incredible forward thinking of the men and women who set these places aside forever. They saved a sense of good, even in this city.

She turned and followed the path back to Georgetown. A breeze filled with garlic and fresh bread hit her nose. She was close to the beginning of the canal again. She slipped into a small grocery store on M Street a block from the canal and bought a bottle of water.

Roots from the trees along M Street pushed up the ruddy bricks on the sidewalk. Leaves stacked up next to the curb as cars whizzed by. She passed the Foggy Bottom Metro Station and the man with the Jack Daniels sign was sitting outside the entrance. She tipped her water bottle to him. He was free, and she was stuck with Mobley and Greaves.

But maybe she'd been too quick to judge Mobley. Her degrees proved she was smart. A woman doesn't get through Harvard Law without some brain cells and guts. But her attitude, she needed to lose it.

ॐ

After a shower, Madison dressed in the non-work clothes she had thrown into her suitcase, jeans and a T-shirt. She grabbed her briefing book and the Grizzly Park file out of the safe and took the elevator down to the lobby. The desk clerk gave her directions to Pete's Café. She hoped Greaves' recommendation was good.

Pete's faced M Street. Polished mahogany booths lined the front windows in full view of the open kitchen. Madison liked the place, the dark wood to mute the space, the grease and hint of smoke in the air. It reminded her of a cop's bar, a place for masking sorrow and protecting partners. After all these years she still saw the image of Imelda's body lying at the base of those red rocks. Her restoration work at Yosemite hadn't dulled that picture.

A young woman with a baker's apron motioned for Madison to sit at the last booth along the wall, then filled her coffee cup.

Madison took a long, slow sip. "That's much better, thank you," she said. "And I'll have the Grilled Vegetable Scramble with pesto hollandaise."

The waitress nodded. Madison waited for her to move away, then opened her briefing book. She took the map out and spread it across the table.

She should have looked at the map before she ran along the C&O canal. One red mark next to the canal had "1906" next to it. She didn't have to worry about that murderer at least. The text that Roy had failed to point out that morning "For a complete list of incidents since 1900, see Chapter Seven," gave her pause. She flipped through the pages of the book and found no Chapter Seven. Only short summaries of the most recent deaths. Whoever wrote them used a style Madison used for her police reports. Short, sweet, to the point. She checked the summary for the death in Grizzly National Park:

"Male Caucasian, 42 years old, body found at base of cliff. Scene reviewed by county coroner. No foul play suspected. Scene not inspected by FBI crime scene investigators until two weeks later. Crime scene likely compromised. Information sent to Operation Leon September 30, 2010.

The following items were found at or near the scene:

1. one small gold button
2. one Asolo hiking boot, size 12, gray
3. five pieces of a broken beer bottle..."

Why hadn't Roy told them about "Operation Leon?" Need to know basis, would that be his answer? Her first thought was to call him up and call him out on it. But something told her to start off with this case, start small, before taking on the big picture. She'd like to discover more before she confronted him.

Madison heard Greaves' footsteps before she saw him ambling toward her, his gait off just a hair because one of his feet turned out farther than the other. The cuffs of his khakis covered the top of his hiking boots.

Greaves sat down without being invited. His *University of Pennsylvania* T-shirt looked new. Madison could've sworn his profile had said Greaves graduated from Penn State. She'd file that small detail about him.

"Lt. Soto let you shoot?" she asked.

"He certainly did," Greaves said. "We went out to Andrews Air Force Base for some rounds. I quite surprised myself. Bottom line, I'm ready, Chief."

Madison could have sworn Greaves widened his eyes and pumped up his chest. His god-given face was attractive enough, with sandy hair and steel blue eyes to create interest, too bad he ruined the appeal with his personality.

He leaned over her pages. "Find anything else interesting?"

"Not yet. Just got started."

The waitress came over with a pad of paper. Madison pulled the book closer.

"What can I get you, sir?"

Greaves tilted his head. "I'm watching my weight." He winked at the waitress and patted his abdomen. "I'll have the Lobbyist's Asian Salad, hold the pork."

Madison was sorry she had to share the table with him. She needed time to think about their "mission." "Don't you have some packing to do?"

"I packed in 30 minutes. Half my stuff's still in my bag from my last trip."

She wasn't getting anywhere.

Greaves leaned back in the booth. "Mobley's the one who'll hold us up. She'll want to bring a trunk full of suits."

Madison didn't bite. She didn't need to defend Mobley.

A series of thunderclouds slipped overhead and light disappeared from the windows. The small light fixture in the booth cast a golden round circle on the map.

Greaves smile changed into a concerned frown, like the expression a therapist once gave Madison to get her to talk about a shooting. "You're not too happy about all this either, are you?" he said. "Let's change that 'glass half empty' mind-set you have."

"I'm not really the pep talk type, Greaves."

"Oh, don't get all cynical cop on me, Madison."

She took a slow drink from her coffee.

"Have I hit the mother lode?" Greaves said. "Me and Mobley, we're just bumbling bureaucrats who have to follow your lead. Miss Indian Law Princess might not like it, but your experience has her cold on this one. Exploit her to your advantage. And me, too. Without guilt." Greaves leered. "Besides, you could use this to make your career. You won't want to be sticking willows into streambanks the rest of your life."

He had her there. She loved her work in the park. And she wasn't ready to kick Henderson out of his job, but when he retired, she wouldn't mind calling the shots.

"You could get your own favorite spot declared a national park, the President could do it by Executive Order," Greaves said. "And if people can't feel safe in a national park, where can they?" Greaves started waving his hands.

Madison picked up her fork. "Quit playing the cheerleader. I'm in. Now tell me all about yourself."

CHAPTER 8

Buffalo, New York

September 10, 1901

IN THE CORRIDOR outside the room where President McKinley lay with two gunshot wounds, Vice-President Theodore Roosevelt sat with the President's secretary George Bruce Cortelyou. Large crowds waited outside, anxious for word about the President's condition. McKinley's doctor finally emerged from the President's room and gave Roosevelt good news: the President would recover. The deep wrinkle on Roosevelt's brow, a constant since he had been summoned from Vermont, finally relaxed.

He stood up from his chair, and shook the doctor's hand. "He has a strong will," Roosevelt smiled. "No anarchist can stop him."

After Roosevelt discussed the details of McKinley's continued treatment with the doctor, Cortelyou laid a hand on Roosevelt's shoulder. "A word please, Mr. Vice President."

"What is it?" Roosevelt said.

"Sir, since the news of the President is hopeful, the

administration suggests the people need to see that the national emergency is over."

Roosevelt knew what was coming, but let Cortelyou finish.

"We kindly request that you leave Buffalo. We will, of course, keep you informed if anything changes."

Roosevelt nodded. Again he was dismissed. He was so used to taking action, but as Vice President, he could not take charge. At least the assassin had not succeeded. He did not share the love others felt for McKinley, but the Republic must be protected.

Roosevelt strode toward the end of the hall where his own staff waited. "Our prayers are answered, the President rallies," he said as if the public could hear. "And so we may leave for Mount Marcy as planned." His secretary handed him his hat and coat as he marched outside without looking back.

The train ride from Buffalo, then the long carriage ride to Camp Tahawus, tired Roosevelt, but once at the camp, the mountain air revived him. Leaves dropped slowly to the damp ground through the remains of fog. Tahawus was an old mining town, caught in the ups and downs of resource prices until one of Roosevelt's friends had turned it into a destination where men could scale the highest mountain in the Adirondacks.

Roosevelt strode into the camp's lodge. A fire burned in the hearth. Mullioned windows cast boxes of gray light across the worn floorboards. He signed the guest book and surveyed the massive timbers supporting the roof. He loved that the lodge and the land around it would now be preserved.

Roosevelt asked the clerk to enlist a ranger to guide him up Mount Marcy.

"Certainly, Mr. Vice President," the clerk replied. "I'll take care of everything."

The morning broke cold and damp. A dense haze covered the mountain and dropped in waves on Roosevelt and the park ranger leading him up Mount Marcy. The trail crossed stretches of ancient rocks and fresh mud, both slick from the mist. About noon, Roosevelt reached the top of the mountain, cleared now of fog, and he could see the changing fall colors across New York reflected in the lakes below.

Roosevelt agreed when the ranger suggested they travel back to Tears-of-the-Clouds Lake for lunch. The water was calm and they rested along the tree-lined shore.

A crow squawked in the distance and Roosevelt looked down the trail. Another ranger scrambled on loose rock, his face red. The ranger ran to Roosevelt and held out a yellow telegram. Roosevelt stood. He feared what it must say. His expression did not change as he ripped the telegram open. He breathed in cool air and closed his eyes. Then he looked long at the two rangers and the silent lake around them. He did not want to leave such a peaceful place.

"The President fails," Roosevelt said. "I must return to Buffalo."

CHAPTER 9

Grizzly National Park

October 2010

GRIZZLY NATIONAL PARK Superintendent Corrigan wasn't going to be happy about their investigation, Madison knew that much. At least Roy arranged to give him a head's up so he knew they were coming. No park boss likes surprises.

Madison's lungs filled with cold pine air as she took a deep breath. She pulled her green ranger's jacket around her shoulders. Mobley and Greaves were already out of the car, headed toward the trailer housing the temporary Superintendent's office until Vista Lodge and the adjoining new park headquarters were rebuilt.

Construction crews were preparing the unfinished lodge for winter, with tape across the windows and the entrance drive marked with orange poles for the snowplow. Mobley and Greaves were introducing themselves when Madison came through the door.

"Thank you for welcoming us, Superintendent," Madison said as she shook Corrigan's offered hand. "We'll try not to disrupt things too much."

Corrigan took a deep breath. "I hope you can find your way around the park. My staff and I have a hell-of-alot of work to do." He folded his arms across his chest.

So much for the heads up phone call. She ran her hand along the bronze buttons on her jacket. She had hoped wearing her uniform would help them gain some acceptance with Corrigan, but she was afraid it was working like her police badge had, helped her with some people and put others on the defensive. Corrigan appeared one of the latter. The stuffed head of a grizzly on the wall behind him could have been his brother.

Madison was just about to speak when Greaves beat her to it.

"Not a problem, sir," Greaves said. "We'll just follow our fearless leader. No worries, eh Captain?" Greaves tilted his head towards Madison. "Quick look around and we're out of here."

Madison wanted to slap him, playing the fool, making inane promises.

Greeting cards with pressed Indian paintbrush, avalanche lily and other wildflowers from the past summer were for sale at the front counter. They were another reminder of the natural things she'd rather be dealing with now. Even Corrigan, under better circumstances, might be preferable to share a beer with than Greaves and Mobley.

Madison moved slightly in front of Greaves. "We'll take as long as we need, no more. We'll keep out of your way."

Corrigan took his hat off a hook near the door. He caressed the broad rim with his hands, then set it on his head. He opened the door a crack and appeared to concentrate. "We gave this accident a full look. You won't find anything new here."

"You're probably right," Madison said. "We'll keep you informed." Corrigan nodded and went out the door.

The closest lodging was the Moraine Motel, a typical mid-century one-story lacking any interesting architectural details, with a wide parking lot in front. It was down the hill from the lodge site, in the only commercial area allowed in the park.

Madison opened Room 5 and dropped her bags on an orange and red bedspread right out of the 1960s. She tossed the room key on the wooden table next to the window. A small paper tent in the middle had a drawing of a brimming pint filled with dark "Moraine Madness" beer on tap at the local bar and general store, "30% off for Ladies" in large angled script across the pint. They didn't know how many pints she could put away.

She opened the Keller file. Keller's picture was paper-clipped to the first page. In the photo he was standing next to a split rail fence grinning, his arm around his young son. Old Faithful was beginning to explode in the background. The light in his eyes was as bright as the sun on the geyser behind him. His face looked as if he could feel the great pressure of the earth being released and he wanted to witness it. He was as excited as his son next to him.

Similar faces were the reason she wanted to be a detective in the first place. Keller at Yellowstone with his son, smiling at someone else he loved taking the picture, in a magnificent place, not knowing someday he would die in another park as exquisite. She wanted to find out what happened between those two moments in time. And who injected evil, if there was evil, in between.

Mobley and Greaves passed her window and knocked on the door.

"Captain," Greaves saluted. Mobley rolled her eyes.

Greaves raised an eyebrow. "Trying to keep it light."

Madison decided to ignore him. She set the file on the table with a slap. "I read the file. Keller's been around job sites all over. Trained the younger guys. Happily married, loved the outdoors. Probably always wore his seat belt. Doesn't seem like the type to take a header off a cliff."

Mobley flipped through the pages of the file. "So, Keller has an accident. It happens, he's not a young man anymore. Maybe he forgets his glasses, gets disoriented and that's it."

"Maybe," Madison said. "But he's younger than me, fit, just a few more wrinkles than someone with a desk job."

Greaves sat on the bed. His legs almost reached the door. "This guy is the poster kid for normal."

Madison agreed. "But everybody has secrets. We'll take a walk around. Most of Keller's stuff was sent home, but there's one box still at the construction office we should go through. Then you can buy your captain a Moraine Madness at dinner." Madison picked up the paper tent and tossed it at Greaves.

When they got close to the single-wide trailer behind the lodge that Hamilton Construction used for their office, Greaves didn't wait, he ran up the wooden steps and opened the door.

A radio crackled as two men sat at a conference table looking over timesheets. The construction schedule was written in black marker on a white board on the wall. Someone had written a cell phone number for "Tex" in slanted text next to the schedule.

Fresh coffee filled the well-used pot on a small table next to the door. Mugs lined the windowsill: "Things you can't do after forty…World's greatest bowler…Stewart Lumber…"

Greaves held out his hand. "Name's Greaves."

"I'm Ward and this is Del." Ward got up and nodded his head toward Del as Greaves introduced Madison and Mobley. Both men wore blue denim work shirts with Hamilton Construction stitched in red on the front pocket. Ward tucked his shirt into worn blue jeans. Del favored suspenders and his eyes lingered a bit on Mobley, then looked down at his heavy leather work boots.

"You must be the fresh Feds," Ward said.

A large clear bowl filled with bite-sized candy was next to the coffee pot. Madison picked up a Tootsie Roll and unwound the ends. "I see I'm not the only one with a sweet tooth. Always loved these things."

"Help yourself," Ward said. "We have a construction inspector who keeps us supplied. Cute kid. The guys like her."

Madison popped the roll into her mouth. Ward and Del were older than Keller, doubtless seasoned by similar big projects around the West. Joints a little stiff in the morning, still in pretty good shape. She could relate to that. She rubbed her jaw. "You guys are up to your necks in work, but we have some questions. You must have heard we're following up on Mr. Keller's death. How well did you know him?"

"Worked lots of jobs with Henry," Ward said. "He loved this park. He visited the old lodge with his dad when he was ten. You get him talking, he would go on and on about how incredible the lodge was…. Watching it burn broke his heart. When we got the construction contract, he was the first one to sign on."

"Crew's takin' his death hard," Del said. "There's not a soul who didn't like him. Someone of his caliber, he'll be tough to replace."

"Anyone seem eager to try?" Madison asked.

Del shook his head.

Madison pulled the last bit of candy out of her tooth with her tongue. "Unusual on a job this size, you know what I mean Del, lots of pressure, people away from home, a few hotheads. No one had a gripe, got a trip to the woodshed for a little attitude readjustment, was let go?"

"I know where you're going," Del said. "We got a couple of knot heads here, this work ain't for everybody. But I don't know of anybody giving Keller grief." Del looked as if he was going to ask Madison for the candy back.

"We would've known about it right away," Ward said. "And put an end to it."

Madison grabbed another Tootsie Roll. "I can see you would."

Mobley fingered a union magazine that had a photo of men scrabbling up a steel tower on the cover. "Your company have many accidents?"

Ward folded his arms across his chest. "You think this kind of thing happens every day? Construction's dangerous. But Henry's accident was off the job. We haven't lost anybody on a work site in 20 years. Idiots try to air nail their fingers sometimes, but our safety record's one of the best in the country. That's part of why we got this contract. Just check it out."

"We will," Madison said. "And we are truly sorry for your loss." At least she knew how to use that tired phrase, something Mobley seemingly hadn't learned in law school. Madison let everyone have a moment to check their emotions.

After a minute she broke the silence. "Says in our file there's a box of Keller's things here. We'd like to see it."

"It's in the next room," Del said. "Mostly work stuff."

He went in and took a large cardboard box off a metal shelf filled with other boxes, long map tubes, a black steel lunchbox with *Tom* scratched on the outside, and an assortment of hammers and extra hand tools. He set the box on a conference table in the middle of the room.

"Not a lot in here, blueprints, his daily work log, that sort of thing. We just left it as we found it. The rest of his personal stuff, Corrigan said we could send it to his wife."

"If we need it, we'll talk to her," Madison said. "Thanks."

Del left the room and Madison closed the door behind him. A calendar advertising construction sky cranes hung on the back of the door. The room smelled of wood smoke mixed with stale cigarettes.

Mobley pulled a paper towel from a roll on a shelf, wiped off the seat of one of the chairs, took off her jacket and sat down. Her pressed jeans and starched cotton blouse had survived the trip from D.C. without a wrinkle. She lifted a book that had "Permanent Record" embossed on its green cloth cover from the box. Dust coated her fingers as she turned the pages and she grabbed another paper towel to wipe it off.

"I suppose it would be easier if we knew what we were looking for," Mobley said. She set the record book down and picked up a blue spiral notebook out of the box. She leaned on her hand as she flipped through the contents. It was the first time Madison could say Mobley's posture was bad. The substance of the pages must not have been too enlightening, and her eyes started to glaze over. Mobley put the notebook back into the box and rubbed her hands together.

Madison bit her lip. Mobley must have clerks doing her grunt work. Madison couldn't afford that from her. Most of the cases Madison solved, unless the criminal was incredibly stupid, turned on some small detail. The same should apply to the slightest word change in a legal document, something Mobley was supposed to understand. Maybe she could only work in the abstract. Maybe Madison would have to test Mobley's mettle in the field.

Greaves grabbed a set of blueprints by its long aluminum fastener and spread it out on the table. The title page showed an architectural sketch of the front of the lodge. Next to the sketch was a long list of firms that had worked on the design. The next page showed the overall footprint of the lodge. Miniature images on the third page showed the contents of each of the following pages: views of the lodge from each side, close-ups of construction details, pages of notes to explain the details. Greaves turned a few of the pages and looked as if he understood them.

"Can you read those things?" Madison said.

"I get the general idea," he said.

"I couldn't build a birdhouse, so you go through them," Madison said.

She looked at the objects left in the box: a coffee cup, more notebooks, hand cleaner, etc. This could be a royal waste of time. Madison had the beginnings of an old familiar feeling. Even after she became a detective, when the whole point was to sift through all the minutiae of lab results, of photos of the crime scene, of the victim's background, where all the connections you think about lead to other connections you never fathomed, even when she knew the answers were almost certainly right in front of her, she was still the street cop, 'prone to action,' the old cliché for describing getting outside, walking the streets, getting off your butt, bustin' some chops. In those days it was always a struggle between sitting in the office and filtering the valuable information from the extraneous, or grabbing her partner and physically going to the crime scene again. Or just walking somewhere together. She didn't want to think about where that had led her and Stan. But she still wanted to get out of this room.

Greaves turned pages back and forth. He held the first page separate from the other pages.

His face had changed. Gone was the "everything is funny" expression he had been wearing almost every minute since they met. He pored over the blueprints, his long frame twisted like an old pine over the table. Any interruption looked futile until he checked all the pages. Madison now pitied the poor artifact smuggler who had Greaves opening his container. He looked downright blissful in the sunlight that crept across the conference table.

"Greaves," Madison said. "Greaves!" She waved a hand in front of his face.

"Huh?" Greaves turned his head up, but didn't move his eyes from the blueprints.

"Think you'd miss us for a couple hours?" Madison asked.

Mobley raised an eyebrow.

"What?" Greaves tried to swat Madison's hand and missed. He raised his chin, but his eyes wandered back to the table. "No."

"I didn't think so," Madison said. "Mobley, I'm going to check out where Keller fell. You with me?"

Mobley was already up.

"We'll meet up later," Madison said as she moved into the front office.

Greaves never looked up.

Madison changed out of her ranger's uniform so people would think she was a tourist. She opened the back of the government SUV and dropped in her backpack and the hiking boots Henderson had managed to pack along with her clothes.

Mobley jogged across the parking lot to the car. The pockets of her buff-colored fishing vest bulged. She held her fishing pole in one hand, a backpack in the other. Madison expected one of those inner tubes with waders attached to roll out of her room behind her.

Mobley's face smoothed around the eyes and mouth as she raised her head to catch the sun. "Perfect day!" She beamed. She stored her belongings in the back of the SUV without another word.

Mobley gave no logical, reasoned explanation of the fishing garb, but Madison let it go. She picked up the map of the park from the dashboard and handed it to Mobley.

"Could you check which road we take to Beargrass Mountain?"

Mobley opened up the map and folded it so that Road 62 was in the middle. "Take the road south along the lake, then we'll have to turn east. It's about 20 miles to the trailhead."

The deep blue sky to the south glowed between the dark silhouettes of the mountains at the end of the lake.

Closer evergreens stood out against scoured layered cliffs of red and burnt orange along the water's edge.

Interpretive signs next to the road pointed to named peaks and described Native-American history. Road 62 led to the eastern prairie, the world of broad meadows and a large marsh the Kowaho Tribe used to trap bison. Beyond the marsh the road looped back through the mountains just as Indian trails once did.

They crossed a small pass and poured onto the plains without warning. Giant grasses stretched for miles. Small patches of willows and trees defined wetlands and creeks. Mobley's eyes widened when they drove on a bridge over a large river edged with lush grass, scattered pines and cottonwoods.

"I can almost feel the wild cutthroat trout down there."

"I'll bet."

"What?"

"You brought your pole." Madison stared ahead.

"Just in case. I thought we might get a break." Mobley rubbed her hand on her pants. "Besides, I'm not much for cliffs."

Madison didn't want to tell her she'd had her moments of panic following criminals up on roofs. One time she leapt from the top of a concrete wall and broke her ankle. She couldn't run for 6 months, and that about killed her. "Hey, I love the mountains, but sometimes I avoid cliffs myself."

"Don't tell Greaves, okay?" Mobley adjusted the seat belt across her chest. "I'll never hear the end of it. Christ, men can be annoying."

"You got that right," Madison said. "I may have to shoot him if he calls me Captain one more time."

The road looped back. The Rockies this far north had no gradual foothills, just endless piles of glacial debris, then steep mountainsides jutting up from the piles. Madison turned onto a side road and climbed through a deep canyon next to a river that tumbled over gentle rock steps. She pulled into a small campground in a broad meadow at the river's edge. The trailhead to Beargrass Mountain was across the road.

"How's this stretch of river look to you?" Madison said.

"You serious?" Mobley asked.

"Sure, it'll only take me a few hours to get to the top and back. I'll make you a deal. You get some fishing in and then when I'm good and tired, you look over whatever arcane details in Keller's box of goodies I find. Okay?"

"Deal." Mobley bounded out the door.

The trail up to Beargrass Mountain, according to the trail guide, was a moderate hike, with an elevation change of about fifteen hundred feet. Madison knew trail guides were always wrong, usually in the difficulty or length of the hike. Most "moderate" hikes were fine if you were a marathon runner with five percent body fat. Anyone else might amend it to 'moderately difficult.' She'd heard that from tourists all the time, as if she could change the ratings. Madison kept in shape, the trails in Yosemite saw to that, but the desk time also took its toll. At the first switchback she stopped and saw Mobley standing in the middle of the river, flicking her fishing pole. Her line caught the sun as she cast a peaceful arc in the air. The fly drifted gracefully in the slack water.

Madison took a drink from her water bottle and followed the trail as it turned away from the river and into a constricted side canyon. A small creek followed layers of twisted shale covered with vivid red and green crystals and patches of moss. Water swirled in small undercut caves and potholes along the stream.

The wind flowing down the canyon cooled her. The wide trail was well maintained; she was glad of that. After about 30 minutes, the trail moved away from the canyon, grew steeper, and twisted through a patch of old growth pine. The sun was still bright through the boughs. Madison rounded a bend and the trees began to thin out. Another steep mile and the trail went across bare rock at the top of the mountain. A finger-like ridge of layered rock jutted from the trail to the south, and dropped off to the river below. Someone had stacked round rocks on top of each other to form a cairn at the very end.

The edge was not quite as scary as the aptly named Diving Board at Yosemite; she'd been as afraid as the tourists to climb up and gaze through 3,000 feet of nothing. This ridge seemed more stable, but just as heart stopping.

Madison pulled photos from the Keller file out of her backpack. They identified the end of this ridge as the place where Keller fell. All the crime scene tape, if there had been any, had been removed.

The full glory of the Rocky Mountains spread out in all directions — snowcapped peaks above classic U-shaped glacial valleys. Keller had picked a beautiful spot for his last hike. Madison grabbed a granola bar from her pack and took a bite. The gentle fall sun warmed her face. The silence, then the sound of the wind below, was music to her.

The trail guide said the Kowaho treasured Beargrass Mountain as a place for honoring spirits, at least the Park Service thought so, though the Kowaho wouldn't directly confirm that. Madison knew Native-Americans were reluctant to talk specifics about their traditionally hallowed sites.

"We can't trust our places will be kept confidential," a tribal elder named Harold told her one day in a high meadow in Yosemite.

She'd gotten the go ahead to spend money to restore the meadow after years of too many tourists. She wanted to move a popular trail, and bring back native plants local tribes valued that would also provide food for wildlife. Nothing she said reassured Harold. He wouldn't even tell her that the tribe had used the meadow, though there was evidence they had. He gave her a full smile, because he was a polite man, but his eyes didn't soften.

The Beargrass Mountain main trail continued back through the trees, off toward the next peak. Layers of transformed sediment held up the ridge, and the most resistant buff-colored limestone formed the top. Madison inched across the uneven limestone toward the rock cairn. She stayed in the middle of the thin ridge and watched her step. It was a long way down.

The largest rock on the bottom of the cairn was dark basalt, different from the nearby layered rocks. Someone had carried that rock up the trail from far away where basalt was prevalent. The smaller rounded rocks on top of the basalt glinted red and green, made of the same minerals as the canyon below. At the edge there was just enough room for one person to sit, anyone else would have to stand or sit behind the other. The cliff dropped about 200 feet before the next rock ledge would slow a body's fall.

Park staff had found a number of items near the cairn after Keller died, including one of his Asolo boots, as if he had slipped out of it as he fell over the edge.

Madison checked the list of things found at the scene again. Pieces of a broken beer bottle at the bottom of the cliff could have been there for months. No one dusted the pieces or noticed if anything other than a label was on the bottle. Keller was sober when he died, at least his blood work said so.

Same with the gold button. Madison looked at the picture of the button stuck in a crack in a rock near the cairn. It could have popped off anybody's coat. Not much else had been found at the scene, a few eagle feathers thought to be from a nearby eagle's nest, empty trail bar wrappers, nothing that seemed connected to Keller, nothing unusual for a viewpoint at a park. Cleaner than most she'd experienced at Yosemite. Grizzly got fewer visitors because it was so remote.

Some red marks were carved into the limestone on the next finger of ridge, a face on the side of the cliff. Two dark rings surrounded broad eyes. A wide nose ran down to what might have been a mouth. The red against the limestone, even weathered, stood out. The face seemed feminine. High over the river, watching everything from grizzly bears to people, this face saw Keller's last day. Madison took a step and the eyes on the rock seemed to follow her.

Some local tribal elder would know her name, but might not tell. Madison took a camera from her backpack. "Smile, sweetheart. If you could only talk."

Trees lining the river below moved with the wind and Madison rubbed her temple. The air pressure had changed, the way it used to in Denver when a front was coming in. Telltale bluish clouds formed sheets like waves and surged over the far western mountains in a broad arch. A Chinook wind. She'd been caught in Chinook winds before, as thick warm air lifted over the mountains and flooded onto the prairie. Perfect for making her head ache. She and Mobley should get back before the winds blew trees across the road.

The cloud-wave grew across the mountains to the west and pushed up against the last of the blue sky. Dust blew across the eyes on the petroglyph as they watched Madison hurry back down the trail.

Halfway down the trail a high-pitched screech ricocheted against the walls. Madison knew it was a hawk, but they didn't call the park "Grizzly" for nothing. She was downwind of anything behind her, but she'd never take safety for granted. Trust your instincts, take suggestions "under advisement," then do what your gut tells you.

Her gut was giving her fits. She set her pack down on a flat rock that reflected the remains of sunlight in its scarlet crystal faces. She pulled the Beretta out of her pack and strapped it in the shoulder holster. The gun rested easy against a familiar spot, the slight pressure on her skin a comfort. She picked up her pace. The hawk screamed again behind her, she'd have to check her birding life list, but it sounded like a zone-tailed hawk, out of place for the Rockies. Blown in by the Chinook, or global warming, a species taking a wrong step. No one was on this trail, she knew that, but she unsnapped the leather strap covering her gun so that she could get to it easily. Trust your instincts.

A young man looking over the edge of the canyon smiled as Madison stopped along the trail to adjust her holster. He snapped a dead branch from the small pine tree next to him and threw it across the gorge. His throw carried the branch up, then it hit the opposite wall and slid down the layers of time into the creek next to the trail, innocent.

The wind spiraled downriver, bending pines and grasses along the bank as Madison reached the trailhead. She put her gun in her pack and put it in the back of the SUV. She waved to Mobley to hurry. They needed to get out of the area before the storm hit.

Mobley reeled in her line and sprinted to the SUV. "Beautiful trout in this river. Real fighters. And the sun on their backs when you release them…."

Madison pointed up. "Those gorgeous clouds might turn on us."

Mobley nodded. The brim of her fishing cap blew up, almost flipped off her head. She lifted her gear into the back of the vehicle. "Find anything up top?"

"I found out why Keller hiked there. It's stunning. But it would be easy to take a spill off the edge. I didn't find anything the park staff might have left behind, it was pretty clean. And there was this interesting petroglyph. Carved right into the side of the cliff. It looked like a woman to me."

Madison pulled the camera out of her bag and showed Mobley one of the photos.

Mobley nodded. "Looks like the Wind Woman from an old legend. I should have climbed up with you."

"It was a sheer drop off."

"Please, I would have been fine." Mobley climbed into the car and looked straight ahead.

That Mobley was a hard one.

The sky darkened and wind shook the SUV as they drove back across the prairie.

As they pulled into the motel parking lot, Greaves stepped out of his room with his hands on his hips. They got out of the SUV.

"Ladies," Greaves said. "I certainly hope you had a lovely day. It's been grueling for me." He dropped his arms. "Come see."

Madison and Mobley followed him into his room. Loose papers covered every horizontal surface. He cleared off space on the chair and bed so they could sit down.

Madison slumped in the chair. "What's all this?"

Greaves made a big circle with one hand. "Keller's wife called while I was talking to Del in the office. Keller had asked her to send all this stuff, but he'd never picked it up from the post office. It's full of magazine articles he clipped about electrical schemes for different kinds of commercial businesses. He wanted to be ready for any kind of job that might come up, that's what his wife said." Greaves pointed at Mobley. "And that spiral notebook you browsed at the construction office?" He twisted one side of his mouth and arched an eyebrow as if he was ready to rap Mobley's hand with a ruler. "I took a longer look at it. There was a strange note in a margin–'second set of prints'–and then power flow calculations. Del let me borrow his construction calculator, which lets you figure out anything related to construction, rise and run, angles, have to get one of those ..."

"Greaves, the point?" Madison said.

"The point is that while you two were out enjoying the

sun, I've been studying his calculations trying to figure out what was so fascinating." Greaves waited.

"And did you figure it out or do we have to leave again?" Madison asked.

Greaves pushed his lips together. "Really, boss, I'm hurt. Of course I figured it out. Keller was trying to estimate the power load on the lodge."

Finally. Madison was impressed, but she wasn't going to let Greaves know that. It might distract him.

Mobley took off her fishing cap. "Why would he be interested in that?"

"That isn't clear yet," Greaves said. "But I did notice some of the pages in the set of blueprints are missing." The blueprints covered the small table next to the window. Greaves leaned over the first page, the one that showed what the front of the new lodge would look like when it was finished.

"The new lodge will have this huge room in the front, just like the old lodge did, but bigger." He turned the page. "Look at the size of this, and the verandas lining the upper floors... But the pages with the details for this room, and the electrical plans for the lodge aren't here."

Madison flipped through the magazine articles in the box. The articles were filed by type of project. This guy was as prepared as a boy scout. "What's the connection? If he was worried about overloads or whatever they're called, wouldn't he just talk to the architect or construction manager? They must have had an engineer do the original calculations."

Greaves held up his hands. "There aren't any notes in the file that he talked to anyone about it. Maybe he was going to and didn't get the chance. If he thought they'd made a mistake, he sounds like the kind of guy who would've mentioned it before it created a problem. That would save the contractor from eating extra costs later."

Madison bent forward. "*Saving* money doesn't seem like a good reason to kill someone. Most crimes involve greed, sex, or control. Assuming Keller was a good family man, a crime of passion is out. And the President wouldn't care about that. Building the lodge was worth a lot to someone, but what did that have to do with Keller? What do you think, Mobley?"

Mobley ran her finger along the edge of her hat. "I can pull financial records. Maybe we should start following the money. I don't remember any controversy about rebuilding the lodge, but I'll check the legislative history, call some of my colleagues."

"Good," Madison said. "Let's see where that leads..."

"What about your hike, find anything?" Greaves asked.

Madison showed Greaves the photos of the face carved into the limestone.

"Man, I missed it," he said. "So many petroglyphs close to trails get destroyed. There are similar ones in the Southwest. A woman, eyes watching everything, everyone, using the river. *She* knows what happened to Keller."

"Mobley said she might be like the Wind Woman, from one of her tribe's legends."

"I'm not a member of any tribe," Mobley said.

"Sorry, my mistake." Madison smiled. If someone mentioned Mobley's heritage, Mobley let a small tell slip, like gamblers do. A wince, a tic, a look at her polished fingernail, small enough most people wouldn't notice. Her file listed time on the Creekakee reservation, but she didn't claim a Creekakee connection or maybe the tribe didn't claim her. Why spend her life working tribal issues, but for the government? With her background she could have gone anywhere.

Mobley put on her hat. "Why spend any time on this petroglyph if it has nothing to do with Keller? I need to call DC while someone's still in the office."

"Thanks," Madison said as Mobley left the room.

"One of you beat the other to the top of the mountain?" Greaves winked.

"Not exactly," Madison said.

"Two tough women, bound to happen," Greaves said.

"I'm not taking your bait," Madison said.

Madison pulled the photo of the gold button from her backpack. "I was thinking on the way back down the trail that most hiking jackets these days don't have buttons. They have Velcro and zippers and snaps. Maybe it's nothing."

"Let me see." Greaves held the photo close to his face. "A crow might have dropped it, they like shiny objects. It's awful clean for being out in the elements. If we had a digital image we could look closer for markings."

"Roy's the man who said he could get us anything." She dialed the number he had given her that first day in the conference room.

"This is Ranger Madison, sir."

"It's good to hear from you. How's the investigation going?"

She heard his question drift at the end, as if Roy knew the answer before he asked. She wasn't sure what to say, but if this administration operated anything like her old police department, admitting no real progress could be a career-stifling move. The game was to give the boss something for him to give his boss, no matter how creative you had to be with the facts.

"Going over the situation, sir. No firm conclusions yet, but we have some interesting leads."

"Wonderful, Madison. I hope your partners are proving helpful?"

She looked at Greaves doing calculations on the motel notepad. Time would tell. "Certainly, sir."

"I appreciate the call Madison, but I assume you're not just checking in."

"No, sir, I need some digital photos of the gold button found at the scene here at Grizzly. It could be nothing, but it seems out of place."

"Trust your instincts, Madison. You'll have images within the hour. Have a good evening."

She started to say goodbye, but he hung up. She'd so like to know his story.

Madison looked up from the blueprints Greaves had spread across the table and saw Mobley crossing the parking lot with a notepad in her hand. Madison leaned back in the chair and noticed the way she marched, even in her fishing clothes, as if every moment was an inspection. Mobley reminded her of a younger version of herself, when Madison had her gun on her hip, bulletproof vest keeping the back straight, patrolling with her partner on the night shift. She knew what it was like to be scrutinized all the time for the slightest screw-up, the chance for one of the good old boys to bounce you out of the play. Mobley was in a whole other league with white-collar heavies who had eyes everywhere. She couldn't trust anyone either.

Mobley held up the notepad as she came through the door. "I got through to a friend at the Interior Department.

There's a long list of contractors working on this place. The way my friend told it, Senator Brumley promised to hire companies from every state in the country just to get the bill passed."

"I remember Brumley masterminded the funding for the new lodge after the fire," Madison said. "He created this coalition of environmentalists, tribes, construction companies and historic preservationists and got the appropriations passed. He even invoked the ghost of Teddy Roosevelt, since Roosevelt made Grizzly a national park, and castigated anyone who was against it."

"The budget was lavish by national park standards, too," Mobley said.

"So the local tribes supported it?" Greaves asked.

"Yes," Mobley said. "The only conflict was between the Kowaho and the Teton Bird tribes. They disagreed about who made 'usual and customary' use of the land before Euro-Americans came."

Greaves shook his head. "Typical. No offense intended, Mobes, but you know how it is, sometimes our red brethren hate each other as much as they hate the white man. They care as much about territory as the rest of us. Can't blame them."

Mobley didn't blink. "The name's Mobley."

Madison sighed. "Thanks for your enlightened opinion Greaves, but did they get anything out of the deal?"

Mobley didn't look at Madison, but kept her eyes on Greaves. "The government agreed to add a new wing to the lodge for a cultural center. The tribes will use it for education, and it will generate some tourist dollars."

"Right," Madison said. "So, the tribes get something

out of the deal and appear okay with the plans. That leaves the contractors."

"It'll take a while to study them. Hamilton Construction is the general management company, but then there's all the subcontractors."

Madison scanned the list. Mobley wasn't kidding. The travel expenses alone for these companies would deepen the national debt. Madison wanted to throw the notepad on the bed with the rest of the loose ends. Greaves and Mobley needed a referee and some direction. She needed a shower and something to stop her stomach from growling. She sighed.

"Okay, what do we know? Everybody's getting something out of this beautiful new lodge, money, cultural spin, political points. Then we have a happily married man who likes to do power flow calculations in his spare time. Everybody loves him, he's a hell of a good guy. The good guy takes a hike and goes over the side of a cliff. He leaves a boot, there's a button, a broken beer bottle, eagle feathers and paper trash at the scene. Who would really care enough to kill him? And what does this have to do with the other so-called park accidents? And why does the Executive Branch care?"

Mobley and Greaves shook their heads. The connections weren't obvious. That would be too easy. What was Roy not telling them? He said to trust her instincts; her instinct said Roy wasn't giving them everything he had.

Something banged against the side of the motel as the wind thrashed outside. The overhead light dimmed, then brightened. Madison could kick herself. She had made a serious mistake taking what Roy had told her without question. He never gave her the letter about Keller's killing. It wasn't in his file. And she didn't ask for it. It had to be key. If there was a good reason for her not to have it, she didn't know what it was. He should have known they needed it. He knew.

"The letter, the one the President got about Keller, we never got a copy."

"It might be classified," Greaves said. "Why else keep it out of the file?"

"Something too sensitive for us to know," Mobley said. "National security?"

"But we're vetted and cleared," Madison said. "We're on the same team. Damn it, Roy needs to treat us like it."

CHAPTER 10

MADISON LEFT GREAVES to wait for the close-up of the button and try to figure out if Keller was just a frustrated electrical engineer or if he was on to something. She had to think about what she was going to say to Roy before she called him. She hated it, but Mobley was closer to the top of the federal food chain than she would ever be and Madison needed to pick her brain. She had asked Mobley to walk with her to the Vista Lodge General Store.

A warm wind swirled around the exposed construction site near the lodge. Madison wiped an ancient bit of Canada out of her eye as she and Mobley headed across the parking lot.

Madison opened the store's heavy fir door. The smell of fried Jojos, fresh trout cooking and wood smoke made her stomach growl. Collectible park patches with miniatures of the old lodge lined the wall. A glass case of revolving hot dogs and burritos waited right above the kid-level candy bars next to the front door. She had seen a million park stores with the same layout, ready to take money out of kids' hands. She'd been a sucker for Milk Duds and red rope herself.

Madison grabbed a bag of barbequed potato chips and canned lemonade, gave the clerk her money and sat in one of the rustic pine chairs next to the window. The last petunias of fall swayed back and forth in the window box. She ate two potato chips and licked the barbecue stain off her fingers. Field work nutrition.

Mobley took off her baseball cap, scratched between the gelled strands of her hair with her fingernail, then lingered at the glass case at the back of the store. The case held the trappings of fishermen: lures, reels, maps to secret fishing holes, and hand-tied flies. "Could I see that fly?" she asked.

The clerk retrieved a caddis fly from the case, and Mobley laughed as the clerk exaggerated the way it would attract a fish. Seemed to Madison that catching fish might be the only thing Mobley enjoyed.

Mobley declined purchasing the fly, then opened the freezer section and pulled out an Eskimo pie and added it to her can of herbal iced tea on the counter. She got her change and sat opposite Madison.

Madison leaned close to the table. "Let me ask you something. Before I ask Roy for the letter about Keller, why do you think he didn't give it to us in the first place?"

"What do you know about him?" Mobley looked out the window.

"Not much," Madison said. "I guess we should have asked for his profile."

"I doubt there is one." Mobley took a slow drink from her ice tea and started unwrapping the ice cream sandwich.

"What do you mean?"

"For starters, I couldn't find him on any federal employee lists on the web."

Madison's last chip was gone before she even tasted it. "What employee lists?"

Mobley took a small bite of the ice cream. "Department employee lists. I checked the web. Every federal employee is on one list or another, along with lots of information. For instance, anyone can find out you're a GS-11, that you started with the National Park Service in 2005, and have earned two commendations. Good job saving that little kid in the river."

Madison gulped some lemonade. Henderson should have taken that old press release off the web by now. But what about the rest? "I didn't know you could get those details on the web." It made sense, but she didn't like it.

"We're public servants after all. But Roy's not in there anywhere."

"CIA?" Madison half joked.

"I'd say some special agency not on the official books."

That was a theory Madison would expect from Greaves, not Mobley, but she wasn't going to point that out.

Roy might be a special assistant to the President, but he should be just as transparent to the public as the rest of them. And Madison didn't like the suggestion there was an agency nobody knew about while her life appeared to be an open book. "You find out *anything* about him?"

"All I know is this guy's pretty invisible, even within the Beltway. I didn't ask anyone point blank, but I couldn't find anything in my sources."

Madison hadn't learned any more about Roy, but she'd found out something about Mobley. She did her homework.

A pint of Moraine Madness would be perfect for this conversation.

"You do any other research on me?" Madison asked. Might as well get the playing field defined.

Mobley turned from the window and unfolded the foil wrapper from the last of her Eskimo pie. She licked chocolate coating off a red-polished nail and took the last bite of the bar. Her eyes squinted as if the ice cream were too cold.

Madison waited and tried to keep her face blank.

Mobley looked straight at her. "Of course."

Madison knew before she asked. If she hadn't been sitting down, she would have sworn her knees buckled. As it was, she heard her pulse thump faster than normal in her ears. She broke eye contact with Mobley. The photo of Imelda's body flared in her mind. There was disgrace in that vision, even though she didn't deserve it.

"I didn't get that girl killed." Madison couldn't keep her cheeks from flaming.

Mobley didn't answer back.

Madison didn't need to justify herself, but she couldn't stop. "If you read anything different, it's not true." Madison shifted on her chair. "That case was the biggest thing that had ever happened to Denver. It was complicated—."

"Looked simple in the papers."

The image of Madison's tired face on the front page of the sunrise edition of the Denver Post was the beginning of the end. Stan had his arm around her back to steady her. The whole case against their suspect was falling apart, and little Imelda had just been found. After months of working day and night, their desperate love affair had made them miss something.

How many times had Madison played those months

over in her head? It was years before she had a good night's sleep. Now she'd have to prove herself all over again.

"There's a lot the papers didn't say. You know how they can spin the truth. Especially at an unsuspecting target."

Mobley took a long sip of her tea. "It can happen." Her eyes drifted upward.

Madison had interviewed enough people to know Mobley might be calling up an old memory and Madison saw an opening.

"Well, it happened to me. Like an avalanche slid right over me. The men at the top, they stepped away just in time. The papers didn't talk about that."

"You were their *scapegoat.*"

"Skinned, grilled and served up on my polished police shield."

"Quaint."

Madison leaned toward her. Mobley had the same look on her face she'd seen on her asshole bosses when the news hit the papers and the deal was done. Madison was going down and the big boys' expressions said it was a shame she hadn't played the game better. She wanted to slap that look off Mobley's face, but a park ranger wouldn't do that. "You got that right. A quaint way to cover their well-connected asses."

Mobley raised her hand from the table and turned her palm toward Madison. "Settle down."

"You listen to me," Madison said. "I didn't get Imelda killed, and I don't care what you think." She wiped sweat from her upper lip. So much for getting over it. Her hairline was wet. She talked too much.

Mobley fingered the remains of the ice cream wrapper on the table. "I really don't care what happened to you,

Dana. We don't have time for personal problems." She slid back in her chair with a tight-lipped sneer.

The wood stove pumped out too much heat. Madison drained her can of lemonade. She'd lost whatever edge she'd had in Denver. Mobley's daily tangle with other lawyers kept her sharp. And she was just young enough to think the strides she made were all of her own doing, like some of the younger policewomen who seemed to forget who and what had paved the way for them.

A dusty whirlwind twisted toward the lodge. Madison wished the storm would blow the damn world away or at least the person sitting opposite her.

Madison turned back to Mobley. "Did you tell Greaves?"

Mobley tilted her head and looked across the lot. "Of course not."

Madison wasn't sure she believed her, but if Mobley knew, Greaves would soon enough.

Across the parking lot, Greaves closed the door to his room. It blew open again, and he shifted some papers from his right hand to his left and closed the door with a hard pull. He covered his eyes with his hand as he started toward them.

Warm dirt blasted in as Greaves opened the store's front door. He lumbered over to their table and pulled up a chair. "I hate to interrupt tea time, but look at this." He placed a color picture of a button on the table. The enlarged button, its surface clearly shown, rested on a black background.

"Damn." Madison picked up the photo, then put it down. The number *1* was in the middle of the button, with

United States written in script along the circumference. Not a scratch on it.

"Interesting, huh?" Greaves said.

"Damn." Madison said again. It had to be a replica. It couldn't be original, not stuck up on the top of the mountain.

"What's so special?" Mobley said.

Madison noted a hint of flush on the surface of Mobley's cheek. Clearly Mobley didn't like not knowing everything. "The markings would make it U.S. Army, First Regiment, circa 1800," Madison said.

Mobley shook her head. "Clearly a reproduction."

"Won't be sure until we get our hands on it," Greaves said.

Greaves lifted his eyes from the photo and smiled at Madison. It was the kind of thing he obviously loved, old things in odd places, no trace of how they got there. He seemed neither surprised nor concerned that there were no notes in the file about the type of button it was, nor any evidence that anyone except them had considered it important. Roy must have known Greaves would recognize it or at least be curious about it. And that she loved the history of the American West. For god's sake, he conceivably knew that Greaves would be happy to tackle Keller's power flow scratchings.

Mobley ran her tongue over her teeth, looked disinterested.

Madison knew Mobley could have easily glossed over the button, as others must have done. Mobley didn't seem to want to have anything to do with what she thought were mundane objects from Keller's last few days. Madison had that photo of Keller plastered in her own head, but Mobley probably took one look and couldn't give a description beyond a middle-aged white man if pressed. And she was a bit impatient for someone who worked on cases that referenced treaties and other commitments that went back over a hundred years. Maybe she missed her status in D.C. She wasn't interested in the physical environment, except to fish, at least from what Madison had seen so far. Madison had made a typical leap about Mobley without any facts to back it up, that her background in Indian law and her own DNA gave her some special access to the collective memories of the land. That she might be curious about what happened in this place that had so much meaning and history. Madison knew better. Mobley could smell those ill-placed assumptions about her. No wonder she had an attitude.

Black clouds with swirls of green rushed behind the half-finished lodge. Mobley shook her head as she looked out the window. "Am I the only one here who thinks this is bullshit? You two seem to be getting awfully excited about something that's obviously a fake, that has nothing to do with Keller slipping off a cliff. You must've really pissed off your supervisors to be here."

Greaves took his eyes from the photo of the button. "Back at you," he said. "Why's someone of your caliber stuck here with a couple of morons like us?"

Mobley's flush deepened. She crossed her arms on her chest.

"Hold on," Madison said. "Anything and nothing is possible now. Keller's death…we just don't know. It's too soon to dismiss anything. People can get blindsided by little things."

"Hope not Keller," Greaves said.

"Let's trust he slipped, not slipped up," Madison said.

"For now, Roy's got a few more questions to answer, number one being if the First Regimental cavalry was already here, why he needed us."

CHAPTER 11

A STRONG WIND gust hit Madison as she left the store. Greaves and Mobley had taken off separately to do more research. Madison had to call Roy again, but in another hour the quality of light would fade and she needed to walk around and in the lodge and get a feel for what Keller might have seen.

She followed the curve of the road up to the top of the terminal moraine. She ran her hand over the tumbled and rounded granitic rocks sticking out of the roadcut. Veins of quartz filled the weak joints of the boulders, taking advantage of the opportunity to seal any void. She flicked off some of the ground-up jumble of rocks and dirt packed around the boulders, whatever had been in the glacier's way. Geology took no prisoners, and left a mess behind. Kinda like life.

Warm wind flowed over the top of the moraine. It picked up loose motes of soil and leaves and lifted the mix over the lake. Smoke from the store's chimney blew toward her and blended with the smell of pines. One light burned in the Park Service's temporary office near the lodge. As Madison rounded the top, Superintendent Corrigan stepped out of the ranger's office carrying a briefcase.

"Superintendent."

"Ranger." Corrigan touched the brim of his hat.

"Taking work home?"

"You know the drill. Always more paperwork." He started toward a lone car parked in a graveled area.

"That I do." Madison walked next to Corrigan. "Sorry about our intrusion. I'm hoping we won't need much help from your staff."

"We can handle it."

"I'm sure you can." So much for giving them a break. "At least this warm wind will help get a few more construction days in."

"We could use 'em. It'll be 30 below before we know it." Corrigan stopped next to his car. "Have you confirmed our conclusions?"

"Not yet."

Corrigan nodded a humph.

"We did find something, it's probably nothing. But it got one of my partners worked up."

Corrigan didn't respond.

Madison put her hand on the roof of his car. "It's just an old Army button from the ridge where Keller fell. If it's real, it might at least have some historic value."

Corrigan slipped into the driver's seat. "Army button? That ridge's been checked and rechecked by our archeologists and tribal elders. We've documented everything up there. You know the rules. Especially with the tribes. We don't get to cut a tree that's fallen across the trail without their okay that it's not sacred. I can't imagine we've missed anything."

"I'm sure it's nothing, but we'll check it. You know, to

satisfy the D.C. boys. Have a good evening, Superintendent." Madison tapped the top of his car.

The sun had slipped behind the streaking clouds, but Corrigan squinted as he closed the door and started the car. He backed up, then drove down the road.

Corrigan didn't seem to know about the button, he just seemed angry. Madison couldn't blame him. He had to protect his park kingdom from idiots who wanted to love it to death by trampling fragile meadows or by speculative drilling, while keeping everyone else happy. Their intrusion only added more stress. He had a right to be testy.

And Grizzly, his kingdom, was truly magnificent. The high Rockies and deep woods rimming the lake, the golden light of quaking aspen leaves rippling in the water, Madison wouldn't mind another assignment here that didn't involve murder.

Workers' silhouettes moved across the light beaming through the lodge's long windows. As Madison moved toward the lodge she wished she had her uniform on, so slipping in and out wouldn't raise any eyebrows.

She neared the interpretive sign the Park Service had erected to keep tourists from getting too close to the construction site. The photos of the lodge on fire were heartbreaking. The huge Douglas fir logs that supported the building streaked orange torches into the sky. Tourists and rangers huddled as the third floor veranda slid into the inferno. Madison and the other rangers at Yosemite had been glued to the TV coverage. The worst image was of an old man breaking through the Park Service's barricades and running into the flames. They turned off the TV when they brought the tribal elder's body out.

Vista Lodge had been one of the grand ladies of the

national park system, built in the same majestic style as Glacier Lodge in Glacier National Park. The building rested on top of a terminal moraine pushed up by the flow of glaciers during the last ice age. The moraine backed up Vista Lake into the heart of the Rocky Mountains. High winds, strong enough to blow the windshields out of tourists' cars, frequently came across the lake and hit the lodge head on, but the lodge stood firm, its floor-to-ceiling picture windows flexing with the force.

Madison had stared out those windows before, during a training class. She had climbed up the wide wooden staircase to look at the buffalo and moose heads ringing the second floor veranda. The Kowaho had made the blankets, bows and arrows that adorned the walls under the animal heads.

The new building would never be the same, the huge timbers weren't available anymore. But the Park Service sign stressed the effort to find and use something as close to the old materials as possible, even if it meant pulling a few old-growth trees from wilderness areas, something that had taken an Act of Congress.

The sign had a picture of the President and Senator Brumley and representatives of the Kowaho Tribe cutting the ceremonial ribbon last spring, Vista Lake glistening behind them. Members of the cabinet attended, including Secretary of State Meyers. The Middle East could evidently wait, again. Madison could understand that might have been protocol, but now with this assignment, what was his connection?

The whine of a power saw overwhelmed the intermittent voice of Johnny Cash drifting out the back door of the lodge. Madison stepped over the unfinished threshold through a mixed haze of sheetrock dust and the steeply angled light shafts of the setting sun. Gray globs of spilled adhesive and spatters of tobacco juice adorned the plywood subfloor. She could lift a wealth of DNA from it.

A chaotic stack of plastic pipe and lumber filled one corner of the room. Portable workbenches ringed the walls, set-up for cutting studs. Half-empty nail strips, crushed soda cups and candy bar wrappers littered the floor. The air tasted of chalk. Men's deep voices jumbled with the thud of hammers and whirr of power tools. Madison surveyed the mix of construction workers: hardhats covering some long hairs; older guys with a bit of roundness in the belly; the big guy in the worn canvas overalls who spit and acted as if he could break a beam in his calloused hands, even with a finger missing.

A young guy noticed her and straightened the 4x6 he carried on one shoulder so it was parallel to the floor. His grimy, once-white T-shirt fit tight over his flat stomach, his hips slim the way only a young man's can be. He strolled in front of her. Madison wasn't dead yet, and her eyes followed, but she still kept her mind focused on Keller as Mr. 4x6 finally left the area.

She crossed the room, and avoided the roughed-in gray electrical conduit evenly spaced in the subfloor. An air compressor with blotches of blue, white and gray paint connected a yellow hose line to a nail gun held by a worker squatting next to an unfinished wall. A hardhat covered most of his hair, but a long black braid ran down the back of his Tartan plaid work shirt. He pulled on the nail gun's trigger, and nailed wood braces around a plastic pipe in the wall.

He set the nail gun down and measured along the wall

with a tape. He barked "9 and 3/8th" to his helper at one of the workbenches. The power saw threw sawdust as it glided through the wood, and the helper flipped the piece to the man.

She stepped around a pile of wood scraps and made her way closer to him. He might be 40, but just. Close to Keller's age. It wouldn't hurt to see if he knew Keller.

The man rose up out of his squat. He was a tall drink of something cool. She liked the look of this one, his long legs filling out dusty jeans. Maybe a runner.

She walked up to him. He set the nail gun down and took off his safety glasses. His face had lines of experience around the outsides of his eyes, but they hadn't found their way down his high cheekbones yet. He ran tanned hands over the stained denim on his thighs and faced her.

"You should be wearing safety glasses in here." His tone was clear, not angry, but his voice dropped at the end. He sounded tired.

"Yes, I'm sorry." She held out her hand. "Madison, Park Service."

"Dodge," he said.

Madison saw the smallest downturn of his mouth, as if she was going to lecture him. She supposed the truth might be the best strategy, since it might be unexpected.

"I suppose you heard about the Keller investigation."

Now the lips moved, tightened, then let loose a sigh. He turned to the younger worker at the saw. "Go ahead, Billy, take a break." The worker shrugged, took a pack of cigarettes out of his shirt pocket and headed off to a group smoking outside the doorway.

"Word spread that someone was poking around. Guess that would be you?"

"Yes."

He snapped a measuring tape from his belt and gauged the distance between the floor and top of one of the pipes.

She moved closer to the wall. "Thought I'd look around, talk to someone who worked with him. Maybe learn a little more about him, about what might have happened."

Dodge took a thick construction pencil out of his shirt pocket, and wrote "16" on a scrap of wood. "He slipped on the rocks, that's what they said."

She nodded. "That's what they said."

He turned and met her eyes. "He was alone, that's what they said." He pulled the tape out and pushed the button of the silver case, and just as quickly released it. The tape clattered back into its case.

"That's what they said." She needed to go easy, but not give him anything. She pulled an empty white bucket over to her, turned it upside down and sat on it. "I hiked up to the cliff where he fell this morning. It's catching up with me. That and too much desk time."

His chin lifted a bit and his shoulders relaxed. "Henry loved that view. He must have climbed up there ten times since we started this project."

Madison put her hands in her lap. "You were friends?"

He nodded. "He had more on his mind than beer and women, unlike the rest of this crew. Sorry if I'm a little frank." He eyed the group of men at the door.

She shook her head. "I used to be a street cop. You won't upset me."

His eyebrows lifted as he leaned over to pick up another piece of wood.

She was sorry for blurting that out, especially when those endless eyes held some promise behind them. Brother, she was out of practice around attractive men. She held up her hands. "I'm not a cop anymore, they just wanted someone with experience looking at Keller's accident. I drew the short straw. Been trying to get away from all that since I left it years ago, but it keeps coming back." She needed to shut up, as she should have done with Mobley.

Dodge moved to the saw, measured 16 inches along the edge of the stud and let the saw glide through the fir.

She put her hands in her pockets. She waited for the noise to fade. "So, Keller. Tell me about him."

Dodge picked up the nail gun. He held the wood against the wall, pulled the trigger, and the nail flew like a bullet into the wood. He moved the gun to the next stud and pressed again. "He was smart, not a dumb ass like half these guys. Loved the old lodge and the lake and the mountains." Dodge stood up and pulled the tape measure out of the case and just held it. "And he was old school about work and doing a job right. We used to talk."

"About what?"

"The usual. How the world was pretty messed up. He wanted his kids to have these kinds of places to come to, unspoiled. He respected the history here."

"Not everyone does?"

"Hell no, what do you think? It's just a nuisance to them. They think all the cultural permits and inspections are a waste of time and money. They spit anywhere, leave garbage all over. Don't take care of their tools. Typical young jerk offs."

"I'm sorry."

Dodge folded his arms across his chest and stared with darkening eyes to a place behind her. She'd seen that far off look before, in the faces of victims' families. She'd let him have his memory for a moment.

"You knew him well. Do you think he fell from that cliff?"

Dodge looked from side to side before staring directly at her. "You know what you're asking?"

"Yes," Madison said.

"I had already made up my mind that I wasn't going to talk to anyone about Keller before you showed up. And don't say I can trust you."

"I suppose there's no keeping our conversation a secret." She observed the blur of pounding and sawing across the room.

"Look, the word went out about your little threesome before you crossed the park boundary. Everybody already knows I'm talking to you."

She followed the outline of his leg to his hip, up the red thread in the plaid of his shirt to his eyes. "Then we might as well make it worth something for Keller. I'm in Room 5. Come see me when you get off."

CHAPTER 12

FROM INSIDE THE lodge, the tape protecting the lodge's windows made six black Xs against the haze of the late evening sun. In the dusty light, the room felt as if it could hold thousands of people. It would one day all magically come together. The workers she passed acted busy, but she caught more than one lifted head out of the corner of her eye. Dodge would get the treatment from some young jerk trying to mark territory when she left. Maybe he'd show up later at her room, maybe not.

She went through the oversized French doors flanking the picture windows as the last bit of light drifted off whitecaps on the lake. She shoved her hands in her pockets and crossed to the line of boulders between the lake and the lodge. The rock she sat on still held a bit of the sun's warmth. Its smooth surface contradicted its violent history. Unlike the cliffs where the glaciers had clawed against the country rock, this mammoth boulder had been ground down as it rolled and rolled along, caught in the glacier's assault, until it stopped when retreat was imminent.

She leaned back. A hawk circled high through the

pine-scented air. Its red tail caught a shaft of fading light as it turned upward. Nice night for a stroll along the lake. Maybe with a tall man, good with his hands. She shook her head. Ridiculous. Sure sign of low blood sugar. Her laugh echoed off a nearby pine.

She breathed in the fresh air and let it out in a long sigh. Back to business. She had to call Roy. She opened her cell phone and scrolled down to his number.

He picked up on the first ring. "Dana, how nice to hear from you again." He hadn't called her Dana before. "Enjoying the great outdoors?"

How the hell did he know? "Not a priority, Roy." She sat up.

"Ah, don't be afraid to waste a day. After this is over, of course." He paused. "But you called me, again…"

Across the lake the mountaintops had enough snow to stay bright while the sun set.

"What do you know about the cavalry?" she asked.

Roy didn't answer right away.

It sounded as if ice slipped in a glass near his phone.

Roy cleared his throat. "Why do you ask?"

Answer a question with a question. "Pertains to the case," she said.

"Do you need, how would you say it, some backup?" A small laugh seemed to catch in Roy's throat. He coughed the rest of it up, then coughed deep.

"Been reading detective novels, Roy?"

A chipmunk skittered across the gravel in front of her and stopped, his eyes glued on her, body shivering. A power saw groaned, then changed pitch behind her and the chipmunk scrambled under the boulder, scattering dirt as it dove to safety.

"There is enough intrigue in Washington for me. Now, what's this vague question about?"

"The button, Roy, in the enlargement you sent, it's First Regiment cavalry. Surely you knew."

"On the contrary. I don't waste my time on such details. We asked *you* to investigate."

Better let that go. Game face on, he couldn't see her sweat over the phone.

"Roy, the park's superintendent says that the ridge where Keller fell had been combed over and over for artifacts. Then the initial investigation team finds what could possibly be a 200-year-old Army button, but doesn't identify it. They disregard it. But Greaves and I, we know what it is. Is this a coincidence? That doesn't pass the smell test."

"I assure you I didn't know the significance," Roy said. "It wouldn't be logical to keep anything from you."

A lone jet's contrail separated into rippled gauze across a jagged peak at the end of the lake. In a few minutes someone might think that it was just a cloud broken by high winds across the sky. What's logical depends on your perspective and the outcome you want.

"I need that button authenticated. Send it and I'll get Greaves to work on it."

"We have competent people."

"No. This investigation stays here." A stiff breeze lifted the smell of grilled meat past her. She turned toward the lights coming from the motel and the general store. Roy wasn't the only one she didn't trust, but she was stuck with her team. Maybe they'd surprise her; she had to take that chance. "One more thing. Send the letters."

"The letters?"

"The very first letter and the last one that the President received."

"What could the first possibly…"

"The first and the last one, about Keller, that's the deal."

"You know I can't send you the originals; I'm not sure I can even send you copies. You don't have that kind of clearance."

"Anything I need, that's what Secretary Meyers said. Whole government at my disposal."

She got up and paced.

"Very well, Dana." Roy's voice lifted as if she had suggested going for ice cream. "You will have hard copies of the letters by tomorrow. Please keep them under your protection at all times. Don't hesitate to call again if you need anything."

"You can count on it."

CHAPTER 13

THE FIRST EVENING star flashed through fast-moving clouds overhead. Madison closed her cell phone. She'd pissed off Roy. Not the first superior she'd done that to. All she had ever wanted to do was make the world, no, just one city, a little bit safer. Interrupt an armed assault in progress. Talk gang wannabes out of taking the wrong path. Clear Imelda's homicide.

Was it asking too much? She'd given it her best shot, accepted that the cottage with the white picket fence wasn't in the cards. Most cops are divorced cops. Most men don't like their wives carrying a gun. She'd almost broken up a marriage herself.

The gravel under her feet slipped a bit as she walked down slope toward the motel and general store. She rolled her shoulders. Nothing was certain but uncertainty. She didn't believe Roy for a second. Neither would Henderson. He was a good judge of character, but she couldn't ask him.

As she got closer to the motel, she flipped open her phone and called Henderson.

When he answered, the nightly news was on in the background.

"I hope you have plans to take Jeannie out to dinner tonight. I could enjoy the food vicariously."

"Dana. Checking on my marriage again?"

"Of course."

"Sorry, but I'm cooking my famous butt-kicking chili tonight," Henderson said. "I've been wondering how you're doing."

"Surviving."

"I wish you would at least fake some sincerity."

"That obvious?"

"Statistics getting you down?"

"Seems I'm not hiding my boredom; I might have stepped on some toes."

"That's not news."

"No, I mean it."

Henderson laughed. "We need a secure line?"

"I should have called you collect from a pay phone in a bar but that wouldn't be right on government time."

"Just your luck the phone'd be wired anyway. What can I do?"

"Nothing really. I was on my way to eat some dead cow with enough grease to end the energy crisis, and I don't know, it just seemed a good time to share it with you."

"Whatever is going on, you can handle it. It's only a few days. And we'll be here when you're done."

Madison's hands felt the approaching night cold. Never let your fingers get too cold or you can't think. Or hold a gun. They told her that at the academy.

"Dana?"

"It's starting to cool off a bit, even for DC. I could use a bowl of your chili about now."

"Well, get yourself a warm one before you have a cold one. If you really piss someone off, I'll take you back."

"Do something for me? Take Jeannie to The Ahwahnee tomorrow. Have the bay scallops with white sauce on their house made pasta. Side arugula salad and that fabulous soy dressing."

"We'll go when you can pay for it. You take care now."

She closed her phone. Henderson was right, she could handle it. She had to follow the leads, listen to her instincts, question everything and everybody. She was trained to do just that. If Keller was murdered she'd figure out who did it and why.

CHAPTER 14

AS MADISON REACHED the motel parking lot, the wind stirred up dust mixed with the scent of pinesap. Greaves came out of his room at the end of the motel at the same time. He looked as if he had just left his shower, hair wet and face flushed. His khakis had been freshly pressed.

"Hey, Chief." Greaves' face wrinkled around his eyes. His shoulder twitched as he adjusted his coat.

"You're looking spotless. Makes a girl feel grubby."

"Dirty is more what I'd like." He winked.

She shook her head. "Stop. I have a gun in my room."

"Not the only one, el Capitan. Lt. Soto ran me through the whole shooting drill, remember? Armed and dangerous, that's what he said."

She took a deep breath. Nothing could be closer to the truth. The whole gun thing, she did it mostly to get Mobley's goat, and it got over blown, at least that's what she thought afterwards, but now she wasn't so sure. She was glad to have her gun on the trail. And Roy wasn't the first superior who had kept things from her or had it in for her, just because she was digging a bit too deep. But he was at a much higher level. Before she never felt as if someone might take her out, not literally. She might need Greaves to cover her back after all.

She started to rub her eyes, but stopped. Grit from the construction site came off on her fingers. "I need a shower; leave any hot water? Meet you for dinner?"

"Mobes and I will see what the 'fresh catch' might be over at the store. I would treat, but I believe it's already ladies' night."

She closed her eyes and shook her head. "We should go over whatever you two learned while I was sweet talking Roy."

A small grove of quaking aspens bordered the circle of grass next to the motel. In the fading light the yellow leaves grew gray as they floated in the wind.

Greaves smiled at her like he was trying to sell her a used car.

"Greaves, you *did* do something in the last few hours?"

"Ten four, absolutely."

Madison nodded to the bartender and worked her way across the room. Ladies' night had failed to bring in many of the gentler sex. She'd been in plenty of taverns where no special draw was needed. She'd seen too many smoked-stained bars where the number of broken veins on your face gave away how many straight shots you'd had. Black and white close-ups of similar faces were considered art by those who never stepped in places like that. What they really said was misery.

She supposed there weren't as many visitors to the park without the lodge being open, mostly day trippers, the kind who bring their own lunch and supplies, the kind the concessionaires hate because they come for the views, not to shop. Construction workers would keep the store in business, part of the deal making for the project. The way lodging and food contracts were doled out by the past few administrations, no money was left to replace the sagging bridges or seasonal workers' quarters slowly giving way to the nature everyone came to see. An invisible Asian conglomerate probably owned this store and supplied the video games.

Greaves and Mobley sat on opposite sides of a booth. Watercolor landscapes by local artists filled the wall behind them depicting the former lodge in every light, available for purchase at the bar.

Madison ran her hand across deep cracks in the red vinyl as she slid onto the bench seat next to Mobley. Mobley smiled. Seemed as if she'd checked her attitude at the door.

Greaves held up a pint half full of dark beer. "The 'Moraine Madness' isn't so bad. Game for one?"

"Just one?" Madison said.

"That's the spirit," he said. "As I was telling our comrade here, no reason we can't save the nation and have a good time simultaneously."

Mobley put her chin down and opened her eyes up wide to look at Greaves. "I don't believe work had exactly come up in the conversation yet."

"Mea culpa cuz I'm jovial."

Mobley held up her hands to give up. She twisted around on the bench and pushed a menu over to Madison. She grabbed her pint and lowered her eyebrows. "No French wine." She glanced at Greaves and lifted her pint slightly.

A ketchup stain covered part of the appetizer section,

so the first listed said "urly fries." The rest was the usual pub fare, jalapeno poppers, onion rings, individual frozen pizzas. The house salad promised fresh tomatoes and hard-boiled eggs.

The special was "locally caught" cutthroat trout, but Madison could have sworn they were about to be listed as an endangered species so she passed. When in the Rockies, it had to be a thick steak.

The waitress was the only other woman in the place. Greaves waved her over. "My boss, the lady here, would like one of these fine pints. Could you bring her one, darling?" He put his hand on her arm.

Her nametag said Becky and she was old enough to be his mother. She lifted his hand by the middle finger and placed it on the table. "Sure sweetie, I'll see if I can bring in another without spilling the foam. Anything else?"

Madison wasn't going to make anyone handling Greaves wait for even a second. "New York steak, rare. Baked potato, with everything."

"Rare'll be bloody." Becky's whole forehead wrinkled. She didn't want anything going back to the kitchen. "But it's your party."

"Perfect." Madison smiled. "And bring him one too, I know he wants it."

Mobley pulled the menu back towards her. "The bison burger under 'House Specialties,' is that free range?"

"Ain't nothin' free about the range anymore, not since the government closed it in 1934." Becky tapped her pencil on a finger.

Mobley squinted up at her, started to say something, then looked at the menu again. "I'll try it, with a salad instead of the fries."

A couple of construction workers leaned on the bar as Becky moved behind them. As one lifted a beer bottle he smiled at Madison and Mobley. Madison wondered if he was the type who took off his wedding ring as soon as he was outside the city limits.

Madison pushed a wet hair behind her ear. It had been a long day. Mobley's flip was perfect. Madison never quite understood how some women could look as if they never left home, all hair and nails and clothes in place.

Becky safely left Madison's pint on the table. The "Moraine Madness" carried a scotch-like smokiness and a hint of chocolate. A nice porter. She would have more than one. "So," she said. "Learn anything from the files?"

Mobley lifted the ends of the fingers in her right hand and stared at her nails, then closed her hand. "Of course."

She was going to make Madison work for it. "I'm all ears."

The cook slapped the steaks on the hot grill and a flash of steam rose into the air behind the bar. Mobley looked past Madison at the empty booth behind them. "I could teach those so-called detectives something about keeping proper files. That would make it easier."

Madison wasn't a detective anymore, but she still wanted to take Mobley's perfectly manicured hand and slip it into some of the butchery she'd seen and see how neat her files would be. "Can we look beyond the coffee splatter and cruller grease?"

Mobley frowned. "It wasn't just that, I would expect that. Everything is disorganized, it makes it impossible to make connections."

"Conspiracy, I knew it." Greaves lifted up from his seat and leaned toward them. "They'll be framing us next."

Madison leaned into Greaves' face. "Let's not jump to any conclusions, Columbo."

Mobley held her lips tight, then released them. "I hate to say it, but he might have a small point. There is big money behind the lodge project. Tracing it is another matter. That's going to take more than a day."

"What do you know?" Madison asked.

"It starts with millions for design, then more for redesign. The actual construction the most, of course. There is one general contractor and any number of subcontractors. The firms with the biggest financial ties have doled out pieces of the work to constituencies all over the map, to get votes."

"It takes more than patriotism to pass appropriations." Madison lifted her glass in toast and took a long, slow sip of her beer. She turned to Mobley. "What's next?"

"I know forensic accountants at DOJ who might be able to help. Without knowing why, of course."

Madison had no doubt Mobley was cool enough to get information without divulging anything.

Becky set three steaming plates and a condiment dish with sour cream, bacon bits, and chives in front of them. "Enjoy," she said.

Mobley shook the ketchup above her burger. "The information about Keller, that surprised me."

Madison waited until Mobley got the ketchup going. "What about him?"

"He was quite the saver. He had no money problems, at least that I could find. A small mortgage, and quite a nest egg."

Madison looked over to the construction workers lining the bar. Most moved around from place to place to work on these large projects, the kind that started and stopped with the economy. Living paycheck to paycheck, not worrying about the future. Keller would have been older, the exception, saving money for his wife and kids.

"Did he have enough to remove finances as a reason to sail off a cliff?"

"Do you have $400,000 in the bank?"

Greaves whistled.

Madison shook her head. She couldn't imagine ever saving that much. "A rich uncle die recently?"

"I didn't get that far." Mobley grabbed the bison burger with both hands and took a small bite. She set the burger down and wiped her mouth with her napkin. Even her lipstick stayed perfect. "But I'll find out."

Madison picked up her knife and slid it through her steak. Wine-red juice ran across her plate and surrounded the aluminum foil cocooning her baked potato. The first bite proved again she could never be a vegetarian.

Greaves chomped with a broad smile across his face, like an anxious kid waiting to be called on for show and tell.

Madison unwrapped her baked potato. "Greaves, pass the sour cream, would you?" His face dropped a little. "All right, tell me about the button."

"Thought you'd never ask," he slid the serving dish from the end of the table over to Madison. "What a day I had! Calling in some favors from historians, and this old friend of mine who is also an archeologist…"

"Greaves …" Mobley tapped a nail on the pine table.

Greaves squinted. "Oh, all right. Stop and smell the proverbial roses would you two? What I found out was the First Regiment has been in on everything. The Lewis and Clark Expedition, the Indian Wars, the whole Manifest

Destiny movement. They chased Chief Joseph, caught him before he got to Canada."

"He should have signed the Treaty with the rest of his people." Mobley pulled the ends of her shirt down as she sat up straighter. "It turned out the same anyway."

"Mobes," Greaves eyes opened wide. "You surprise me. Not so politically correct. The First Regiment wasn't too kind to the Creekakees on the Trail of Tears."

Mobley's face lost its earlier smoothness and tightened. She glared at Greaves as if she could see right through him. She pushed each of her thumbs against her index fingers. Madison watched her slow her breathing, while keeping her gaze on the top of Greaves' head. "Stay in the present, Greaves. The past has nothing to do with me."

Madison sliced another piece of steak. Wherever Mobley was coming from was another mystery.

Roy's map had marks across the United States thicker than the flood of stars in the night sky. They had to determine why. All the jewels of the park system, Yellowstone, her beloved Yosemite, Carlsbad, even obscure parks like Wind Caves were in the tragic mix. And now Grizzly, one of the last protected by Teddy Roosevelt. If some group had been disturbing the peace of the national parks since then, then Mobley's personal feelings and what was behind them didn't matter much.

"Mobley, the past has *everything* to do with this."

After dinner, they decided to meet again at 8 a.m. the next morning. Madison told them she would wait for her credit card receipt and Greaves and Mobley headed back to the motel. Earlier she'd seen Dodge come in, and lean against the end of the long bar back toward the restroom. He was still there in his work clothes, holding a beer, talking to a younger worker. She slid out of the booth and skirted the bar, brushing by the men who acted as if they were going to drink their dinner.

Dodge sipped from his beer and watched her as she passed. She eyed him and raised her eyebrows. He lifted his head as she opened the door that said "Ladies."

She didn't look at him when she returned to the booth. She signed her receipt and made her way toward the front door, turning once to nod at Becky and catch Dodge watching her leave.

Madison untied her shoes and slid them off her feet. She checked behind the padded headboard for her gun. Important old habit, easy to slip into again: always know where your gun is.

It was after midnight and she was poring over some notes Mobley gave her at dinner when someone tapped on the door. She pulled her gun out from behind the headboard and tucked it under her pillow. She peered out the slit in the drapes. Dodge. She slipped the gun back behind the headboard and opened the door.

"Thanks for coming. I wasn't sure you would."

"I'm here for Keller."

"Understood," she said.

Dodge took a step into the room, but his hunched shoulders told her he didn't want to. She bent to take her jacket off the chair near the window. "Have a seat. Sorry it's so cramped."

"I'm not going to be here long enough to sit." Dodge shifted his weight from one foot to the other.

"Suit yourself, but I'd rather not have to crane my neck at you." She pointed to the chair.

Dodge looked around the room, at the file folder on the bed, then back at her. He stretched the fingers in both of his hands, then sat down.

She breathed deep to steady a floating feeling in her head.

She waited. She fixed her eyes on his.

It was her move. "Now, what is it you don't want to tell me?"

CHAPTER 15

THE NEXT MORNING, Madison watched Mobley and Greaves cross the motel parking lot toward the store for breakfast. Mobley's hands were in the pockets of her sweatshirt, her stride straight, as confident as a quarterback. Greaves' long legs seemed disconnected from his big feet. He stopped in front of the store, his head barely missing the elk rack above the door. He pointed to the white porcelain urinal filled with yellow mums on the wall.

Madison shook her head. She needed to make a call before she caught up with them. She flipped open the Keller file and turned the pages to the list of objects found on the cliff where Keller fell. This list, and something Greaves said about keeping track of artifacts, made her think of another list. The list for Imelda. But she wasn't sure, they'd never recognized the small numbered purple piece of paper as being significant.

"Damn, I have to do this." She pulled her cell phone out of her pocket and sat down on the edge of the bed.

The phone rang three times and she almost hung up. She couldn't leave this message on voicemail.

"Detective Hailey."

"Hey, Stan."

"Dana." Hailey said her name slowly, his voice like a flat timeline of the years since she left Denver.

Madison shifted her weight on the bed, heard a slow breath. "How are you?"

"We're expecting in February."

She couldn't help but sigh. He didn't have to blurt it out.

She heard his fingers drumming on the side of his desk, the way they used to when he was on the phone and he'd said too much to a potential suspect.

"I'm sorry," he said. The drumming stopped.

She stared out the motel window at the mosquitoes trying to break through the screen. She knew he was probably holding his hand in a shape of a gun pointed at his temple. His turned-up mouth always looked so good when he did that, knowing he had made a dumb move, said the wrong thing.

"No problem. Ancient history. I'm happy for you both, really." She leaned back against the pine headboard. Men are forgiven and allowed to start over, not women.

"I just hope I don't screw the kid up."

"You'll be great, Stan. Just don't go all gaa-gaa if it's a girl. Frilly crap and all that Barbie doll nonsense."

"Well, that'll be Mary's department," he said.

Mary, stunningly beautiful, perfectly coifed all the time. She knew how to accessorize. Likely had a pink Barbie car when young.

Madison knew this was a bad idea. She should have called somebody else, but no one else would do what she needed done.

Stan took a breath. "So, how are you doing? Keeping those bears at bay in the high Sierra?"

"More like throngs of people who can't behave. No staff and no money, same as the Denver police department. But I love the park. It was a good move." He would never understand how hard it was to leave him. She wasn't sure how to get to the point, so she just said it. "Stan, I want to see Imelda's file."

"Jesus, Dana. I knew this couldn't be a social call. Why go through it all again?"

"It's not for me. I don't care about clearing my name anymore."

"I don't believe that. Why else?"

"I really can't go into it."

"That figures. Call me out of the blue after five years, but can't tell me anything. Nervy as hell."

"I'm sorry. It's not about you either."

"Sure." He drummed the desk again. "I can't send the file to you. I could lose my job. I have other people to think about now."

Madison sat up on the bed. He could go fuck himself. She wanted to say that he should go home to that bimbo of a wife and wait for her to want more money, start harping about him getting a promotion, wanting him home more with the baby. She'd never understand his work the way Madison did. She'd end up divorcing him and get his pension. Madison had never asked him for anything.

She got up off the bed and paced in front of the TV.

"O-kay, Stan. But do I have to say it? You owe me." She was the one run out of town, and he didn't even try to protect her.

"But they'll know I checked the file out, if that matters to you at all."

"That sweet little thing who had the hots for you still working in Records?"

"I don't know who you mean."

"Give me a break."

"Yeah, Brenda's still there."

"Then use your magic on her and keep it unofficial. Just copy the evidence list and I'll let you know where you can fax it. That's all I need. "

"And call you when I have it, before internal affairs takes my balls out of action? Or call you then, too, just for grins?"

"Yes on both counts. But call this cell." She hung up.

Madison lay down on the bed and closed her eyes. It was too early for a drink. The last time she saw Stan he wouldn't look at her, he let her clean out her desk and carry her career in a box to her car alone. His world was falling apart too, he had to protect his job and get his wife Mary back. She didn't blame him, she only wished he could have been more courageous.

Her cell phone rang. "Madison."

"It's Stan." His voice was low. "There's a problem with the file."

"What problem?"

"First, someone put a hold on it, somebody I don't know in the department, so no one can check it out until he says okay. Second, the file's already checked out."

"Checked out?"

"Brenda said it's gone."

"Crap." Madison shook her head.

"You still there?"

"Yeah, I'm just trying to figure out why it would be gone."

"You and me both. Not to mention what Brenda might think now that I asked for it. She wanted to call the contact and tell him I wanted it before I stopped her. I had to put my charm into overdrive."

Madison's head hurt. A hold on the file. But why? Who could want such an old file?

"Stan, please don't tell anyone I called. Brenda won't remember anything but your baby face. Call me if anyone says anything to you."

"Don't worry, Dana. I haven't bucked the system for a while. It's good to stay in practice."

The desk clerk ran out of the motel office and headed toward Madison's room. He carried a large padded envelope in his hand. He peeked in the window, tipped his baseball cap and handed Madison the envelope as she opened the door.

Madison turned the envelope over, looked at both sides. No return address. She opened it and pulled out a thick manila folder held closed with rubber bands. It was Imelda's original file. A yellow note was clipped to the folder.

"*Thought you might want this. Good luck, Roy.*"

CHAPTER 16

ROY. THE BASTARD. How the hell did he know she wanted this file? She was tempted to throw the cheesy table lamp against the wall. Not that it would do any good. She had to stay focused if Roy knew her thoughts before she did herself. She had to snap back into her old detective habits pronto. Go over what you know. Check your information again and again. Think like a killer.

The file exposed more about Roy. Oh, it was coming clear why they picked her. They knew the end of the story already and were waiting for her to get there. Was Keller's death connected to Imelda's? What could possibly... Madison's legs felt drained, the way they did after a marathon, but this time it wasn't fatigue, it was Imelda.

She pulled her copy of the briefing book out of her luggage. She flicked her ranger's hat from the small table to the bed and spread out Roy's map. She didn't want to look anywhere near Denver, hadn't since Roy went over the material in the book. Now she had no choice.

There were the green boundaries of Rocky Mountain

National Park, 50 miles from Denver, where she used to find solace after a tough case.

Her first thought of a new life after Denver, after Stan, had stirred during time she spent among the old growth still left in the park. Hiking along Fall River, she came upon a group from a local Outdoor School watching greenback cutthroat trout spawn. A school counselor corralled a rowdy bunch of sixth graders behind him, and Madison had to smile, as even the hard-core class clowns stopped shoving each other and looked in awe. She wanted to be able to make that happen, give someone a spark of life's magic. Wildlife recovery could save more than fish.

Henderson called it her hatching day when she told him about it. "You just started a bit later than most, you'll make a fine ranger because of it," he had said.

On the map she traced the drive from Denver to Rocky Mountain National Park through the lower elevations of Roosevelt National Forest. The national forest butted up against the national park. She thought Imelda must have been killed there before she was left in Red Rocks Park, closer to Denver. But Madison and Stan and the search team found nothing. After no more clues, they didn't think to look at a higher elevation in the national park.

But there it was, the symbol for a murder on the map next to the Park's identifying script.

The symbol was labeled #53. Madison flipped to the back of the briefing book at the list of numbers found on the map: "#53, Imelda Sampson, 2003, unsolved. Letter delivered October 2003."

She rubbed her temples with the palms of her hands. At that moment she wanted to rip the map to shreds, rip the cartographer who casually placed #53 in the park, not knowing who #53 was. God, she needed a drink.

She had failed Imelda. If it was just a game to the powerful, how should she play it this time? What about Mobley and Greaves? Greaves probably wondered if the package was the button or the letters. And where were the letters? Roy could get her this file at the same time as she was putting two and two together, why not what she asked for?

She had to either tell Mobley and Greaves and trust them, or keep them in the dark as she had about Dodge.

She had to run to clear her mind. She should have told them to meet her at nine.

Madison pulled the evidence list from Imelda's file. Down near the end was a notation: "One (1) purple piece of paper, 1 inch x 3 inches, with the number 4798, see file photo #72." The purple paper had a string running through a hole at one end, similar to a small luggage tag. As she went through the stack of photos, she tried not to look at the pictures of Imelda, lying in an old campsite, near soaring red rocks the same color as the dried blood on her head. She didn't need pictures to see Imelda crumpled in her tiny jean jacket. Her memories of the scene were sharp, they always would be.

She looked back through the file for any recent information. Just a few notes written by another detective who told Imelda's parents every six months that nothing was new. No fresh leads. No one was actively assigned; Denver didn't have a cold case unit.

She needed Greaves to look at the tag and see if it triggered anything. Mobley, well, she had so many contacts she seemed to be ahead of everyone else.

Madison checked her gun again. She stuck it in her holster, and tucked Imelda's file under her arm over it.

Madison nodded to Becky as she pushed open the store's door. Greaves threw his hands above his head, like he was swatting flies. Another smuggler story no doubt. Mobley at least looked amused, if that slightest upturn of her mouth was real.

They hadn't waited for her to eat; she was 30 minutes late.

Madison slid next to Greaves this time, and waited for his hands to calm. Becky filled her cup from the coffee carafe. Madison waved away the menu. "Bacon, eggs up, hash browns. That'll do it."

She put Imelda's file on the table.

"I have something for you to look at." Madison opened the file and slid out the photo of the tag.

"Guess we're on the clock," Greaves said.

"I don't remember this from Keller's file," Mobley said.

"It's from another case that Roy just sent." She wanted to say "sent me," but she caught herself.

Greaves picked up the photo. "Looks like an early collection tag. Nothing I've used; the writing is old-fashioned."

"What's the case?" Mobley said.

"It's from Rocky Mountain National Park, 2003."

"Isn't that outside Denver?" Mobley said.

"Yes."

"Your old stomping grounds, Chief?" Greaves said. "Ghost rearing its proverbial ugly head? Interesting."

She'd have to go over the whole story again for Greaves and in front of Mobley. She would have to suffer Greaves' snide remarks. She did not look at either of them, just looked at the photo. "For some reason, this might be connected to Keller." If only she knew, if only she could have come to the table with her own theory, instead of a hunch, that the tag might be something they could trace back to whoever killed Imelda and Keller.

"I worked on this case," she said. "The victim was found outside the national park, at Red Rocks. Denver Homicide handled it. And the tag, if that's what it is, we never thought it had any significance. It was mixed in with other loose papers we thought were windblown trash around the body."

Mobley turned the photo around to face her. She bent over it and pulled her hair behind her ears. "What about the rest of the file? Can I look at it?"

"I wouldn't recommend it before breakfast." Madison pulled the folder closer to her. "It's brutal, a child."

Mobley's left eyebrow arched.

She could see Mobley had made the connection, that it wasn't just any file, it was Madison's last case.

"Did Roy highlight this photo for you?" Mobley said.

"No, he sent the whole file. I think he knows these cases are somehow connected, but why is he keeping us in the dark? Greaves, when you said something yesterday about labeling artifacts for shipping, I thought, that's what we do with forensic evidence. And this tag jumped into my head. Then Roy sends the file to me, without me asking for it. He's pissing me off."

"What else could be significant?" Mobley leaned back into the bench.

"I don't know. We looked at everything a hundred times. We had the killer in jail. He was primed to spend the rest of his life assuming the position for Bubba. We drank champagne, practiced answering questions for Denver's morning shows. Then somebody sends a letter claiming responsibility. Party over."

Madison could almost see the gears turning in Greaves' head, just as she had that day in the Denver situation room, when every detective on the force, the mayor, the police chief, stared back at her and Stan, the pictures of Imelda on the wall behind them, waiting for her to explain how someone had outsmarted them. They wanted an explanation that held water, so they could give each other high fives, then face the press and public, and keep the killer they were so sure of in jail. She had no victory for them. There was nothing to tell.

Madison opened the file and flipped through her own paperwork. She folded over the bulk of interview transcripts and lab reports and showed them a scanned copy of a letter that someone who claimed to be the killer had delivered to the mayor.

Greaves' eyes widened as he read it. Mobley's finger traced every line.

Greaves pushed his coffee cup away and grabbed his water glass. He took a long drink. "Man, I feel sick."

"He said he planted the evidence, told us details only the killer would know. That's why we believed him. Then he sent messages to the media that made us look like fools. We had to release our perfect suspect."

"The shit hit the fan then." Mobley wasn't scowling this time.

Greaves scanned the letter again, then turned away. "I'll take smugglers any day. They're just greedy. This guy is psycho."

"You know the worst part? We never found out if our suspect really killed her. With this letter, we had reasonable doubt, no way to convict him, even if he confessed. We had to let him go and he disappeared."

"Christ, I'm sorry, Chief," Greaves said. "All the more reason to find out if there's a connection."

Mobley nodded agreement.

Madison exchanged her empty plate for the check as Becky walked by. If they could figure out why Imelda had to die, and who did it, then it would be worth it. That was a mission she could get her arms around. Maybe then she could clear her name, get it out of her mind, move on.

Outside, as the wind calmed, yellow quaking aspen leaves fell from the trees and settled up against the motel's mossy wall. The sky was one the Rockies were famous for, the deepest fall blue in the gaps between the mountains.

The door creaked as two men came into the store. Madison noticed the way they carried themselves, trying to be casual, as if they were hunters trying to get the big one. But their posture and short haircuts said military or FBI. They were hunters, but a different kind. Madison pulled her jacket onto her lap and slipped her hand into her front pocket. Until she knew who they were and what they wanted, she'd trust her instincts.

The two men took off their new caps as they sat down in the booth behind them.

Madison took a napkin from the holder and wrote, "Don't say anything more, let's go" with an arrow pointing to the booth behind them. She moved it slowly in front of Greaves, then in front of Mobley. Mobley was cool, said something inane about the weather. Greaves' eyes went a little too wide, but at least he didn't draw more attention to himself.

Madison dropped cash on the table and they left.

"A bit jumpy there, boss," Greaves said as they crossed the parking lot. "You think they were, like 'G-men?'"

"One thing I know, when two guys march in with backs that straight, they're either local assholes who want a fight, or they've been through some military or police training."

"Better safe than sorry," Greaves said. "I'll start packing my gun."

"Keep the safety on," Madison said.

Mobley shook her head. "Why should we assume anything about them? Maybe they're tourists or hunters."

"You may be right. But there's no hunting in the park and I'm suspicious, especially now, with this file just showing up. I don't trust Roy."

Greaves scowled. "My jury's still out on Roy, too. But I'd like to give him the benefit of the doubt."

"His whole demeanor gave me pause in D.C.," Mobley said. "I would have expected the President to have someone less absurd brief us."

Greaves shook his head.

Mobley might think the whole set-up absurd, but Madison had to take it seriously now, if Imelda was just a pawn in someone's game.

Madison looked over her shoulder. The two men were still in the booth, chatting up Becky. She could have sworn one of them looked her way. If he did, he was quick.

They'd have to split up in a minute to go into their rooms. Greaves was already taking out his key when she touched his arm. Those guys could easily find them, but she wanted them to work for it.

"Listen, indulge my paranoia. Let's not show these guys which rooms are ours quite yet. Follow me."

They continued past the last motel room, through the circle of grass under the aspens. Behind the building the forest quickly closed in and the trail to Maiden Falls and Upper Falls began. Madison led them toward the trail and within minutes they were out of sight of the store.

The wide trail wound through patches of scorched trees, spindly against the backdrop of an area of pines unaffected by fire. As the lodge burned, the inferno tossed blackened pieces of history into the air and forest beyond. No one could save the lodge, but the Grizzly Hot Shots kept the fire from destroying the other commercial buildings and most of the surrounding forest.

Through breaks in the trees, they could see how the layers in the towering rocks had turned on themselves. Pushing and pulling, the earth's pressure had contorted the strongest bonds into folds, the sediments curved but not broken.

Madison held back an overhanging branch and let the others pass. The trail to the first falls was flat and wide and smooth. She looked behind them on the trail.

They skirted a rock outcrop and falling water roared ahead. Maiden Falls tumbled over a miniature of the larger folds in the distance, the gray and green layers forming stair steps to momentarily stop the flow, then release it as it gathered over the lip. The last water of autumn pounded into the pool at the base of the falls and misted the air.

Greaves stopped to sit on a boulder near the water.

"Boss, can I ask you a question? Did you leave the force after this case?"

Madison took a breath.

Mobley sat against a pine, checked out the pool, said nothing.

"We, I, blew that investigation, and I planned never to investigate another homicide."

"No wonder you didn't want to jump into this." Greaves pulled his knee toward his chest with his hands and stretched. He looked off toward the falls. If he had known her history before, he hid it well.

They sat in silence while water slipped over the rocks.

Pine needles on the trail dampened the sound, but in a minute, a figure appeared farther up the trail. It was Dodge.

Madison hadn't told them about her meeting with Dodge. He'd told her what kind of man Keller was, and in the process she'd learned the same about Dodge. She didn't want Mobley talking to him, pissing him off like just about everyone she'd come across when Madison was around. Dodge was too good an opportunity to waste. And that wasn't the whole of it. Maybe she wasn't sure what else she wanted.

She put Imelda's file under her jacket and kept her face as blank as she could, to let him know she wasn't going to say anything. He slowed his pace before he got to them. She didn't want him to stop, didn't want to talk with him here, in front of the others.

He stopped right next to her. His chest rose and fell under his loose T-shirt.

"Ranger," he nodded his head to her, then wiped a bead of sweat off his brow as he looked at Mobley. "There's a tree down about two miles up this trail. Couldn't quite move it out of the way." The creases at the corners of his eyes deepened slightly.

Madison touched the rim of her hat. She'd always hated the cut of her uniform; tailors couldn't make a woman in it look anything but sexless, same with police uniforms. But right now, it served a purpose.

"Thanks, I'll get it taken care of. It looks like a good trail for a long run, other than the tree." Why say something so dumb?

"Especially just before sunset, with the views of the upper falls and lake. Might do it again tonight, if the weather holds." He nodded and ran toward the motel.

She'd get her run in after all tonight, regardless of developments. Maybe he had more to tell her. Maybe he only wanted a running partner. Either way, she'd find out.

CHAPTER 17

Rural Pennsylvania
September 17, 1901

THE TWO BLACK-DRAPED locomotives of McKinley's funeral train bumped back and forth as they slowly pulled the cars out of yet another station. McKinley lay in the final Pullman car, his flower-covered casket visible through the floor to ceiling windows.

Roosevelt sank into his black leather seat as the transformed Pennsylvania countryside rolled by. What was once lush old growth forest of white pines was now a sea of stumps, like fallen soldiers left on the battlefield. Nothing grew on the scarred land. This kind of damage was always off limits as a topic when Roosevelt talked to industrialists as Vice President. But at this moment, with his new role before him, Roosevelt had renewed hope of making these men listen.

On either side of the railroad tracks, scattered loggers working where there were still a few trees put down their saws, took off their hats and bowed their heads as McKinley's railcar passed. Roosevelt had worked with men like these on his ranch and knew they were the ones that kept the country going. They kept the industrialists, including the owner of this very rail line, wealthy, and able to avoid this violated landscape. Roosevelt must speak for these men too, now that he had been given the chance.

The last remnants of recent rains flowed through fresh gullies on the barren soil. Roosevelt hated the short-sightedness of this resource game, and he and others were starting to plant the word "conservation" into public discourse. More than once in his life a swift hike through towering trees had humbled him and healed his despair. He wanted great woods left so his children might find the same comfort.

The train slowed as it approached another small town. He closed the black curtains against the rows of people lining the depot platform. Rushing out and shaking hands was what he wanted to do, but he would wait, for this was not his time, it was McKinley's. The nation needed to grieve, and witness their new president as solid and calm. In the meanwhile, he would make his plans.

CHAPTER 18

THREE STORIES UP workers leaned against steel scaffolding and stapled building wrap over exposed plywood on the lodge.

Madison knew she should go in and talk to a few more workers about Keller. It would look better for Dodge if she did, wouldn't look as if she singled him out. She could ask them the same questions, make sure what she heard from Dodge was the whole story. She used to be good at getting information out of people, playing the good cop to Stan's bad cop, switching roles for the hard core cons used to dominating their women, taking them by surprise in the interrogation room.

But it was different here, no partner, Mobley not the type to talk to these guys; Greaves better suited to research. She was on her own.

The scale of activity on the lodge couldn't push that image of Imelda out of her head, Imelda's tight pale fist lying against the remains of an old campsite, bits of charcoal and unburned scraps of pine bark in her skin. Why, years later, did that purple tag creep into her mind? Why had she and Stan missed it?

She knew why. They had thought they'd been so discreet, thought no one in Homicide would figure out what was going on between them.

No wonder they overlooked something. No wonder the real murderer doubled their investigation back on itself and squeezed them as tight as the folds in the Rockies.

She would not make the same mistake again.

She rounded the corner of the lodge. Superintendent Corrigan stood at the back waving his hands to a group of rangers. Wrinkles crossed his forehead. The ranger next to him shifted from one foot to the other, shuffling and reshuffling papers in his hands.

Corrigan turned and his staff scattered in different directions. A man Madison figured for the head construction manager came up to Corrigan. His khakis and flannel shirt were clean, and his yellow hard hat shined. He tucked a set of plans under one arm. Corrigan motioned to one corner of the large room inside the doorway, then shrugged his shoulders. They shook hands, the manager never smiling.

When Corrigan turned and stormed toward the cyclone fence, Madison approached him.

He pulled his hat onto his head. "Not the best time."

"Some emergency brewing?" Madison walked alongside him.

"If you call another visit from Senator Brumley an emergency, then yes. It's almost as bad as hosting the President. The construction crews are fighting the calendar as it is, we don't need a reelection sideshow."

"What's the official reason?"

"Says he just wants to check progress. Christ, he was here last month. He want miracles from these guys? Now they have to stop work and clean up as if their mother-in-law's coming."

"When politicians come to Yosemite to get votes, it screws the whole week."

Corrigan shook his head. "Listen, you folks about done here? I got enough going on. We need to put that accident to bed."

Madison stopped in front of Corrigan, physically slowing him down. His eyes were inflamed.

"Superintendent, with all due respect, we've barely scratched the surface. It may be an inconvenience to you, but if this was an accident, no one needs to worry about us."

His arms rested against his sides. He looked off to the right, down the road that led in and out of the park, then back to Madison. "Sorry, but Brumley will be here any moment."

Senator Brumley had Corrigan worried. She'd like a good look at the senator, to take his measure. Maybe Brumley knew about the Keller investigation; maybe that's why Corrigan looked as if he'd been up all night. Brumley was on the powerful Senate Energy and Natural Resources Committee in charge of park operations and expenditures, maybe he was also on the national security committee. He'd have clearance, have a need-to-know, if anyone outside the Executive Branch's loyal staff knew anything. If he didn't know, it wouldn't be the first time a Senator didn't have access to information.

"Good luck," Madison said.

Corrigan's shoulders lifted; he took a deep breath and headed toward his office.

Madison saw a slight slouch as he moved quickly across the gravel. What would Henderson do in his shoes? Swear a lot. Send somebody lower on the totem pole to be tour guide, feigning some family emergency. Then show up as the political caravan left the park, to say what a competent staff he has and do come again, anytime. At least he would buy the beer after.

Maybe the guys in the store at breakfast were advance men for the Senator's visit. That would make sense. Maybe they weren't interested in them at all. Just maybe. Until she was sure, she'd stay armed.

CHAPTER 19

WITH THE WORKERS too busy to interview, Madison wandered by the lake. Two elderly tourists near her nodded their heads in unison, then smiled at her. She tipped her ranger's hat, wanting to trade places with them as they made their way back to the motel, the woman lifting up the man's collar against the wind.

The sun was as high as it could get in the fall, listing to the south as if its rays couldn't make it over the rugged country. Too weak to burn, strong enough to cut the edge off the chill in the wind. A gift.

She sat at a far picnic table under tall pines and pulled the official Grizzly National Park map from her pocket. The big map was the kind with shaded relief that she loved as a kid. If she squinted the map was in 3-D. The buff colored shades of the prairie changed to dark sage and forest green on the ridge tops. She'd spent a lifetime poring over maps, mastering the elusive folding, tracing the paths of rivers and streams. Now with almost every inch of the planet covered by digital satellite images, she could go on-line and see every detail. But she liked the feel of paper under her hand.

Madison traced the route from the lodge to Beargrass Mountain. Only one lonely two-lane paved road snaked through the opposing terrains of the park, the rows of mountains stacked one on top of another, and the sweeping openness of the prairie.

The front of this year's version of the map showed the outline of the old lodge in brown, with the footprint of the new lodge and outbuildings superimposed in red. Even at this scale, the difference was clear. There would be a larger main lodge, more parking, and a separate cultural center for the local tribes to house their artifacts. The text said all construction would be done in the style of the original lodge, in keeping with the historic architecture. A banner along one side of the map gave a slogan: *A disastrous fire restores cultures lost.* Even the map had the political spin required to get the money to do good.

She flipped the map over. Madison hoped it would give her insight into why the President and his staff thought there was some tribal connection to Keller.

Madison read through the short prehistory section. Many tribes wandered through the region, hunting bison, elk and bear, using the mountains to escape each other before using them to escape the white man. On the eastern edge of the park, in the open prairie, the Kowaho fought the U.S. Army for the last time, when the military massacred women and children in a mistaken attack on a friendly village. The blurb didn't dwell on the Army's atrocities; people at national parks are on vacation after all.

The recent history section didn't provide much: the first white man to see the lake was named, but his native guide's name was lost; Teddy Roosevelt's creation of the national park for the American people led to visits by millions who treasured it each year.

Around the edge of the map colored photos touted the local flora and fauna, some extinct everywhere else. The grizzlies were increasing in number, thanks to the park's protections. And soaring over the majestic Vista Lake, a golden eagle, with a western cutthroat trout in its talons, was finally making a comeback.

There were eagle feathers found where Keller fell. Many tribes revered the eagle, but Madison knew that finding one might not mean much because there was an eagle nest close. She could probably find more feathers on any nearby cliff, including the one with Wind Woman.

Wind Woman. Too bad she didn't have a video camera behind those eyes. Petroglyphs didn't provide interviews. Any link might be no more than a coincidence. The Park Service hadn't put a sign about the carving on the trail, possibly to preserve it from vandals. Madison hadn't noticed it until she was making her way back to the trail.

The sun's warmth on her back faded. Two shadows reached out beyond hers toward the lake and grew longer. She took one leg out from under the table, turned and straddled the bench.

The faces were hidden in their own shade, but Greaves' out-turned foot gave him away.

He grinned like a kid wired on sugar, hair awry in the wind, wool jacket buttoned crooked. Madison was ready to grab him if he overshot the picnic table. Mobley followed behind him, arms tense, ready in case he stopped abruptly.

"You should leave your cell phone on." Mobley slid by Greaves, stood at the end of the bench. "We've been trying to find you for an hour."

"Sorry. Senator Brumley is coming to the lodge

and Corrigan is panicked. I couldn't talk to any workers. What's up?"

Greaves lifted his long legs over the opposite bench and leaned across the map. "You're not going to believe this, Chief."

Madison tilted away from the top of the table. If Greaves leaned any farther, he might land in her lap. "Believe what?"

"Remember a couple years ago somebody at Harvard opened up a box in the back of the Peabody Museum and found a bear-claw necklace?" Greaves nodded his head and his hair rearranged itself.

He waited for her to remember. She looked away from Greaves, caught Mobley's lips turning down.

Madison took a deep breath. "What are you talking about?"

"Now don't give me that look, it made the national news. They found a bear-claw necklace, an old one, of course it would be old. For god's sake, somebody almost threw it out."

He stopped, but his mouth stayed open. He wanted them hanging on his every word. An osprey squealed in the distance as Madison pulled her coat around her.

"Okay, Greaves, I'll bite. What does this have to do with us?"

"Turns out the necklace was from the Lewis and Clark Expedition." Greaves came close to clapping his hands, then there was that smile again.

"Really?" Madison thought she remembered that news report and Henderson making some reference to Easterners thinking the country stopped at the Mississippi. "I remember something about that. I still don't know how it relates to us. Don't make me guess." Madison put her hands on the map.

"Well, contrary to the opinion of some, you appear to have good instincts. That purple tag, the one you remembered from that young girl's file, isn't just a luggage tag someone lost at Denver International. That little tag could be related to the necklace." Greaves leaned back.

"What the hell are you saying? Mobley, you got this?"

"Hardly." Mobley couldn't be more unmoved. She tried to flick an errant leaf off her boot. "He dragged me off the computer to find you. I know nothing about a necklace."

"The necklace had a purple tag on it," Greaves said. "Just like yours from Denver, from that girl's file."

"A museum tag, near Imelda?"

"No, no, not a museum tag."

He was going to wait for her to beg. He was enjoying figuring this out ahead of her and Mobley way too much. If he worked for her under any other circumstance, she'd think about slamming him against a wall.

"I give, Greaves, the tag is an evidence tag. The necklace was tagged, not by the museum."

"Exactly, but it's not an evidence tag, not in your sense. More like an artifact tag. Filled out in the field, by the person who collected it."

Mobley sat down next to Greaves and grabbed his arm. "You *are not* saying the tags originated from the same place."

"Oh, but I am, Mobes. Same type of tag, same handwriting. Bingo, the country's greatest road trip across the infamous Louisiana Purchase."

"Please." Mobley waved him off.

Madison shook her head. "Lewis and Clark? That makes no sense." Recommended or not to the President, Greaves now seemed capable of a hoax. Madison couldn't get her brain around it. One look at Mobley's rolling eyes and it was clear she shared the thought.

"Is this just your speculation or do you have some kind of proof?" Mobley held her palms open.

"I'm a professional." Greaves pulled a folded stack of printed web pages from his coat pocket. "Look for yourself." His hands flattened out the stack on top of the map.

There was the necklace, the museum director holding it in his white gloves, a small tag at one end, possibly written in the hand of someone on the most famous expedition in the United States. The mythic opening of the West, changing the landscape and peoples forever. The similarity to the tag found near Imelda hurt the top of her stomach. She rubbed her side.

"You're saying the purple tag is old enough to be from the Expedition? Written on by someone on the Expedition? How could that be, and better yet, Greaves, what could this possibly have to do with Imelda?"

"That's the 200-year-old question."

Madison moved the web pages off the map. Maybe the answer was on the map, somewhere between the folds.

The breeze shifted and pushed ripples across the lake from the north, their crests lightening with the sun, then plunging into deep blue. Over and over the light exposed the water, up and down, a rhythm so familiar. The same water, different angles.

CHAPTER 20

IN ONE CORNER of the map an inset showed the park in relation to the region around it. National forest bounded the park on three sides, with part of the Kowaho Reservation to the east. Beyond the reservation open grasslands transitioned into private wheat farms. The Missouri River bent in a half circle from the mountains through the prairie then flowed toward the country's breadbasket.

This small map traced how Lewis and Clark followed the Missouri, but never made it north to land that would become the manmade boundary of Grizzly National Park.

"Look," Madison said. "Lewis and Clark didn't make it this far north. If we have a connection to Keller, it's not jumping out at me."

"Jump being the operative word, Chief," Greaves said.

"That's right," Mobley shook her head. "We have no proof that Keller didn't jump, trip, or lose his balance. We don't know it was murder. This guy was experienced in the mountains and survived 20 years around construction sites. But anybody can get careless, doesn't mean it's murder."

Dodge had told Madison he truly believed Keller had

been killed, but Madison questioned Dodge's judgment. Nobody wants to believe a smart friend can do something stupid, maybe Dodge let grief blur his thinking.

"I'm not convinced either, but I know one thing for sure, Imelda's death was clearly murder. And if there is a link here, we have to follow it." Madison needed to find out why Imelda was dumped outside the national park and at the same time, why Roy and his underlings knew that when Madison didn't.

"Greaves, did that damn button ever get here?"

"Thought you'd never ask." Greaves pulled a plastic bag with a shiny button from his coat pocket. "Arrived about two hours ago. Took a quick look at it, and I believe it's an original. Made about 1800, just as we thought." He raised his eyebrows. He held up the plastic bag and the button caught the light.

"You positive?" Mobley's eyebrows mirrored Greaves'.

"No, I'm not saying definitively it is. I can't really know that, but the markings are accurate, the material and quality of the work appear to be from the right time. It's the kind of button that officers like Lewis and Clark had on their uniforms. Not that it just popped off; I believe they gave them away to the locals on the return trip when they ran out of beads. So, if this button is real and is one of theirs, I'd say we made a major find. But then again, to be clear, these kinds of buttons were used for years after their trip, as government surplus through the Civil War."

"How do you know that? I thought you specialized in Pre-Columbian fertility dolls," Mobley said.

"Hey, now, I hiked a bit of Lolo Pass one summer, traced Lewis and Clark's route. And Sacagawea, well…I'm quite the multi-faceted person if you care to know."

Mobley shook her head. "It can't be theirs, we need to rule it out."

Madison smiled. "It's not as if we have a lab here. We can't trace everything in an hour."

Greaves laid the bag with the button on the table. "Exactly, my dear Captain. I wouldn't have thought of it if it hadn't been for the tag. If the paper on the tag is right, if it isn't some cruel, sick reproduction, then I would say it has to be from the Lewis and Clark Expedition. And these two things together, how much do you believe in coincidence?"

Mobley scowled. "Why didn't someone find this out before? Seems they dropped the ball."

Madison looked Mobley in the eye. "Not a lot of time spent on Lewis and Clark artifacts at the Police Academy, even Quantico."

Mobley pushed her shoulders back and flattened the front of her jacket with her hand. "So this is a bit too complicated for most."

She could be such a bitch. Madison thought about the commendations she had received before the Imelda case, the list of cleared cases. She'd used forensic techniques, all that Denver could afford, to put people away and give victim's families some sense of justice. Not as immediate as pulling a drowning kid out of the water, but she was proud. Mobley was doing everything to make her feel stupid. It was true, she and Stan hadn't given the tag a second thought. They were looking for DNA, a cigarette butt, something. They missed the handwriting on the tag, or worse she couldn't remember them thinking about it at all. By the time the case was blown apart everything happened so fast, she was removed from the investigation and had to defend herself.

That damn Mobley was right, this was complicated.

But she wasn't about to let a DOJ lawyer think she couldn't solve it. She let the remark float out over the lake.

A pinecone slipped from the branch above the table and hit Mobley's shoulder. "Damn it." She brushed it off the table.

"Hey, it's just a pinecone, Mobley. Your jacket remains pristine. Somebody's a little…bit…tense." Greaves gave her a big smile.

Pine boughs strained together as the wind brushed through them.

Mobley took a deep breath and closed her eyes at the same time, then rubbed her forehead. "You just don't get it do you? I thought you might be more sensitive, being an archeologist, but then your field hasn't done Indians any favors in the recent past, Kennewick Man and all."

The grin that shaped Greaves' face fell and his head moved back as if Mobley had struck him.

Mobley stood up. "Lewis and Clark, your 'greatest road trip,'—flip to the other side of the Jeffersonian coins they gave the Indian chiefs. Trinkets for the savages. If you spent as much time and money protecting older, more valuable artifacts and the people who revere them, it would make more sense."

"Hold on." Greaves held up his hands, then grabbed the pages trying to fly off the table. "You can't call me insensitive and just walk away. Like it or not, explain that remark."

Mobley shoved her hands in her pockets. "Are you so smitten with these two icons that you need an explanation? Undaunted courage, my ass. More likely freezing to death without the help they got from the Indians. Why be enamored of people who brought the end of a world, not the beginning? Don't either of you know anything?"

"Whoa, slow down before you drag me into this." Madison wasn't about to take any of the evils of the last two centuries on her head.

"But you *are* in this. The President says tribes are involved and you don't blink an eye. Accept it, as if it's truth. And these *clues* as you quaintly call them, don't you think they may be leading us to just the conclusion the President wants? Unbelievable."

"Okay, you're right." Madison knew better than to tell her to calm down. Better to go ahead and agree with her. "We're insensitive morons, so sit down and help us figure this out."

Mobley's eyes moved left and right, as if checking off a long list of arguments ready to prove her point, as if she were unaccustomed to anyone agreeing with her. She tucked the bottom of her coat under her and sat next to Greaves.

Whitecaps forming on the lake sparkled as a bullet tore into the bark of a pine tree just behind Mobley's head.

CHAPTER 21

Washington, D.C.

October 1901

PRESIDENT TEDDY ROOSEVELT hiked out of Rock Creek Park, flanked by two Secret Service operatives. His Secretary of the Interior, Ethan Hitchcock, waited for him at the trailhead connecting the park with the lock at the start of the C&O canal. Since McKinley's death, Secret Service officers had been his constant companions. It gave the American people some sense of security.

Regardless of the concern, Roosevelt wasn't about to let so-called anarchists keep him from his daily exercise. He needed to get away from the White House and get close to the working classes, men who did real work, like the cowboys in the Badlands. He loved politics, but the personalities tired him. Hitchcock at least shared his passion for conservation of what was left of the country's resources.

The canal was busy, with mule-led barges winding their way along the towpath. As Roosevelt approached, Hitchcock ran his hand over his gray mustache.

"Mr. President." Hitchcock's slight drawl had Alabama

roots. He took an envelope from inside his jacket pocket. "This just arrived."

"President Roosevelt" was written on the envelope by a practiced hand. The letter inside had three lines in the same script:

> McKinley tried to exterminate us.
> He failed to meet our demands.
> Now it is up to you.

Roosevelt turned the letter over, looking for something more. The back was blank.

"If they think I will be intimidated by this, they are mistaken." Roosevelt's jaw came up, and his voice rose the way it did when he tried to gain the floor from another politician. He walked faster along the canal, striding toward a mule coming the other direction. The eyes of the small boy controlling the mule grew large.

The Secret Service officers smiled at the boy as they ran around him to catch up with the President.

Wind drifted up from the Potomac and Hitchcock covered his balding head with a hat.

"What have you learned about this?" Roosevelt took a short step and turned right into the wind.

"Mr. President," Hitchcock said. "Whoever wrote this letter also wrote the others, at least that is what we believe. The others, as we presented in the cabinet meeting, related to what is going on in the West. None appeared to directly threaten President McKinley. We believed he was safe from this group. We always assumed that specific tribes were behind certain killings, but the killings didn't target politicians. We restructured government bureaus directly for their benefit. We thought we were making progress."

"Obviously, we are mistaken." Roosevelt's voice drifted

with the wind. He leaned closer to Hitchcock. "They know I share many of their views, but not assassination!" Roosevelt pushed the letter toward Hitchcock. "Find them."

Hitchcock retreated from Roosevelt's reddening face. "Yes, Mr. President."

Roosevelt continued up the canal, the Secret Service officers scanning the landscape around him.

CHAPTER 22

MADISON SLID DOWN next to the bench and pulled her gun out of her holster.

Mobley had the wide eyes of those unacquainted with gunfire. Greaves shoved her into the dirt.

"Hey!" Mobley whipped her head around.

"Stay down, and shut up," Madison said. She took the safety off her gun and moved to the end of the picnic table. "Get behind the table. Now."

The web pages drifted toward the lake. "Crap," Greaves said.

"Forget that stuff," Madison said. "Do you have the button?"

"In my pocket," Greaves said.

"Then stay down." Right now she wished her partners were cops using hand signals and knowing nods. But these two she would have to protect.

Madison scanned the area for any sign of sun shining off steel. To the east of the lodge the slope climbed about 1,000 feet to the top of Mt. Badger. A trail along the face of the mountain snaked through rock outcroppings. Plenty of places to hide. A high-powered rifle could reach them from there.

Near the lodge a shooter could stand behind equipment, stacks of construction materials, piled rocks, many places out of view. But it was risky. Too many people around. But exposed pipe, steel beams, sun bouncing off windows would obscure something unusual.

Madison held her gun ready. "Anybody see anything?"

"Nothing," Mobley said.

Greaves kneeled and put his arms and head on the top of the picnic table. "Binoculars would help."

"Yep, and a very large rock to hide behind. I'm thinking a rifle either somewhere on the construction site or up on a cliff behind the lodge. "

"Maybe Brumley's the target." Mobley squatted next to Greaves. She breathed fast and her eyes scanned back and forth. A gray jay swooped over the table to a nearby branch and she ducked. "Jesus!"

Greaves looked Madison directly in the eye. "What should we do?"

Madison's heart pounded in her head. Adrenaline and fear a powerful mix. Made for bad decisions. She could take off herself, try to draw fire and see if the shot was meant for them, or try to get them all back to the motel in one piece. But moving from a safe place too soon could mean a quick end. So could waiting behind a picnic table with rotting wood for protection.

Thick clouds skimmed over the mountains. In a few minutes, the sun would slip behind them. They were about 50 yards from the main road that went down to the motel. A roadcut sliced through the terminal moraine. It provided a much better place to wait until someone somewhere issued an all clear. If there wasn't another shot, maybe the shooter was gone or captured. If there was another shot, then, well, she didn't want to go there. At least Mobley and Greaves were in good shape. It would take them a couple seconds to get to the roadcut. A couple seconds.

Madison turned from Mobley to Greaves. "This table is no protection. We're out of sight maybe, but vulnerable. That roadcut could hide us from view." Madison pointed down the road. "It's a short run. But if the shooter's smart, he knows the layout, knows it's the best place for us to go. We can hope maybe a U.S. Senator is the target–though I don't like the way that sounds. If we want to chance it, we all go together. If not, we sit and wait until someone comes or we know it's safe."

"You recommend going?" Mobley said.

"If it were just me, I'd go. But I can't make you take the risk. It may have been an accident, we may be safe. Or the shooter may be waiting for us to move."

"For once, I wish I was short." Greaves tried a half smile. "I'm for getting away from here."

Madison studied Mobley. She wanted to say that the bullet came closest to Mobley, that at the last minute her sitting down saved her life, so she might have the most to lose. Why she might be the target was too much to think about now. She was a real piece of work, but it takes passion or greed, a real good reason to kill another person in cold blood. She doubted that anyone singled her out.

Mobley took a deep breath. "I want another chance to land a cutthroat. Let's go."

Madison took a last look at the terrain to the roadcut: exposed rocks and gravel interspersed with a compacted layer of soil. Not too steep or slippery if you're thinking straight.

"On my count—you run, head down. I'll try to stay between you and the line of fire." Madison buttoned up her jacket. "Don't stop for anything. Understand?"

Mobley and Greaves nodded.

"I mean anything!" Madison said. The sun slid behind the clouds and the light flattened. They'd be harder to see from upslope. Madison made herself breathe as she scanned the landscape. Fear could sap the air right out of the most-tuned muscles, but there was no time like the present.

"Go!"

The gray jay flew up from a pine branch with a loud *pwee-ah* as a wind gust lifted it toward the lake.

CHAPTER 23

MADISON SIDESTEPPED IN a half crouch in front of them, her gun out, pointed up. Greaves grabbed Mobley around the waist and pushed her straight ahead.

Mobley's boot caught on the raised lip of a buried boulder, but Greaves carried her right out of her fall. They rounded the edge of the bank, and their feet slid on the road's loose gravel. Greaves and Mobley leaned against the rough surface.

"Everybody okay?" Madison said.

"Fine," Greaves said.

Mobley nodded as she breathed deep. She looked at Greaves. "Thanks."

"Old football move," Greaves said. "Get the quarterback off his feet, you've got him pushed back another 5 yards."

"Didn't have you pegged for football," Madison rested her gun on her thigh.

"So much you have to learn about me, Captain. Though I like a little mystery."

That was an understatement. Greaves was much too

thin for a linebacker, unless he had lost a lot of weight. He had the thick head for it, but not the thick neck. Madison would have to check the briefing book again.

"Just stay down." Madison scrambled up the side of the bank, sending dirt and gravel onto the road. At the top, she looked through tufts of dried grass to the east. Clouds thickened across the sun, and colors muted together. Two rangers came out of the Superintendent's office and ran up to the lodge.

The sound of tires made Madison turn around. Two Park Service SUVs tore up the road from the general store toward them. The tires on the first car skidded as it pulled up next to Mobley and Greaves. Madison slipped her gun back into her pocket and slid down the bank. She went over to the SUV.

A park ranger leaned out of the car window. His nametag said Pennella. The radio scratched in the background.

Madison flashed her government badge.

Pennella pushed his wire-rimmed glasses up on his nose and scanned her badge and face. He gave Greaves and Mobley the once-over.

"They're feds too," Madison said. "Corrigan knows us, call him if you need to. What's going on?"

He hesitated.

"We just had a shot fired over our heads, down by the lake," Madison said. She didn't have time to wait for him to trust her. "What do you know about this?"

"People heard two shots. One came damn close to Senator Brumley," he said.

"Anyone in custody?" Madison said.

"Not yet. We've got helicopters on their way to search the area."

He might be park police, but he seemed inexperienced to Madison. "These two, they're not Park Service, could your partner take them to the motel? I'll go up to the lodge with you and see how I can help."

Before he could answer, Madison nudged Greaves toward the second car. "Keep your heads down and work on that problem we discussed."

Pennella radioed the second car, said a few words about civilians and nodded back at her.

Mobley put a red nail up to her mouth. Her eyes left Madison's face and she looked at Greaves and back again. She started to say something, but no words came out.

Greaves put his hand on Mobley's back. "Sure, Chief, we'll get on it." He walked her down to the second vehicle.

Madison was glad Greaves had a cool head. Mobley might have been in shock. Having a bullet take the flip out of your hair was a whole lot different than facing another lawyer's opening salvo in a courtroom.

Madison slid into the vehicle next to Pennella. The thick leather strap over his revolver was unsnapped on his hip. He gave her a quick look, then gravel flew on either side of the road as he gunned the engine and drove toward the lodge.

CHAPTER 24

PENNELLA PULLED AROUND the back of the lodge next to two black SUVs with government plates. One of the men Madison had seen that morning at the store was getting out of another SUV, this time not dressed like a hunter, but in a suit. Madison scanned the area to the east and walked into the lodge, keeping the stack of wood planks, shrink-wrapped circuit boards, and other building materials in front of her as much as possible.

A small group of construction workers smoked in one corner of the grand foyer in front of a No Smoking sign, a few more leaned against the wall.

"Where's Corrigan?" Madison said to a ranger she recognized from Corrigan's office.

"In the basement, with the Senator." She pointed to the partially finished steps along the west wall.

Madison nodded thanks and hurried over to the stairway. The finished lodge would have a grand staircase to the second floor and veranda, even grander than the original, but there were only temporary, roughed-in wooden stairs for the workers to use to get to the basement. The sawdust-covered steps flexed as she ran down.

At the bottom a bank of steel electrical boxes filled the northern wall. The basement had no insulation or sheetrock installed yet and pipes and wires ran up and through the stud walls. There was no time to clean up before the Senator's arrival and bits of electrical wire wrapped in insulation, plastic pipe, sawed off wood blocks, empty soda cans and old newspapers littered the floor.

A large group of uniforms and suits filled the other end of the room. A few expletives and other bits of agitated conversation bounced from wall to wall. Everyone had a cell phone to an ear, except for the Senator. He stood next to a green plastic patio chair set in the middle of the room. Madison knew him well enough from the nightly news and newspaper photos, even from the back she could tell it was him. His shoulders moved up and down and she heard a laugh. She moved halfway across the room and the Senator nodded as he offered his hand to someone. One more step and Madison saw who it was: Dodge. He and the Senator were face-to-face, and shook hands. The Senator put his left hand on Dodge's upper arm. Their easy body language said they knew each other.

Dodge had appeared anything but connected, especially with someone like the Senator. She wanted to think he must have been near the Senator when they heard a shot, why else the apparent friendliness. Dodge seemed on her level, hard-working, not bonded to anyone in the mover and shaker class. That could change things between them, not that there was a them.

The Senator dropped his hand and Dodge stepped toward an adjacent room.

"Madison!" Corrigan tapped her arm. He looked even worse than the last time they spoke. They could name a new national park for the deep wrinkles around his eyes. "What are you doing here?" He headed in the Senator's direction and she followed him.

"Since a shot almost hit me and my team, I thought I might find out what the hell is going on. . . ." Madison leaned her head toward Corrigan. "Sir."

"Almost hit? Jesus, where were you?"

"A place any tourist could have been. Picnic table next to the lake. Anyone hurt here?"

"Thank god no, not that we know of. Geez, the Senator just rolled in, barely got out of his car and we heard two shots. Where the hell were his advance men? We thought they took care of security. It's probably streaming on CNN right now."

Madison was glad no one knew where she was. She could see Henderson, getting the news from the Park Service grapevine, quicker than any news organization she knew of. Shots fired at a US Senator at Grizzly. The office buzz would include a couple conspiracy theories about the senator's next likely political opponent; then somebody would bring in the Kennedy assassination. If the public and other Park Service employees only knew about what her little team was working on. They might send out a press release to write-off the national parks as too dangerous.

"This is a frigging nightmare," Corrigan said. He looked as if he could use a drink. He might not know that average folks had met untimely deaths in national parks for over a century, but he most definitely did not want to be the point man when the nation lost a Senator.

She gave him a blank look. "Nobody's dead yet," she said.

He blinked hard and slowed his pace. "You're right." He smoothed the front of his uniform and walked toward the Senator.

⁂

Madison stuck next to Corrigan as he approached the circle around Senator Brumley. Brumley smiled to his staff. Someone gave him a cell phone.

The Senator held up his hand to his staff for a minute. "Fine, they have me stuck in a dusty basement. No one is after me. Some errant hunter. They'll take good care of me. I have to go now. Don't worry dear."

Madison knew there's only one letter difference between dear and dead.

Brumley's face changed as he flipped the phone shut. The second of the front men they saw in the store walked up as Brumley said, "What the hell is going on?"

"Sorry, Senator." His face didn't move.

"Sorry? I could have been killed. Do you have anybody yet?"

Corrigan stood next to him. "Senator, we have helicopters on the way. They should be here within the hour to help in the search."

"Within the hour? Where the hell are they?"

"Fighting fire north of us across the border, sir."

"For Christ's sake," Brumley said. "What are our people doing in Canada?"

"Reciprocal agreement, sir, for fire fighting." Corrigan's face paled.

"Screw them. Pull those men off that fire and look for this hunter."

"No hunting in the park allowed, sir."

"Perhaps the man trying to kill me didn't read the regulations." Brumley noticed Madison. "And you are?"

"Ranger Madison, sir. They took a shot at me too." She put her right hand out.

Brumley didn't take her hand, but closed his eyes a fraction and pushed the end of his chin out, curling up his bottom lip. "You?"

"Close enough, sir. Maybe you weren't the target. Though I don't want the honor myself. Anyone threaten you recently?"

Brumley's security guy stepped in. "The FBI is handling the investigation. We'll find out who is responsible."

Madison was right about this guy and his perfect posture; he had a wild hair and a rod up his butt. The suit made it more pronounced than the fake hunter's outfit. And Mr. FBI loved wearing his badge on his belt.

There was no love lost between local law enforcement and the Bureau. That went for the Park Police too. Any time Madison met FBI agents in Denver they treated her as if she flunked out of grade school. Sure, who wouldn't want the status of the Bureau, but local goings on were enough for her. Even after what went down in Denver, she could say she knew folks who were as good as any feds.

"Always get your man, isn't that how it goes, or is that the Mounties?" Madison grinned.

The faintest hint of a smile broke across Corrigan's face.

"Senator, we'd like you to leave the area," Mr. FBI said.

Brumley shook his head. "For Christ's sake, I just got here. How is it going to look if I cut and run? I'll decide when to leave." Brumley waved the man away, but the man didn't move.

"Senator, this is now a crime scene. We need to secure the whole area and interview everyone. This will take some time."

With the immediate threat gone, the flush was leaving Brumley's face. Madison saw a different kind of stress in the way he cracked his neck. Brumley grabbed Corrigan's arm. "What does this do to our construction schedule?"

Corrigan stepped back.

"I don't have to remind you that the President is firmly behind rebuilding this lodge as quickly as possible," Brumley said.

What was it in the way Brumley mentioned the *President* that made Madison notice the extra weight of an already heavy word? Anyone of Brumley's status could use his connection to the White House, but the tone in his voice, the slight wrinkling around his eyes when he said it, made her wonder if the threat had a hint of desperation in it.

Corrigan looked at a loss. Madison didn't think he had noticed anything but the hammer in Brumley's name dropping, and unlike Brumley, Corrigan didn't have anyone next to him to back him up. Madison stepped closer to him. He might want her gone under normal circumstances, but in a crisis, she was in his club, and he was outnumbered. Besides, she wanted to test something.

"With all due respect, Senator, this is no construction accident, no one fell off a scaffold." Madison paused. Brumley looked away and back at her.

"Surely you know there's a lot of crime in parks these days," Madison said. "But this is unusual. Might take the FBI some time. There's lots of people to talk to, not to mention finding the guy with the rifle."

"I agree with Madison, sir," Corrigan said. "The workers have been busting to get the outside ready for winter. There was never any extra time in the schedule, but with any luck ..." He looked at the FBI man.

Ball back in the FBI's court. Mr. FBI shifted his weight.

A young woman talking into a cell phone came through the opposite door and trotted in wearing a short skirt and high heels toward the Senator. The conversation stopped around the room until she was at the Senator's side.

"We have a press strategy when you're ready, sir."

Madison smiled, young staffers all looked the same, dressed the same. The young woman could have been in that strange room where they met Secretary Meyers. Maybe she was, maybe Brumley was informed. If Madison hadn't just gotten off a plane, if she'd had more sleep and more of her wits about her, she would have noticed how many people were in that room or asked for a list of them, and why they were there. Madison could still ask Roy. If he would level with her.

Brumley brushed dust off the front of his gray suit jacket. "Fine. Corrigan, bring your staff, we better coordinate everything we say to the press. We need to keep a lid on this." He flicked his hand at Mr. FBI and started moving toward the stairway.

Corrigan nodded toward Brumley and looked at Madison.

Madison shook her head and mouthed a "no" to Corrigan and smiled. "If anyone wants to ask me about *my* part of the crime scene, I'm at the motel. But then you know that." She touched her forehead in a faint salute to Mr. FBI and left.

CHAPTER 25

MADISON LET THE Senator and his group leave before she made her way toward the stairs. A tumbled mess of colored wires and coded tags filled the electrical banks along the northern wall. The arrangement made sense to an electrician, but not to Madison. She and Greaves needed to revisit the blueprints. The key to Keller's death might be hidden somewhere in that chaos.

She'd have to add "organize the chaos" to her list of things to do. Her list was a long one, and she had to get back to it. Right now it was in her head and she needed time to sit down and write out all the connections, even the more fantastic ones, to keep it all from slipping away to the void that was her memory. She used to scoff at department veterans who used a notepad for everything. Not anymore. Even in Yosemite's dead of winter, when the pace slowed, she practically needed a tablet taped to her head to remember anything.

Ranger Pennella rushed down the wooden stairs, skipping the last one. Madison stepped out of his way and waved him on. Soon more feds would be swarming in to surround Brumley. Even a little rusty at the police game she could add some value to their investigation, but at the expense of her own. And it was only a matter of time before they would be knocking at her motel door, wanting to know about the shot that almost got Mobley, and asking by the way, just what were the three of them doing in the park? The questions would come. Their cover was fairly thin.

Corrigan didn't know their whole story, she was sure of that. But who knew what Brumley and the FBI would be clued into now. And how she might have to work with them.

It could get sticky.

Her cell phone rang.

"I hope you're safe."

It was Roy.

High on the fractured crag east of the lodge a young man blended into a grove of trees stunted by high winds and snow. Far off, helicopter blades sliced a low whoosh, whoosh, through the rarified air. The man whistled the vivid notes of a bird song as he slid his rifle into its leather case and threw it over his shoulder. On a nearby boulder, a petroglyph of a warrior cut across natural cracks in the rock. The man leaned his shoulder against the boulder while his fingers traced the warrior's outline. Then he nodded to the sky and ran along the cliff deeper into the park.

CHAPTER 26

MADISON ASKED ROY to hold as she moved away from the lodge and its uproar. Anything she said to Roy she wanted to be private, as private as possible. She leaned against a storage shed. She scanned the area on either side of the shed. The sun wove in and out of the broken clouds, bouncing then retrieving light off the hard surfaces. The dust from government vehicles rose into the air. "We're all fine, Roy. Though it was close."

"What?"

"A pine tree took a hit right behind Mobley. Made me think we were the target."

"I'm sure you weren't."

"Are you sure, Roy?" Madison stood straight and walked around one end of the shed. Nothing on the other side but a stack of 2x4s. "Maybe it was meant for Senator Brumley. You know he's here?"

Of course Roy did. He knew everything. Madison looked in the window of the door on the side of the shed. Stacks of boxes of nails, hard hats, the mundane small elements of new construction, but no one hiding. "Do you think he was the target?"

Madison could almost hear a debate about what to say in the way his breath became shallow. For once, he didn't have his planned cryptic answers ready. The last time they spoke, she made it clear she didn't want to be messed with. Maybe he respected that, maybe it didn't matter if he respected her. Other factors were at play.

"Are Greaves and Mobley with you now?" Roy said.

"No, they're in their rooms. No use putting more civilians in the line of fire."

"Good." He paused. "Good."

Madison heard a thin breath on the other end of the line. "You there?"

"That was smart, getting them away." His voice slowed and lingered a bit, as if another thought would come out. He cleared his throat. "Very good. You are secure. I will report back to the President. He, of course, has others giving him updates since the Senator was involved. Now, then, for your investigation… I hope this has no impact. You have made progress I'm sure."

Madison switched the phone to her other ear. That long list ran through her head again.

"The button might be a key find after all. I'm glad I asked for it." She tapped her hand against her thigh. "I also asked you for copies of the letters. They haven't arrived."

"You'll have them within the hour. I don't need to remind you how important…"

"No, you don't. We'll keep them under our control." One minute Roy seemed to be giving her some slack, the next minute, none.

"Yes, of course you will."

"And us, our investigation, no one should know why we're really here, correct?"

"You can be assured of that." Roy hung up.

A slow breeze rustled the aspens in a patch of undisturbed ground near the lodge. The chill air flowed across Madison's face. Winter was right around the corner, could come any minute. The sun's rays would grow fainter with each passing day. Madison slid her phone back in her pocket and pulled her coat around her. Roy never answered her question about the Senator. Madison wasn't satisfied she'd understood all he was trying to tell her, or worse yet, not tell her. This time his voice seemed weaker, maybe there was worry behind his words. Maybe the gunshot's impact reverberated farther than expected.

CHAPTER 27

THE WIND GUSTED through tall pines, tossing limbs back and forth as Madison walked over to Room 7, Mobley's room. Mobley had trembled as Greaves escorted her into the ranger's rig, her perfect posture left behind with the shattered pine bark next to the picnic table.

Madison shook her head. That was the first slip in Mobley's self-control. But someone shooting at you could do that. One time in Denver, a young punk staggered against a convenience store doorjamb, holding his gun sideways like in the movies, then shot at her. Her Academy training took over, and she shot back. But after, when she became conscious of how close to her the shot had come, she shook from the shock. Taking long runs helped, so did time with a punching bag.

She took the pine-sweetened air deep into her lungs, the smell familiar, the same yesterday, the same tomorrow. A comfort.

Mobley needed some comfort now, but she might take Madison's head off. Madison knocked once.

The drapes parted, then Mobley opened the door.

"Hey..." Madison kept her voice low. She didn't want to sound like those FBI fools, all unyielding force and posture. Not now. She bent her head down a fraction, the way she used to with kids traumatized by their parents' criminal activities. The move used to make her look less threatening, at least that's what she supposed. That and the teddy bear she kept in her squad car.

Mobley's room was neat, her wheeled luggage on the collapsible platform next to the wall. The top of the bag slumped, empty, the clothes hung up or in the dresser. No one would ever confuse Mobley's room with Madison's.

The table near the window held a small portable workshop with an array of miniature tools and materials for tying fishing flies. A small hook clamped on the end of a vice on a stand was wrapped in thread that would be the beginnings of a fly. An open package labeled "Elk hair" rested next to a tool with olive-green thread coming out the end. Lots of fly fishers tied their own flies, but Madison assumed Mobley would have been too impatient.

"Wow," Madison said. She couldn't think of anything else to say.

Mobley took a slow turn and looked at the table. She blinked, then sat down in the chair next to it.

"I just thought I'd check in." Madison leaned against the doorjamb. "Quite the scare we got."

"Quite the scare." Mobley's voice was flat. She nodded twice. She looked away from Madison.

Madison picked up the threading tool. "What do you call this?"

"Bobbin," Mobley said.

"Makes sense," Madison put the bobbin back on the table. "Like in a sewing machine; my mom used to sew."

Mobley's eye twitched. She picked up the bobbin so slowly it was as if it belonged to someone else.

Madison knew when there's a close call, some people scream and shake with cold. A blanket warms and subdues them. But others react like Mobley, shut down, move slowly through a routine task, still in shock.

Madison squatted next to Mobley. "What are you making?"

"A Blue Winged Olive, good for this time of year, when we go out again, maybe I can fish again, for cutthroat, I'd like to..." Her voice lowered to a whisper.

"Show me how you do it. I've never seen anyone make one."

Mobley took the bobbin and wrapped the thread around the hook, bit by bit covering the hook to approximate the body of the fly. Her hand shook as she wound, and twice she unwound and rewound the same thread.

Madison picked up the package of elk hair and pulled a small tuft out of the package. She ran her fingers through the coarse strands. Madison knew nothing about the sport, but she admired anyone who could make something with their hands and had the patience for close-up fine detail work, something she'd never had.

"What else do you use?" Madison said.

Mobley opened a plastic toolbox with separate compartments for hooks and copper wire and tiny bags of material, then grabbed a bag of fur and a bag with a feather in it. "This is just my travel kit. I have so much more at home. I use elk and goat hair, all kinds. Rooster and hen hackles, to make tails and wings..." She separated a hackle feather into sections so that it flared out. She stared at it in her hand.

"I appreciate your skill, Mobley. It must be relaxing."

Mobley stared at the feather a second before she answered. "After a day at work …you know how things can get…." She wound another layer of thread around the hook, quickly at first, then slower. She dropped the bobbin and stopped. Her hand fell on the vice and knocked the stand over on the table.

Madison set the stand upright.

Mobley turned toward Madison and closed her eyes.

"It's okay," Madison said.

Mobley's shoulders curled forward. "You don't understand."

Madison paused. "Tell me."

"It's private." Mobley's eyes were moist.

Madison sat on the bed then leaned over her knees. "Not too much I haven't already seen or heard."

Mobley turned away and put her hands in her lap.

Madison put one hand on Mobley's shoulder. She shuddered.

Madison drew her hand away. "Listen, I've been shot at before. Worse than that, I've seen bad things, you know that. It helps to talk it out. You *will* be okay. You'll tie another couple of fishing flies, have a good cry, and then you, me and Greaves will go forward. We'll watch your back. Something like this has never happened to you."

Before she finished her sentence, Mobley's face told Madison it had.

CHAPTER 28

ROY WAS TRUE to his word. As Madison walked away from Mobley's room, the motel manager came out of the office and handed her a shipping envelope. He winked. "Swore I'd place it only in your hands. Important government secrets, no doubt."

Madison smiled. If he only knew.

Madison spread the contents of the package out on her bed and waited for Greaves to join her. A printed sticky note, with "Office of the President" on the upper margin, said "*As requested. Please keep under your control and confidential.*" Roy's slanted handwriting, the lines broken with a frequent quiver, said aging on the page.

Greaves knocked on the open door. "Ah, the Chief's inner sanctum. Now we're talking." He took Madison's jacket off the inside doorknob and closed the door. "Are you going to let Mobes see how real work is done?" His brow lifted.

Madison took her jacket from him and hung it in the small closet, then closed the bathroom door. "Mobley needs a bit of a rest."

"I don't blame her. That shot was close." Greaves slid his long legs under the table as he slumped into the chair. He picked up the *Moraine Madness* beer ad off the table and tossed it to the windowsill. "Makes you crave something stiffer than a beer."

Madison hoped he was talking about whiskey. After seeing Mobley change from a hard-driving woman to scared and broken, Madison had no energy for jousting or anything else with Greaves. Madison's attempt at letting Mobley know they shared near death experiences had raised more questions about Mobley. But it was too soon for Madison to go there.

Madison rubbed her eyes and watched three cars pull into the motel parking lot.

"Chief, hell-o." Greaves waved his hand in front of her face.

Madison batted at his hand. "Greaves!"

"Sorrree. I won't mention anyone being a bit touchy today." He rolled his eyes.

Madison stepped from the window and stood next to him with her feet wide apart over her center of gravity. "One more word, and I'll take you down not in a way you expect. Got it?"

"Yes, Ma'am." Greave's head shrunk into his neck as his shoulders came up to meet his ears.

"All right then." Madison stood straight. "Now let's take a look at these letters Roy sent and figure this damn thing out before someone else takes another shot at us."

Madison passed the copy of the first letter to Greaves. It was as clear as a modern copy machine could make it, but the original must have been faded along the edges. The right top corner had a log number and date in handwritten script.

To President McKinley. September 1, 1901. Three lines. Perfect penmanship.

War against the People fails.
You disrespect sacred Earth
Your bones will feed our children.

Greaves turned the paper over for more text and found none. "They didn't mince words, did they? A direct threat to McKinley--guess he didn't listen."

"That's a leap. We know who killed McKinley, some wacko, not an Indian."

"Ah, Captain," said Greaves. "You're making the leap. One, we are assuming this was sent by a Native American. Two, we are assuming that McKinley's murderer was really caught. We need to find out how soon after McKinley received this warning he was shot."

"Check your conspiracy theories at the door, Greaves."

"You are naïve for one so smart, Madison. History is rewritten all the time."

Greaves had a point. But it was a huge stretch. "We're looking into Keller's death, not McKinley's assassination. My god, I want to get back to Yosemite before I'm eligible for retirement."

"I'm just saying...think of the TV interviews we'd get!" Greaves said.

He made her dizzy. "Let's try to connect some more recent dots, Greaves, you know..., in the country's best interest, not our own."

She handed him the second letter. It was a modern one, unsullied by a secretary's mark. Left pristine for scholars.

To President Eliot. September 15, 2010. Three lines. Computer-generated, common Times Roman font.

One hundred years
And still your people forget
As Spirit falls from the precipice.

"…falls from the precipice–that's Keller!" Greaves slapped his hand against the table.

"Maybe," Madison said.

"Jesus, Captain, do you only get excited when you're about to bust someone's balls? This is the connection. Somebody pushed him off the cliff, just to make a statement. Eliot got the message."

Madison wasn't so sure. It seemed too easy. "Keller the Spirit? He was a good man, loved nature, that's what we know about him, but he was a middle-aged white guy. We don't know that he had any special interest in Indians."

"Think metaphor, Chief." Greaves said. "What do we really know about Keller? Maybe the goodie-two-shoes was a cover. Maybe he *knew* he knew too much."

"And maybe he *was* a plain Joe curious enough to stumble onto something," Madison said.

"Then you and Mobley better get your heads back around this, and soon, while I get on those blueprints."

Greaves made Madison's eyes hurt. What resembled a promising day this morning would end with even more questions. Mobley was a walking ad for post-traumatic stress disorder. Greaves vacillated from serious puzzles to conspiracy theories even the National Enquirer wouldn't publish. And now he was telling Madison what to do.

Shadows of late afternoon bled across the parking lot. In another hour, if Dodge meant what she thought he did, he would be at the trailhead, waiting for her. She wouldn't mention Greaves' theory to him, but if she did, she doubted he would laugh. Madison had never believed the myth of the noble savage, but she still didn't want to think that tribes had been involved in Keller's death or anything as sinister as assassination. She'd come with an open mind, but now? And what had Dodge been doing with Brumley at the lodge? Greaves was right about one thing, the people in power can rewrite history. That meant she had to question everything, and damn it, if there's wasn't anything good left to believe in, what was the point?

She took a deep breath.

Greaves nodded toward the window as he got up from the table. "You suppose they got that shooter yet?"

The muscles around Madison's eyes tightened. "A pro is long gone before anyone figures out where to look."

CHAPTER 29

MADISON PULLED RUNNING shoes out of her duffel bag. It would be good to get some fresh air.

Greaves was right. If you weren't cynical, you weren't paying attention. She never trusted those in power. She hardly trusted herself. Police work didn't help. There was always that temptation to cheat a little on behalf of the good guys.

But she had never crossed the line, not even for Imelda.

She stretched out her right calf muscle and it twinged. In her marathon days, when everything still worked, Madison could warm up, jog a few miles, stop at a sidewalk bakery, drink a cup of coffee and eat a roll, start up again and not feel a damn thing. Sometimes she and her running partners hit a pub instead, and braved hills with a pint in their flat bellies. But those days were over. The hardest part of the years passing, even with all her workouts, was the realization that the effortless 10-mile runs were history.

Madison took a look around the room as she put on her shoulder holster, then slipped the folded photocopies of the letters into the pocket of her fleece vest. She zipped the pocket closed and locked the door behind her.

Crisp air filled her lungs, cold enough to notice, not cold enough to hurt. A thread of wood smoke wound from the store's chimney across the road and spread like a foggy delta over the motel parking lot. There was a local TV news car stopped at the motel office. Before long reporters and cameramen would grab anyone breathing for a sound bite.

She jogged behind the motel and started up the trail. Its layers of decomposed pine needles and worm-worked soil cushioned her feet. She hoped Dodge would show. She wanted to see him again, for more than one reason. He seemed to be playing everything straight, but his chat with the Senator, that surprised her. Maybe it was a random meeting. The Senator could have been angling for a vote.

Madison came around the last bend in the trail before the falls. The October afternoon light blurred the edges of the waterfall against the rocks. If Dodge didn't show, she would chalk it up to her own pride. Maybe he'd been serious earlier when he said there was a downed tree farther up the trail.

And if he didn't show, she was out alone. She should have checked the Superintendent's office before she took off, found out if they knew anything about the shooter. All that talk with Greaves, she wasn't thinking.

She leaned against a chiseled rock outside the waterfall's splash line. In the shade the temperature dropped a good 10 degrees. Deep shadows in the forest hid anything or anyone who might be near.

Madison zipped the collar of her vest up around her

neck and shook off the chill. She'd have to start running again soon.

Pine boughs shifted in the breeze over her head. A far-off hawk called the late sound of approaching twilight. She could see the hawk's faint outline above a distant old growth tree as it sailed through the thin air.

Madison looked down the trail. Dodge was running toward her. Her legs tightened.

He took a last short stride and stopped in front of her. His face was in shadow, but she could see mist in the air as he breathed. "You came," he said.

He wasn't winded. His worn gray T-shirt showed no signs of sweat, only a black number 8 over his heart, some sort of old team uniform.

He grinned. "I'd hoped you could find time." He took a deep breath. He put his hand out as if they were colleagues. As they shook hands, he put his other hand on hers for a moment.

Sweat formed along Madison's hairline.

"I needed a run." Madison pulled her hand away.

He looked toward the waterfall.

She lowered her eyes but caught herself. She needed to look him in the eye, not let him know she was uncomfortable. She had to be wary. But she needed him to talk.

Madison made herself smile; her cold cheeks tightened. "How far do you want to go?" She leaned against a rock and stretched out her calf again, as if this were a casual date between running partners. "We've got an hour of light left."

Dodge pulled his shoulders back. "About a mile up the trail the switchbacks are killers. But at the top there's a birds-eye view of the new lodge. We can see everything from up there."

The trail was wide enough for two people and the only hazards were occasional tree roots across the path. Madison set an easy pace, fast enough she hoped he wasn't bored, slow enough for small talk.

"How is it you get enough time for two runs in a day? You guys start making noise pretty darn early." Madison kicked aside a rock in the middle of the trail.

"I don't every day. Construction is a lot of hurry up and wait."

"That's a cop's typical day."

"You bust your butt meeting a schedule and then the inspector's late or the HVAC guy doesn't want to finish because the sheetrocker's salsa music is too loud. This morning I was waiting on somebody to figure out just what the architect 'intended' when he forgot to specify how he wanted his fireblocking."

"I'll pretend I know what you're talking about."

"Short answer, it's how you prevent a fire from running up a stud wall—ironic since the old lodge burned to the ground."

Madison played along. "Did you talk with him?"

"Not me. The general contractor had to do that. The architect's screwing up someone else's plans, as my boss put it, so we had to wait two hours for him to return the call. I hate sitting around."

"But you got an answer?"

"Typical one. He said the plans are just a 'suggestion.' And 'does he have to specify everything?' We did the wall the way we always do and hope the inspector okays it."

"Reminds me of a captain I used to work with. They get the big bucks because they supposedly know so much, then when they don't, you have to freelance and that pisses them off. I thought Americans were supposed to show initiative."

"Only when it makes other people money." The trail steepened and Dodge passed her.

Madison began to sweat and started to unzip her vest, then stopped. Her gun would be visible.

Madison picked up her pace and ran a bit closer to him. He looked back at her and grinned. That smile could make her lose her train of thought.

The trail traced the edge of a huge boulder, then the switchbacks crisscrossed up the slope to the top of a ridge. Vista Lake loomed dark below. The motel sign seemed to float above the smoke from the store's chimney. Lights from the store blushed on. Headlights bounced along the road on top of the moraine.

Madison sat on a lone rock near the rim and caught her breath. "This was worth it."

The sound of a helicopter carried from across the valley. The sun setting on the eastern mountains burned the bare rocks orange and red.

"If there weren't any lights or noise, it would be perfect." Dodge put his hands on his hips.

"At least Roosevelt protected this," Madison said.

The wrinkles around Dodge's eyes deepened. He didn't respond.

Dodge turned toward the western sky. "We should start back."

"Wait." Madison stood up and stepped toward him. "What did I say?"

"Nothing."

Madison touched his forearm. "What is it?"

He pulled back. "I'm sorry, this wasn't a good idea."

"It *was* a good idea–what changed?"

"Of all the workers at the lodge, why did you pick me to talk to?"

"Maybe because you're about Keller's age, maybe because compared to the younger workers, I thought you'd answer questions without a lot of bullshit. Call it experience, intuition, blind luck? I thought I could trust you."

He stared hard back at her.

She waited.

He grimaced. "Keller was a good person. *Trusting.* It got him killed."

"But why?" Madison asked. "What did he know?"

"I don't know. He didn't say anything to me, except that he was curious about the lodge's electrical plan."

"Did he ask someone else about it?" Madison said.

"He'd have to ask a higher up."

"And if that someone didn't appreciate him asking questions, would they inform someone higher?" Madison asked.

Dodge stepped back. "Such as ...?"

"Senator Brumley."

Dodge shook his head. "Why Brumley?"

Madison faced him. "I'm asking—I saw you in the lodge with him. You seemed close. "

"You checking up on me?"

If Dodge said this to make her feel guilty, it worked. But she wanted him off her list of potential bad guys.

Dodge took a step toward the trail. Deep grooves rimmed his eyes. "When did I become your business?"

She stepped back on the trail to block his way. "Don't tell me not to notice you being chummy with the Senator. Don't ask me to quit asking you questions. So far, I only have loose ends, no connections. Last night I said you could trust me. I know what the word means."

"You think the Senator is involved with what happened to Keller?" he said.

"I can't say one way or the other."

"And the shots? Connected to him?"

"Possibly." Madison loosened her shoulders. "I'd like some help finding out."

Dodge rubbed the tops of his thighs. His muscles contracted and defined the long miles he had put on them. "We need to start back." He took off down the trail.

Madison followed. Something in the way his face changed, the slight deepening of his cheekbones when she mentioned Brumley, he knew more than he let on.

After the last switchback the trail flattened. Two halves of a giant old-growth cedar formed a bridge across the small creek that fed the waterfall below. The wood was slick and Madison and Dodge slowed their pace.

On the other side of the creek bed the trail widened enough so they could run abreast. The broad tree canopy above them blocked most of the day's remaining light. Through a break Madison could see the first star of the evening. It would be dark when they returned to the trailhead.

The trail steepened. Gravity was working on her quads, and her knees began to ache.

"You never said if you would help me." She slowed again.

Dodge turned to her. His mouth was tight. "If this involves the Senator, it gets complicated."

That word again. Everyone's excuse for not doing the right thing. Before she'd had to leave the police force, before her own life got *complicated*, she had always brushed the excuse off. Life is what you make it, she used to tell the people she arrested.

"I'm no mind reader, Dodge," Madison said. "I need you to be specific."

Dodge stopped. He frowned as if she shouldn't need to be told. "Sam Brumley chairs the Senate Indian Affairs Committee. Do you know how powerful he is? It's rare to have a *friend* to Indian nations in that position."

And Brumley must also get something out of it. With all the scandals in DC the last few years, it would be hard to convince Madison that no one had a personal agenda. But she would let that ride until Dodge was ready to tell her more. She nodded her understanding to him as she ran ahead.

The sky was dark when they neared the trailhead. Madison slowed.

Dodge matched her pace.

She put her hand on Dodge's forearm. "We should split up, so we're not seen together. I don't want to put you in any danger."

"I can take care of myself."

Madison pulled her hand away. "No offense meant."

"*Some* taken." He stopped. "Sorry, you're probably right."

"I do need your help," she said.

Dodge touched her shoulder. "Don't worry, I'll find you." He ran behind the motel, toward the construction workers' RVs.

The buzz of a grasshopper sparrow floated above her. It wasn't the only thing that seemed off course at this elevation. Madison stared at the giant sweep of the Milky Way. Its already ancient starlight filled the sky. In the city, the sky was cut off from people. Being removed from nature made people inhuman. Made them do inhuman things. She expected more innocence in a place like Grizzly.

A shooting star burst into pieces above the distant cliffs. She wasn't sure about Dodge, or much else.

CHAPTER 30

THE NEXT MORNING a knock startled Madison as she worked her towel through her hair. She threw the towel on the bedspread and opened her drapes. Greaves was under the porch light, the top of his head inches from the fixture.

Greaves gave a short wave as she opened the door. "Fresh out of the shower?"

"I haven't had my coffee yet, Greaves, don't push me." She stepped aside so he could come in.

"Wouldn't dream of it, Captain." He slid beside her. "But I didn't see you at dinner last night. My god it was a zoo. The place was full of reporters, federal agents and Park Police. The construction crews had most of the day to be at the bar, so they were in fine form. You had other plans?"

"Not that it's any of your business; I took a run."

"Seeing the sights again or just 'thinking.'"

"You ought to try it, Greaves."

"I was working and don't need to run to do it. Want to know what I found out? There's good news and bad news."

Madison rubbed her eyes. She wasn't about to tell Greaves that she was up late looking over files, just in case

Dodge came by. "The good news, and I hope it has something to do with the investigation."

"You are heartless Captain, since I skipped communing with nature to be productive. You obviously are on edge without caffeine, so long story short, Keller, our hapless cliff diver, discovered that the lodge's extensive electrical plans were way beyond what the lodge would ever need. Even with Internet access and tourists wanting blow dryers and TVs and microwaves in the rooms. What I haven't figured out is why Keller was concerned, and who knew that he knew."

"So Grizzly Park gets flat screens, that's the good news?" She grabbed her hairbrush from the bathroom. "And the bad news?"

"Mobley is back to her old self. She's recovered enough to throw me out of her room after a small, tiny really, inappropriate remark. She's ready to work."

Madison's brush ran smooth through her hair. That was *good* news. She needed Mobley.

"Give me five minutes and we'll meet you for breakfast."

Madison knocked softly on Mobley's door. The drapes moved and the door opened.

"We're going to breakfast. Join us?"

"Sure." Mobley had on a starched white cotton shirt and pressed jeans. Her face had her usual look, assured, controlled. The perfect flip was back in her hair.

"How are you doing?" Madison knew the answer she would get.

"Fine." Mobley locked her door and slipped her key into the pocket of her pressed jacket.

Madison stepped away from the door. "Did you finish tying that fly? I'd like to watch you do that again."

Mobley's eyes drew together. She tossed the strap of her black travel purse onto her shoulder. "I'm sure you would find the whole process tedious."

Some people resent you if you've seen them vulnerable. Madison gave Mobley the "piss off" smile she reserved for assholes. Greaves was right, Mobley was back.

The motel parking lot was filled with cars and SUVs. Most of the SUVs had government plates. Madison's favorite FBI agent set a rifle bag on the back seat of the largest black SUV.

Madison nodded to Mobley and stepped next to the vehicle. "Hey, sorry about the crack about the Mounties yesterday. I didn't get your name." She held out her hand.

Mr. FBI didn't shake her hand. "Parker," he said.

"This is Mobley, DOJ. Any news on the shooter?"

"I'm afraid I can't tell you," Parker said.

Madison leaned closer to him. "Come on, we're on the same team. Whoever it was almost took Mobley's lovely head off."

A cold breeze filled with smoke and bacon frying lifted over the parking lot. Parker looked through them and put his black briefcase next to the rifle bag.

Mobley blinked and put her hands in front of her. "Perhaps sir, you have not been informed that we in DOJ have top clearance. Surely this was your supervisor's oversight. Do I need to make a call?" Her forehead remained smooth, without the smallest crack.

Parker closed the SUV door. "The shooter is in the

wind. There's no sign of him. We think he shot from one of those cliffs." He looked to the east.

In the morning light, the sun lit the eroded ledges of the cliff faces and left the deep crevices in shadow. Perfect for hiding.

"Find any spent shells?" Madison said.

"Not yet."

"I'm thinking you won't." A professional doesn't leave any trace. It could be a random act, but she guessed the shooter knew what he was doing. Maybe even planned to miss his target.

"Shells or no shells, we'll find him." Parker grabbed a black duffel bag from the ground and tossed it into the back of the SUV.

"We figure it out, we'll let you know." Madison said. She waved as Parker gunned the motor out of the parking lot. "Nothing would give me more pleasure than to beat the FBI at what they think is their own game." Madison smiled at the settling dust.

"We must." Mobley said as she looked up at the brightening cliffs.

CHAPTER 31

AFTER BREAKFAST, MADISON went back to her room and sent Greaves to charm the guys at the construction office into letting the three of them use their back conference room for the day. Her place was too small and she didn't want the others hanging around there. And the Superintendent's office was out. The FBI would take over any extra space there and Corrigan wouldn't want them getting into a pissing match with the FBI. He had enough troubles. At least Senator Brumley had left as soon as the FBI thought it was safe.

She looked through the drapes of her motel room to check the weather. Dust swirled across the ground. A dark brown pine marten zigzagged across the parking lot, then turned a series of flips. It looked towards her, then ran up the bark of a lone Ponderosa along the road. Seeing a shy pine marten during the day was rare.

She opened the door, then remembering the files on her bedspread, turned to grab them.

Dodge stuck his head into the room. "Hello?"

She jumped back and almost fell onto the bed. "You scared the crap out of me!"

"Sorry, I wasn't thinking."

Madison put the files down. Why was Dodge here now? He seemed to be able to come and go whenever he wanted. "Did they stop construction again?"

Dodge squeezed his lips together and looked around the room. "They're running a limited crew. I volunteered to take the day off without pay. Besides, I wanted to talk to you again."

He closed the door with one foot and reached into the inside pocket of his coat. He looked down at the folded piece of paper in his hand and shook his head. After a moment he passed the paper from one hand to the other.

Madison relaxed her shoulders. "What's that?"

Dodge looked at her, then the paper, then pulled the drape aside and looked out. "Keller gave this to me, the day before… the day before he died. I should have given it to you before. I just wasn't sure."

He unfolded the paper. His eyes moved back and forth as he read. He raised his eyes and Madison could feel the sadness behind them. "I should have gone with him to the cliff. He asked me to go, he was nervous, and didn't want to talk on the job. Something about a petroglyph, something was bothering him. If I had gone with him, he would have told me. This upset him, but I don't know why."

Dodge leaned forward to give her the paper, his large hand almost falling into hers. His fingers shook in the smallest nervous way. Madison reached for the paper and felt sweat as her fingers dragged across his. She wanted to take his hand, then his arm, and pull him closer to her, just to take some of the grief from his face. But she let his hand go and motioned for him to sit down.

The tiny print from the photocopy of a web page was broken by a grainy black and white photo. "Indians greet tourists in full regalia," the headline from 1905 read. The picture showed men in traditional dress, stopping to greet visitors arriving at the new Vista Lodge. Everyone smiled for the photographer. Wildflowers lined the path to the huge front doors. Wooden rocking chairs lined the front façade, ready for guests.

The narrative related how President Roosevelt signed the law establishing the park as a living museum, and a refuge for the native peoples and animals within it. He had made the long journey from Washington for the opening and a second small picture showed him next to an Indian chief.

Madison sat on the edge of the bed. She'd seen similar yellowed articles in the archives at Yosemite, Indians at first the darlings of the national park, photographed making baskets that the tourists paid high prices for. Then the political winds decided that the natives weren't part of the park's wilderness "mission" and they were forced to leave.

Madison set the page aside. "What did he say when he gave this to you?"

Dodge shifted his big frame to one side of the small chair next to the table. He was agitated, grief and rage running adrenaline through the veins straining in his arms.

"He said, as much as he loved this place, part of him wished it was never made a park, that it should have been left the way it was."

"Was that all?" Madison asked.

"He asked me to read the article. His mind seemed

scattered, moving from one thing to another, the article, the hike, then he said something about the new Indian cultural center and moving a petroglyph there. He said the construction was getting out of hand. He wanted me to help him decide what to do. We had planned to talk about it that night."

Madison didn't say anything. She wished now she had put on gloves before she took the page from his hand. "Would Keller have shown this to somebody else? Talked about it with anyone?"

Dodge didn't respond. He bent over and put his hands on his knees. His head dropped.

Madison knew she had to get more from him. "Think. Tell me anything even if it seems unimportant. Was there anyone else at all, his boss, Indians on the crew, a ranger?"

Dodge closed his eyes slowly and the skin across his cheekbones tightened. "I should have gone with him. I didn't even react. The history, it wasn't news to me. Then the shift boss called me and Keller was gone."

Madison moved her hand toward his shoulder. The soft flannel warmed as she felt the muscle tense in his arm.

He turned his head up. The moisture in his eyes deepened as he pulled her next to him.

CHAPTER 32

OUTSIDE HER ROOM, Madison said good-bye to Dodge with a slight nod. She tried to breathe slowly, stop the blood rushing to her ears. He turned from her, his back bent a little as if he aged in that moment. She had to close her eyes.

After he was gone, she walked to the water's edge and leaned against the rough bark of a soaring ponderosa pine. The breeze coming off the lake carried a deep buzz. In the nearby shallows, dragonflies floated one, then two together, hovering above tall reeds, their blue bodies shimmering in the sun.

Years before, in another tranquil space, Madison had wondered how it was that the beauty of dragonflies could mask a scene spoiled by violence. How their mating could continue when Imelda's body was so near, the ground made sacred. Madison had stood there with Stan, watching the dragonflies, sickened by her own predictable actions.

A passing jet's contrail showed moisture in the sky. Change was in the air's sharp smell, storms waiting behind the mountains. Snow-ripe clouds would soon spill over the peaks, swirling drifts across the divide, transforming everything. Covering everything.

Del was filling the coffeepot with water when Madison opened the trailer door. She gave him a thumbs up.

"Thought you might need a cup or two," he said.

"Appreciate that." Madison slid sideways through the door. "And you giving up your conference room."

"No problem. Ward and I picked up a little, but it ain't quite 'pristine.'"

"No worries, we'll be fine."

Greaves had his laptop, long plastic blueprint tubes and the copies of the letters from Roy spread out on the table. "I thought you'd been kidnapped," he said to Madison.

Mobley raised an eyebrow, then looked back at her own laptop.

Madison set her files on the opposite end of the table. "I forgot something in my room. Then my boss called, trying to find out where I am."

Mobley frowned into her screen.

Madison hated lying to them. It was wrong. Trust your partners, they have your back. But this thing with Dodge – she didn't want them to know.

That Dodge pulled her toward him, in what she thought might be a warm embrace. That what she wanted to do right then, as she had done in Denver, was compromise the investigation, let her defenses disappear with the breeze into these mangled mountains, if only for a while. That, if he had wanted the same thing, he could have given her something she swore she'd never let herself have again after Denver. But she couldn't let her team learn that she could desire a suspect, a witness, whoever Dodge was in this investigation, no matter how wrong and stupid it was.

And that instead of getting what she wanted, Dodge's grief about Keller had rushed out in what she believed were waves of deeper losses.

She could tell Greaves and Mobley about her selfish moment, that Dodge had made her face her own weakness, and they would look at her with disrespect or worse, pity. Greaves would likely take a crack at her and compare it to a tragic mini-series; Mobley's silent smirk would show disdain. Madison wasn't up to either.

Madison set a copy of the article that Dodge had given her on the table. In the original, Keller had circled the smaller picture of Roosevelt with the local Indian chief. The pencil line was faint, and she hadn't noticed it at first. There were no other marks on the page, no handwritten notes. It must have been Roosevelt that caught Keller's eye.

She passed the page to Greaves and Mobley as she sat down. "This old newspaper article, something about it upset Keller the day before he died."

"How did you get this?" Greaves said.

"He gave it to one of the other workers." Madison tapped her pen on the table. "But what interests me is that he circled Teddy Roosevelt."

Mobley looked up from her screen. "The great conservation president." She slid the paper next to her laptop. She pointed to the picture of the Indians in ceremonial dress. "There's no defending this."

Greaves looked over her shoulder. "Think of the times, Mobes, think of the times. This article is from another era. Even great leaders made mistakes."

"And defending them is as bad as making the mistakes all over again. You are so predictable."

Madison saw the familiar twitch near Mobley's eye. And so are you, Mobley, so are we all predictable. Madison leaned over the table and pointed at the picture.

"Let's focus on the current battle," she said. "Keller circles the picture. Why? He ends up dead. Why? He loved this park, and was worried something would happen to it. What was so damaging that he lost his life over it?"

"This worker you talked to, did he know anything?" Mobley pushed a loose strand of hair behind her ear.

Sweat formed on Madison's neck. She turned her head away. "He said Keller talked about someone wanting to move a petroglyph to the cultural center. Maybe there's something in the current blueprints."

Greaves pulled the prints out of a long plastic tube and unrolled them across the table.

Madison leaned next to him. "You remember anything in these?"

Greaves turned page after long page. "There is only one reference to the cultural center. It's toward the end. Here." He pointed to a long list of notes. "I'll skip the structural details, but the gist is, there is an underground vault running from the lodge to the cultural center. It's like a tunnel for all the electrical wiring."

Madison had seen similar vaults in large buildings in downtown Denver, with electrical conduits strapped to the walls and along the ceiling. "The buildings are right next door to one another. That doesn't look so odd, especially considering the winters here. But is there anything about a petroglyph, or other cultural artifacts special to the tribes?"

"Nothing on these."

"What did Keller know? He didn't have the prints for the cultural center, at least no one found them with his other stuff." Madison knew whatever had gone on had to be complex. Either the President and Roy wanted the three of them to figure it out because no one else could, or they couldn't trust others to, or maybe they wanted Madison and her team to fail so the higher-ups could pretend there had been no threat and Keller's death was accidental.

Outside, shimmering aspen leaves scattered across the gravel. One by one they caught on the angular edges of crushed rock, then drifted onto the next. The yellow bright against the gray, as the wind took hold and carried the leaves off.

Mobley tapped her keyboard. "In the accounts about the lodge I remember some controversy, but I didn't see the tribes involved, and so I didn't spend any time looking at it. I'll find it." Her eyes never left the screen as her fingers moved.

Madison saw Mobley's face relax, as if the search was a meditation. Greaves noticed the change too, and a slight smile crossed his face.

The laptop screen flickered in Mobley's eyes. "Look, isn't that like the picture you took from up on the cliff?" She turned her laptop screen slightly towards them. A photo of the petroglyph across from where Keller had died filled the screen. Mobley closed the photo to a narrative page. "Says here it *is* the Wind Woman. The architect wanted to cut it from the side of the cliff and move it to the front of the cultural center. The environmentalists made more of a fuss than the tribes, and had a media campaign that invoked the spirit of Roosevelt to get the plans changed."

Mobley enlarged a newspaper article, written by a

national environmental writer. It had a stock photo of Roosevelt decked out in buckskins, riding in the Badlands. They insisted if he were alive today, this rock would not be touched.

Madison heard Corrigan's voice in the next room. She opened the conference room door and leaned out. "Superintendent, got a minute? We have a question for you."

Corrigan turned his head and lost his smile.

"Del's been generous giving us space." Madison nodded toward the conference room.

Corrigan closed the door behind him. "Can we make this quick?"

Madison showed him the laptop screen. "What was the hubbub about moving Wind Woman?"

Corrigan frowned. "Wind Woman? Why do you want to know? That's way outside your purview." He folded his arms across his chest. "Isn't it about time you wrapped this up? Keller's death was an accident." He took a deep breath and stood straight.

Madison turned her body to mirror his. "We've been tasked to prove it was or wasn't."

"I still don't see…"

"Humor me."

Corrigan unfolded his arms and rubbed one cheek with his hand. He slowly closed both eyes, then shook his head. "The architect had this 'vision' to move Wind Woman from the cliff to the cultural center. I thought it had some merit, anything to protect her from vandals. At least at the cultural center there would be security, and cameras on her 24/7.

People protested against moving her for months and in the end, we agreed we'd leave her where she is."

Greaves leaned across the desk. "What do you mean, cameras?"

"You know the drill. Homeland security surveillance–like at headquarters. We needed more security here than we had, but the original plans, my god. You couldn't do anything without being filmed. The homeland boys even wanted cameras in the ceiling of the lodge's grand room."

Madison shook her head. Homeland Security was everywhere. The guards, the public places protected by poorly disguised concrete planters, more a sign of weakness than strength. They were even talking about a card to give out at the parks that had GPS units in them "in case people get lost."

There would be absolutely no way to get away from it all, ever. "What were they expecting to happen, two middle-aged tourists from New Jersey fighting over the size of the log in the stone fireplace?"

"Who knows," Corrigan raised his hands. "It's all 'terrorists and high level targets.' Got to have cameras inside and out. Of course, they didn't give me more staff to watch the cameras. Promised that later, likely after they'd persuaded me to retire."

"Manpower needs aren't sexy enough for congressmen," said Madison. "They have other more important issues on their minds." Madison knew what most had on their minds: their next election and next erection. And all this security nonsense was more Viagra for the scared dickless.

Greaves stood up. "Maybe they're thinking of some sort of attack on homeland soil, similar to when the Taliban blew up the great Buddhas in Afghanistan. Maybe they think it could happen here..." Greaves pointed at Madison. "You all may think it's farfetched, but you don't know what people could be planning."

Corrigan shook his head. He turned toward the door. "Anything else?"

Madison opened the conference room door for him. "If we see the Taliban, we'll call you."

After Corrigan was gone, Mobley looked at Greaves. "You are unbelievable. He already thinks we're buffoons..."

"If you weren't so stuck in a computer, Mobes, you might realize I, too, am trying to figure this out. Outrageous happenings seem to be the order of our days, or is this normal for you?"

A slight deep red rolled across Mobley's cheeks. She pulled her hair away from her face.

"Listen," Madison said. "We didn't have much credibility before, we might have less now, but let's keep the end game in sight."

Whatever the end game was. Madison wasn't so sure she knew. What she did know, in her gut, was that Keller had been murdered, this was more apparent than not, but the more they discovered, the more they didn't know. Every track was more convoluted than the last.

"Something's got to connect the dots," Madison said. "Money, sex, power, that's what drives people, but come on, Keller had no real power, he loved his wife, and didn't owe anybody any money. Who'd want him dead? If not the Taliban, who and why?"

Greaves sat down and picked through the papers on the conference table. "You laugh at my suggestion about the

Buddhas, but their destruction had everything to do with power. It seems to me that these letters sent to the presidents, they're all about power. Indian power, or more correctly, the loss of Indian power in Indian country. Mobley, don't tell me you disagree with that. Isn't that your focus?"

"Of my case work, yes."

"Sometimes you argue for the tribes, but sometimes you have to argue against them, depending on the government's position."

"That's correct." Mobley straightened her back, as if she were on the witness stand.

"That's why the President wanted you, you're good at it, both ways, and because of your heritage, you aren't afraid to push back on their demands," Greaves said.

Madison saw the slight twitch again above Mobley's eye.

"If it's in the best interest of the government, yes. I don't believe my heritage has much to do with it."

"Right. Never threw it back into anyone's face."

"Greaves, that's none of our business," Madison said.

"But it is, O Captain, because Mobes won't hesitate to think the tribes are involved in all this, since the Creekakees decided that those with both Creekakee and black blood didn't belong in their club. I'm guessing Mobley wouldn't mind sticking it to *any* tribe if need be."

"Jesus, Greaves ..." Madison started to speak.

A wind gust from the south shook the construction trailer. A small branch grazed the window. The lights dimmed, then burned brighter.

Mobley stood up. "What I use on a case, and when I use it, is of no consequence to either of you. I am a lawyer, and I win. If you two would take your heads out of your respective asses, you might begin to see how insignificant your opinions about me are. That's what's holding us up, your stupid, personal problems that have nothing to do with real power or this case."

Madison didn't want to admit to Mobley that she was half right. Part of Madison wanted to turn tail and hibernate for the winter. If she had to share a den with a grizzly, it might be easier. But bluster wasn't reserved for the wind.

"Bravo." Madison clapped her hands. "You *are* good. But since we're talking power, let's take a look at Teddy Roosevelt. His name keeps cropping up."

CHAPTER 33

Vista Lake

October 1902

PRESIDENT THEODORE ROOSEVELT leaned against a fractured rock face high above Vista Lake. Late afternoon shadows obscured the intricacies of the mountains ringing the lake. Deer grazed on the still-green bitterbrush growing on the terminal moraine at the water's edge. Roosevelt's Secret Service detail waited there for him. He knew they were nervous, but they wouldn't deny him a solitary walk through the physical evidence of God, not on a Sunday. He'd made it clear the towering cliffs and serene waters were a place of worship to him and he wouldn't be deprived of his time alone.

But it was a ruse. He couldn't conduct this meeting with anyone around. The outcome must remain secret.

The autumn wind blew the lapels of his coat, but he wasn't cold. The wind, and the mountains that shaped it, calmed his soul. He loved the rush of politics, but nature, the one thing he couldn't conquer, gave him a sense of harmony. He understood that about himself, and though he wasn't glad to be pressured to preserve this place, some good could come out of today's commitment.

A tall man moved from behind the twisted stand of lodgepole pines just beyond the edge of the nearby cliff. His opened coat flapped against his flat torso. The man lifted one hand and traced the face of a large boulder, along the outline of a stick figure etched in the rock. "Mr. President, thank you for coming to our sacred place."

Roosevelt nodded and pulled the ends of his coat down along his sides. "It was no hardship to come to such beauty." The Indian looked familiar. Roosevelt waited for him to step closer. Half his face was in shadow, but Roosevelt could see the long line of his jaw. Roosevelt remembered a campfire along a river next to a stand of cottonwoods. "We've met before."

The man looked down the lake. "Sometimes the encounters we have when we are young are the ones we retain most clearly. Once, along a lonely stretch of river in our Badlands, I intruded during your mourning, but you did not hesitate to offer me warmth."

That was a lifetime ago, when the people Roosevelt most loved were taken so quickly, and only the wide plains could revive him. His grief so obvious a stranger could see its depth in the darkness. He dare not speak of it, but he bowed slightly so the man would know he remembered.

The man took a step towards the cliff. "My Indian name is Sky Capture. It is our way, to have grandfather watch us, and when our character is shaped, give us our name. Grandfather did this for me, and I will do it for my grandchildren. My name means preserve the sky. Grandfather knew one day I would meet with the leader of the White Men and try to make you understand."

Sky Capture looked off toward the mountains down the length of the lake. "My grandfather was very smart, he killed many buffalo with his cunning, and many white men also. He's buried in these mountains, right where he died. Maybe I will be buried next to him when it is my time."

He posed no threat to Roosevelt. Both men stood at ease, as if they were discussing the shape of clouds.

Sky Capture laughed. "Grandfather was a great storyteller. 'It is like this,' he would start, and an hour later he would finish his story with an endless grin. You, too, are a great orator. He would have appreciated how you speak about the land."

"Waste of resources is a sin against God and our children," Roosevelt said.

"So we are agreed. The mountain spirit must be preserved." The Indian held his hands out over the cliff. "My borrowed English cannot tell the true story of the mountain spirit. My language has no words for national park, for wilderness, your words for protection. The mountains do not need these names, for they protect us. They cradle the people and take care of us. We believe you, more than others, understand this."

Roosevelt nodded. He *did* understand how high peaks and grasslands in all directions could each in their own way replenish a weary man. He didn't need threats to persuade him. "We must protect these places, but within reason," Roosevelt said.

"Your *reason* has made us a desperate people," he said.

Roosevelt put one hand in his pants pocket, pulled out a handkerchief and wiped his glasses. The flute song of a western hermit thrush floated in slow pitches through the chilled air. Roosevelt knew the timber and mining men would fight him, even his good friend Gifford Pinchot would say timber should be cut and used for the greater good. He relished the fight, for with McKinley gone, he had the power to protect this place forever, and at the same time appease the people Sky Capture represented.

Roosevelt slowly put his glasses back on, folded his handkerchief and put it in his pocket. "You must control your people or I will not make it happen."

Sky Capture turned his face into the wind coming up the cliff. He held his hands out, palms down, and turned to face Roosevelt. "Sometimes it is easier to stop the wind, but I will stop those who know no way but violence. We will save the spirit, and make the rest recognize its value."

Roosevelt nodded and held out his hand. "You have my word."

Sky Capture took Roosevelt's hand. "We are honorable men."

Roosevelt heard the thrush's song again and hoped Sky Capture's words were true.

CHAPTER 34

MADISON TAPPED HER fingers against the aluminum frame of the construction trailer's window.

Greaves and Mobley ignored each other, finally taking a break from exchanging barbs.

Outside the construction workers couldn't take a break. They had bills to pay. They had to keep moving power tools and materials in and out of the construction site, as if shots hadn't been fired yesterday. Still they were exposed. Madison knew the feeling. When she was a beat cop, she couldn't let herself think that someone might shoot her at any time. That would make her a liability to her partner. Catcalls or not, she admired these guys' guts.

Guts, Teddy Roosevelt had more than his share. Madison knew just enough about him to know he had moments when he could have retreated to the life of the well-to-do and left danger behind. He was a Roosevelt after all, with enough business contacts to make millions without any risk to himself. But that's not how he lived.

Mobley might disagree that Roosevelt was a great man, but he did set Grizzly Park aside, and save it from being nothing but second-growth timber and open pit copper mines. Or worse. Madison imagined a gated ring of multi-million dollar homes around the lake. At least Roosevelt protected this place from that slow death.

Madison stopped tapping the cold aluminum and turned toward Greaves and Mobley. "The first letter was addressed to McKinley. After McKinley was assassinated, Roosevelt became president. Anything in our briefing books about Roosevelt? Some killings occurred while he was president, he must have received a letter."

"Roy only sent two of these letters," Mobley said. "You should have asked for all of them."

Madison didn't respond to Mobley's jab. She didn't think Roy would have given them all up, but she should have asked.

Her squabbling team and the dangers out there were a distraction, not to mention Dodge. She couldn't get that last vision of him walking away out of her head. She'd rather be with him than here with these two. She'd lost her objectivity big time.

Greaves looked up from the blueprints. "Roy doesn't trust us, and he should. We've made some progress."

"He knew everything we figured out before he even called us in," Mobley said. "Why did he even ask us to do this?"

"Who's the conspiracy theorist now?" Greaves said.

"Can we focus?" Madison could see the conversation wasting the day. "We've got a long string of unconnected pieces. But the photo of Roosevelt might mean something. We still have the Army button and the museum tag somehow connected to Lewis and Clark. Without something concrete soon, I might pull a Lewis and shoot myself."

Mobley's eye twitched.

"Lewis waited until their mission was completed, Captain," Greaves said. "Don't start talking failure yet."

Mobley slid her chair back from the table. "I need some air."

Madison held up her hand. "Hold on, Mobley, let me get Roy on the phone and I'll ask him about Roosevelt. He's got to start letting us in on more if he wants us to get anywhere." Madison took her cell phone out of her pocket, entered Roy's number, and stared out the window.

Dirt flew up at the end of a pile of lumber. Two ground squirrels faced off with their heads inches apart. She'd seen this elaborate dance a hundred times. More than a hundred times. Madison didn't know if they were about to fight or nuzzle each other. They could fool you.

After one ring, she closed her phone.

Madison stepped back from the window. "Who knows we're in here?"

"Del and Ward out front, and Corrigan," Greaves said.

"And anyone who watched us walk from the motel. Why?" Mobley asked.

Madison lowered the crinkled metal blind over the window. "The last time I talked to Roy and told him how close that shot came to us he paused, then asked if you two were safe. He seemed more concerned about you Mobley, than he did about the Senator. He never answered me when I asked if he thought the Senator was the target. I had a strange feeling then, and I'm getting it back now."

"Roy is our contact, he should feel responsible," Mobley said.

"I wish I could be sure one way or the other," Madison said. "I doubt the shooter would stay around here, especially with the place crawling with feds." She was thinking out loud.

"Unless he was already here, unless he's supposed to be here." Mobley closed her laptop.

"This tinfoil trailer isn't exactly bulletproof," Greaves said.

Mobley's eyes widened, her forehead tightened.

Greaves looked around the room as if he were dissecting the trailer's metal sheeting. Mobley stared past Madison, thinking about whatever in her history made the folds in her forehead deepen. So much about them Madison had failed to learn. Maybe if she had been more trusting of Greaves and Mobley, they would have revealed more. Maybe Roy should have given her all the information that he and the President had on all of them.

Madison's cell phone rang. Roy's number was on the caller ID. He must have seen that she had called. She couldn't tell him that she suspected he knew more than he was willing to give up, or thought they might even be targets.

"Dana?" Roy said. His breath sounded forced and thick.

Madison paused. "Hello, Roy."

"Your call didn't go through. Do you need something?"

"It's these mountains, Roy. Just when you think you're okay, the line goes dead."

Silence. Madison would wait him out.

"What's happened?" Roy said.

Madison wasn't sure how to play it. If there were more to find out about Roosevelt, they'd have to get it from him. But if Roy couldn't be trusted, then telling him they had any clue about what was behind Keller's death would make them more vulnerable. She could gamble and lose big.

"Good news, bad news, Roy. We started figuring things out. We're not sure we like what we've found."

Another long silence. Madison heard footsteps cross a hard surface and a thump as if Roy dropped into a chair. "What is it?" he said.

Madison paced away from the window. "Keller would have made a good detective. Only problem, he ended up dead. The three of us are hoping you don't want the same thing happening to us."

Greaves and Mobley raised their heads.

Madison heard Roy's small cough, then a series of deep coughs.

"Don't say that, Dana." Roy cleared his throat. "Maybe we were wrong to involve you."

Madison walked over to the window, lifted a blind and looked outside. "It's a bit late for regrets."

"You don't understand."

"Enlighten me."

"We had protection for you."

Madison hadn't spotted someone tailing them. Either the protection wasn't there, or she missed it.

"Maybe they lied to you, Roy. Is the Senator involved?"

"I can't say for sure. His trip was sudden." Roy coughed again. Madison could hear him drinking something.

"You should have let us know, Roy, and you should have given us Roosevelt."

"We had to test Greaves and Mobley before we could trust them, Dana," Roy coughed long and deep.

Madison could almost feel his lungs thicken. "Test?"

"It's complicated."

There was that word again. Madison ground her teeth.

"I'm sick, Dana, and Secretary Meyers said he owed you…" Roy gulped hard.

"Owed me? For what?" The phone cut out.

She slipped her phone in her pocket. Secretary of State Meyers? What could he have in common with her?

The wind rattled the window frame and a thin cold drifted over her.

Imelda.

CHAPTER 35

GREAVES AND MOBLEY sat under the glare of the overhead fluorescent light in the dingy conference room. Madison had protected people before, but the danger had always been clear to her. This time, the three of them had accepted the mission with some doubts, but didn't think they were at risk themselves. Roy should have explained the bigger picture to them. And she should have thought it through. Blame sleep deprivation, haste, no time to think. And maybe that had been part of some plan. Still, seeing Secretary Meyers in that subterranean lair of a presidential conference room, she'd had a feeling. When she was running along the C&O Canal, and when she was hiking down from Keller's cliff, she'd had a feeling. If she had stopped to count the times she felt uneasy, there would have been a long list she couldn't ignore. Her gut, for good and for ill, provided the best barometer of a situation. Why had she stopped listening to it?

Now she had to tell Greaves and Mobley that it might be in someone's best interest to have them dead. And Roy had worried about it from the beginning.

"We're screwed," Madison said.

Greaves opened his mouth, but stopped whatever he was going to let fly out.

Mobley grimaced. "What did he say?"

How could she tell them that President Eliot may have considered them expendable? And what about her own part in it? That Secretary Meyers owed her something. A quick bullet was some repayment.

Madison relayed her conversation. "Roy knew we might be in danger. But he said you had to be *tested* for something."

"Damn," Greaves said.

"Damn, is that all you have to say, Greaves?" Mobley's face flushed. "Damn? Yeah, damn that patriotic crap you keep spouting, damn Eliot, damn all the people trying to take my head off." Mobley narrowed her gaze to Madison. "And you, you dragged your mistakes into this, and put us at risk. I'm so tired of getting caught in someone else's fuck up."

Finally something in common. Madison wouldn't point that out to Mobley right now, but it had a familiar ring.

"Hold on," Greaves said. "Madison got screwed a long time ago. Whatever Meyers is trying to pull, we don't know what it is. And shoot me for wanting to do something for my country."

"Nice choice of words, Greaves," Madison said. If a tall lanky man could pull off a pout, he could. One minute macho and obnoxious, the next looking like a little boy ringed by a harem of bullies. Mobley wore some of her baggage on her sleeve, but, Madison thought, Greaves carried a full backpack himself.

Meyers said President Eliot believed he was getting a

trio of the best and brightest, not that they could trust him now either. All people are flawed, Madison knew that, and they can do things they would never dream of when a situation required it.

Perhaps Mobley's stint at the private women's college was her ticket out of an unsafe culture. And Greaves, in his attempt to come to Madison's defense, and fall in step with the President, well, he might just need something to deepen his sad existence. Dusty artifacts are poor conversationalists and don't warm the cold side of the bed.

Madison forced her face blank. She stared them down. "Listen, we can work together or play independent and achieve nothing. Roy sounds as if he's on his last legs. He may be, or it might have been an excuse just because we are getting close to answers. I don't want to invade anybody's privacy, but you know about my experience in Denver. Obviously, Meyers put my name forward for a reason that goes back to Imelda's case."

Greaves shook his head back and forth. "You two are going to tear this apart, but maybe he suggested you for a *good* reason."

Madison lost her poker face.

Greaves took a slow breath. "You're not the only one who can read people. You give up as much as a fossilized rock, Captain. The Imelda case screwed your career. Took you away from what you loved, and the worst of it, the case wasn't ever solved. You feel responsible. If Meyers knew that the killings of Imelda and Keller were related, maybe he thought you deserved to know, even if you'd moved on."

Greaves was too close. When did he get so observant? Maybe he was the one watching them. Madison's face started on fire, the way it did after one too many glasses of wine. "That's ridiculous."

"Maybe not," Greaves said.

"You got Mobley all figured out too?" Madison said.

"Don't start on me," Mobley said.

"But you are so transparent," Greaves said. "Your 'women's intuition' sometimes misses all the cues."

"I don't have to listen to this crap," Mobley said.

"Am I warm? I know you had some sort of close call with a gun, you might as well let us know before we find out." Greaves leaned closer to Mobley.

If Madison knew what had happened to Mobley, it would be one less surprise. "If they picked me because they owed me," said Madison, "then what about you? If there is something in your background that requires a test, tell me now."

Mobley crossed her arms. "Nothing I would discuss with you."

"It might help me protect you."

"Or get me killed."

"Or get us killed," Madison said. "That shot could have hit any of us."

No one said anything.

Madison sat down at the conference table and picked through her files. She pushed two photos to the center of the table: the photo of Imelda in her blood-stained jean jacket, and the photo of Keller at the base of the cliff.

Greaves' grin faded as the photos slid closer to him.

Mobley turned her head away.

Even for October, with the wind throwing pinecones against the thin skin of the trailer, and the windows rattling with cold air, the conference room was what Henderson would call "close." The photos of Imelda and Keller's bodies brought blood to Madison's head. Mobley wasn't the only one who needed to get out of this room. If anyone was after them, they were sitting ducks in the trailer.

And anybody could pick them off as soon as they walked out the door. But that had been true the whole time they were here. There had been lots of opportunities, especially the time she went off by herself to try and figure out what to do.

In DC, when she first asked Mobley if she had ever used a gun, it was only to establish Madison's authority as the leader. She didn't really think they'd need to be ready to use one.

"Look at the photos. We might be next," Madison said. "We're close to the truth. Somebody believes you need to be tested. Someone wants you to fail. Help me make them wrong."

CHAPTER 36

MADISON HEARD A pop then glass tinkling as shards hit the floor, and the bullet's thud into something softer. Someone grunted in the main office next to the conference room.

Greaves arm-wrapped Mobley and threw her under the conference table.

Madison grabbed her gun from under her vest and crouched facing Mobley and Greaves. "Stay the hell down." She scanned the room then looked to Mobley.

Mobley's vocal cords strained. "I'm okay."

Greaves nodded yes.

Madison crawled across the dusty floor to the closed conference room door. She listened. The office clock ticked loudly.

Another muted groan. "Damn it," she said. "Ward!" she yelled. "You all right?"

She sat up and leaned against the door jamb. "Greaves," she whispered. "Your gun?"

"Getting it…"

Madison pointed to herself and then the door. She slid her back up the wall and stood.

Greaves slipped his black leather case off the edge of the table onto the floor. Mobley's eyes widened as he slipped the clip into the gun with a smooth snap and pulled back the slide. Greaves leaned against the table leg and held the gun out in front of his body.

Madison took one step back from the door. She slowly turned the knob, threw the door open and slid up against the jamb. She looked back and forth across the main room of the trailer and crouched, one hand on the floor.

Muddy streaks of coffee drained across the linoleum toward the opposite wall.

Del was behind his desk, plastered into his chair as if someone had thrown him against it. His shirt was bright red where "Hamilton Construction" was embroidered on the front pocket. Madison wasn't sure if life was behind his blank stare.

"Fuck!" Madison looked away to the trailer's front door. It was closed. "Call 911, Del's hit."

"Jesus." Mobley flipped open her cell phone.

Madison heard a groan near Del. Leather boots jerked back and forth underneath Ward's desk. "Del, he's…" Ward mumbled into the floor.

"Ward, listen to me, don't move."

"What's going on?" Greaves said.

Madison didn't answer him.

"Hang on, Ward."

Madison scanned the room. The window next to the front door was shattered. One shot, and Del needed help fast.

Mobley shook her head back and forth. "Damn!" She paused. "At the construction trailer, behind the new lodge. Medical. No, we can't get to him. Didn't you hear the shot?"

Mobley was having trouble, help would take a while. Del might be done for, but Madison had to do something. “I’m going to Del. Greaves, back me up.”

Broken glass dug into Madison’s knees as she crawled across the floor to Del. The smell of fresh blood mixed with coffee hit her stomach hard. Del’s skin was turning gray. Blood dripped off his saturated chair cushion to the floor.

He didn’t have much time. Damn whoever did this. She crawled closer to Del’s chair. His wound was heart level. He was going to bleed out.

Madison ripped an old jacket off a hook behind his chair, reached upwards and applied pressure to his chest.

Ward looked up at her from the floor. A crimson streak ran down from outside his right eye socket. He kept wiping the blood, smearing it over his whole cheek.

“Del’s going to make it. Don’t move.”

The office phone rang twice then stopped.

“Christ. I’m coming over,” Greaves said.

“Stay the hell away…” Madison held the cloth against Del’s chest. She had seen that glassy stare before, when the soul is about to depart.

The phone rang again and again.

“Get the phone. I have to…” Ward’s eyes widened.

The construction warning whistle shrieked. Ward put his bloody hands over his ears. Faint repeats of the whistle bounced off the cliffs. The hum and bang of construction stopped after a few minutes.

Madison pressed Del’s chest harder and looked at Ward. “Help’s coming.”

The doorknob turned. Madison twisted, and saw Dodge come through the door pointing a gun right at her.

Madison tossed the blood soaked cloth. She pointed her gun at Dodge.

"Drop it." Madison scrambled, her feet apart, and held onto her gun with both hands.

"Dana? I…" Dodge's shoulders lifted.

"Now."

Dodge looked around the room and tossed his gun to the floor.

"What the hell are you doing here?" Madison took a step.

"I heard a shot…" Dodge moved closer to Madison and lifted his hands.

Madison loosened the grip on her gun. If she hadn't hesitated when he came in, she would have blown him back out the door. He could have done the same to her.

Dodge looked past her. "Del, Jesus."

Gravity forced Del's limp torso toward the floor. His shoulder slumped against the arm of his chair and caught, his legs splayed out in a V.

Dodge pushed past Madison and grabbed a first aid kit from a file cabinet. The cover snapped as he ripped it off. Dodge looked into the conference room. "Help me."

Greaves still had his gun out. His eyes were on Dodge.

"It's all right," Madison said to Greaves as she moved toward Dodge.

Greaves' eyebrows stretched up as far as they would go. He put his gun down and ran over to Del.

Mobley looked from Madison to Dodge and back to Madison. "Life flight, hurry."

Greaves grabbed thick gauze pads from the first aid kit and applied them to Del's chest.

Madison crawled under Ward's desk and held out her hand. "It's all right. Come out slowly."

A siren screeched outside. Tires slid on gravel. Heavy footsteps strained the wood stairs and two paramedics came through the door. They dropped their medical bags and took over for Dodge and Greaves.

Madison wiped Ward's face as the men worked on Del. Glass shards had sliced Ward's forehead above his eyes, but he would be all right, if he could erase the picture of Del from his mind. Madison handed Ward over to other staff filling the room, now compromising a new crime scene.

Madison stepped behind Del's desk to see if the bullet had gone clear through him. She felt a hand on her shoulder. She threw her shoulders back, then turned around.

"Sorry." Dodge withdrew his hand, dropped his head forward. "I'm really sorry."

"I could have killed you."

"You didn't."

"You're lucky." She took in a breath. She was rusty, not used to reacting that fast. And she had to drop her arm from Del's chest to get her gun. Dodge could have killed her in that split second. Maybe she was as lucky as he was. "What were you thinking?"

Dodge tilted his head toward the medics tending to Del. His eyes rested on Del for a moment, then on Madison. "Dana, that could have been *you*." He wrapped his hand around her forearm.

That slight touch. Madison wanted to believe he came to help her. But why was he so close to the trailer?

Dodge's eyes didn't waver from Madison's face.

If she couldn't trust him she'd be in some deep hole of her own making, again.

She lifted her chin. "You always carry a gun?" He had held the gun as if he knew how to use it.

"Half this crew does, especially now."

Outside rangers held workers back as they came toward the trailer. Madison saw Corrigan coming through the crowd. In a minute the trailer would be filled with prying eyes.

"I've got to go." She slid her arm from his grasp.

She signaled for Greaves and Mobley to go back into the conference room and closed the door behind them.

"Pack up." Madison slid the pictures of Imelda and Keller into a file folder.

"But Del, Ward…" Greaves looked at the closed door.

Madison rolled up a set of blueprints. "We can't help them anymore."

Greaves' picked up his gun and put it on the table. "Who the hell was that out there?"

"Dodge, a friend of Keller's." Madison hated the way her face flushed.

"Looks like a friend of yours, too." Mobley closed her laptop hard. "He could have killed you. How did you know he wouldn't?"

Madison didn't want to answer that one.

"You put us in danger," Mobley said.

"You don't know that," Greaves said. "He came to help."

"Did he?" Mobley said.

Madison handed Greaves the blueprints.

"Why didn't you tell us about this *Dodge*?" Mobley said.

Madison put her files slowly into a box. "You know the technique. Establish rapport. Set him apart from the others."

"You couldn't include us?" Mobley crossed her arms.

"I can now." Madison couldn't tell them her true motives, she wasn't sure herself. Another mistake.

The conference room door opened and Corrigan and Parker walked in.

"We'll need statements," Parker said. He looked across the table. He didn't say any more, but Madison knew he was jotting down details in his head. Blueprints, laptops, map of Grizzly. A photo's edge visible across the top of a file folder.

Madison braced for his request to see everything. She moved next to him.

"We were minding our *own* business." She emphasized own, hoping he would get that what was in this room had nothing to do with him. "We heard a shot. Not much more to say than that is there, Greaves, Mobley?"

They shook their heads.

"Trouble seems to follow you, Madison," Corrigan said.

"Trouble was already here. If whoever did this wanted me, he had many opportunities. He's a lousy shot or made a point to miss."

"Del's paying the consequences," Corrigan said.

"Think he'll make it?" Greaves said.

"Doesn't look good," Corrigan said.

"Jesus," Greaves said.

None of them said anything. Mobley picked up her cell phone and held it as if waiting for a call.

CHAPTER 37

MADISON OPENED THE door to her room and set her files and laptop on the bed. Parker had made them tell what happened over and over. Another hour wasted. By the time they were out of the conference room, the main office was crawling with park police and FBI agents. Dodge was sitting in Ward's chair, answering questions from Parker. She looked away when he searched her face.

She told Greaves and Mobley to meet her in an hour. She needed to change clothes if nothing else. The blood stains would never come out.

She lay down on the bed and closed her eyes. The image of Del slumped in his chair raced around in her brain so fast she grimaced as if someone had turned on a bright light overhead.

Just when she thought they might be getting somewhere, now this. And Dodge. She had told Parker little except the facts about Dodge bursting into the room. She wanted to know what Parker would find out about him.

She rubbed her arm where Dodge had pressed it. Wind rattled the single pane window and she shivered.

Her cell phone rang. If only she could have one day to herself, she might start thinking straighter....

She rolled over to the edge of the bed and grabbed the phone.

"Hey Dana, how're you doing?" It was Henderson.

"Fine, boss."

"Still in DC?"

"Yes." She hated lies. Madison pulled back the drapes and watched the wind swirl dust devils. This place couldn't be more different from DC.

"Thank god. You heard what happened at Grizzly? Friggin 'sniper fire. Twice. Jesus, what does HQ think?"

"Been in meetings all day. Haven't heard much."

"Beancounters will be apoplectic updating those damn numbers. When can you come back?"

"I don't know." Her voice trailed off.

"You sure you're all right? You sound tired."

Madison sighed and held the phone away from her face. Tired wasn't the half of it. "I just need to get back." She let the drapes drop from her hand.

"There is nothing more beautiful than the Yosemite. TR had that right." Henderson paused.

Teddy Roosevelt. He'd been to Yosemite with John Muir. Fell in love with it.

"Dana, I can call HQ and get you out of there."

Madison took a deep breath and forced a laugh. "Please don't, they'll ream both of us. Go for a walk along the river and quit worrying. And thanks, I mean it." She closed her phone.

She drew back the drapes. Outside the wind calmed and the frame of Vista Lodge was in full sun, the cliffs shimmering behind it. Those cliffs the reason the Kowaho and other tribes came here for spiritual renewal, why Teddy Roosevelt made Grizzly a national park.

Madison closed the drapes and sat on the edge of the bed.

If TR wasn't part of all this, then why did his name keep coming up?

CHAPTER 38

Vista Lake

October 1902

AFTER SKY CAPTURE left him high on the cliffs above Vista Lake, Roosevelt sat down on the rim of the rock ledge. Hermit thrushes continued to fill the thin air with their song, and his thick chest swelled with the power of the sacred place. The view before him in the late morning air was holy, as holy as the large cathedrals of Europe, as holy as the soft cheek of his youngest child. This place must be preserved for everyone, for the ages. When he returned to Washington he would set out to fulfill what he had promised, a new national park, where the rights of those who had always used this land could be protected for all time.

The smell of the pine trees mingled with the slightest spit of snow. Roosevelt knew his Secret Service contingent would be concerned seeing the threatening sky, not knowing his whereabouts. He started back down the trail, past the petroglyph of a warrior, something he had missed on the way up. Part of him wished he could be that warrior, able to stay forever.

CHAPTER 39

"DEL DIED EN route." Corrigan called Madison in her room shortly after noon.

"Damn," Madison said. "Ward?"

"Needed some stitches."

"I'm sorry, Corrigan." There wasn't much more for her to say.

"It's just… damn it, Madison, you're a good ranger… but…" Corrigan's words caught and he cleared his throat. "Right now I want you out of my park before someone else dies."

Madison didn't blame him for blaming her. "Again, I'm sorry."

"I've got to go." Corrigan hung up.

Madison picked up the Roosevelt letter Roy had sent. They had to be wary now, and quick, before whoever wanted them gone, in the Del sense, made good. With all the local park law enforcement and FBI still around, she didn't think the shooter would be so bold again, but this morning proved she didn't know the kind of person she was dealing with.

If they had protection, as Roy had said they did, who and where were they? She wanted to get far from the lodge.

As they left the trailer she'd told Greaves and Mobley to meet her at the SUV with their hiking boots. She wanted to be on the move.

The grumbling had started as soon as she drove out of the parking lot.

"We're not safe here," Madison said.

"As if no one can follow us," Mobley rolled her eyes.

"Listen, the prairie is open; we'll see anyone behind us," Madison said.

"Got you there," Greaves said.

"And when we cut back into the mountains?" Mobley crossed her arms.

"A calculated risk. Besides, you haven't been to Keller's cliff. Maybe you'll see something I missed. It's worth a shot."

"Don't say shot," Greaves said.

"Sorry," Madison shook her head. "I got the Roosevelt letter from Roy."

"Jesus, how did he...," Greaves said.

"He must have someone really close by...," Madison said.

"Obviously," Mobley said. "Where is it?"

"Glove box."

Mobley opened up the glove box and took the three letters out. The Roosevelt letter was on top. Mobley read aloud. "McKinley tried to exterminate us. He failed to meet our demands. Now it is up to you." She pushed her hair behind her ear. "It says October 1901 on the top of the page. Two weeks after McKinley was assassinated."

Greaves leaned forward from the back seat. "It doesn't say they killed him, but…"

"Please," Mobley said.

Madison sighed and looked in the rearview mirror. "Greaves, keep checking behind us."

Madison drove down Road 62 way beyond the speed limit. They flew over the small pass separating the mountains from the prairie. Tall grasses filled the horizon, separated by creeks lined with cottonwoods and willows.

"Jesus, it's beautiful," Greaves said.

"Imagine it 200 years ago." Mobley shifted in her seat as the SUV flew up onto an overpass across a small creek.

Greaves leaned forward. "Lewis and Clark said the whole region teamed with fish and bison."

"But they didn't come this far north," Madison said.

"One of their buttons did."

Mobley shook her head. "I still can't believe that button is real."

"Trust me, it is," Greaves said.

"It's got to be a plant," Mobley said.

Greaves shrugged. "They traded buttons for goods throughout their trip. And who would keep an artifact for 200 years then just toss it?"

"Whoever killed Keller," Madison said. "They wanted to send a message."

"About money," Mobley said. "Everything's about money."

Greaves leaned back. "That's a leap. How would that be connected to Roosevelt? Any money there would be, pardon the pun, history. Roosevelt wasn't motivated by money."

Mobley lips pursed. "You are unbelievably naïve."

"He was complex," Greaves said. "Every president is."

"Roosevelt busted up monopolies," Madison said. "That didn't win him any favors with the financial big boys. And why threaten him if he was going to preserve land anyway?" Madison looked at the grasses bending along the road. "It doesn't make sense."

"Look at the date," Mobley held out the letter. "McKinley died, Roosevelt becomes President. With McKinley out of the way, he could do what they wanted. But would you trust him?"

"But these people, they weren't after money from Roosevelt. What's the connection to today?" Greaves shook his head.

"Why am I here instead of doing more research?" Mobley turned toward her window.

"Avoiding the next shot." Madison checked her side mirror.

The road looped back into the mountains across the glacial plain. White-edged peaks rose up straight out of the flatland. In a deep canyon, water tumbled over rocky steps. Farther up river Madison drove past the campground across from the trailhead to Beargrass Mountain and parked the SUV out of sight.

Madison got out of the car and stretched her arms above her head. "Keller's cliff is up there, about 1,500 feet. It's a good trail. I don't think anyone followed us."

Greaves pulled out a hat with a flap in the back that made him look as if he was a member of the Foreign Legion's Lost Patrol. Madison shook her head.

He walked over to the river and pointed. "Too bad you

didn't bring your gear this time, Mobes. I can see fish in there."

Mobley walked over next to Greaves and practiced casting into the river. He tried to match her move with his long arm, but shrugged.

"The fish'll be here after this is over," Madison said. "Let's go."

The patches of moss clinging to the cliffs, the water-worked caves and potholes along the edge of the small creek soothed Madison, muted her thoughts of danger as they followed the trail. In the clear pine air, rich with the smells of centuries of nature instead of man, it was easy to believe nothing bad could ever happen. But her instincts reminded her to be wary.

Near a small cave in the canyon wall Greaves spotted a faded petroglyph of a bison.

Mobley bent close to the image and was quiet. Greaves took pictures and they moved up the trail.

The trees thinned as Madison rounded a bend. The trail continued another steep mile. At the top the ridge was bare of anything but windswept rock and a few contorted trees.

The familiar finger of layered rock jutted out to the south with the rock cairn at its end. "This is it." Madison dropped her backpack.

Long, thin clouds whipped through the tops of the peaks. Greaves crept to the edge and leaned over. "Lord have mercy," he sighed.

Mobley stepped near the edge and touched the rock on the top of the cairn.

Madison pointed across to Wind Woman. "There she is." Carved red abstract eyes stood out against the wall of limestone. The long vertical red line dropping from her eyes was weathered as if in partial shadow.

Mobley squatted. "How could anyone ever think of moving her?"

"What a specimen! Thank god they didn't," Greaves said.

Madison took a water bottle out of her backpack. "Why wouldn't the local tribes have fought for her? Doesn't it seem odd that they didn't?"

"Counterintuitive, Captain," Greaves shook his head. "Goes against my experience."

"Mobley, what do you think?" Madison asked.

Mobley lifted her eyes away from Wind Woman. She looked across the wide gap to the far mountains and back again. "The elders should have protested. Unless they wanted her closer…unless they got something in return," Mobley said.

"They're getting a cultural center," Greaves said.

Madison put her water bottle back in her pack. "And continued funding? Could it support itself?"

Mobley stood up. "As many visitors as this park gets… they could take in a substantial amount, maybe more than costs."

Greaves sighed. "Why does everything have to come down to money?"

"It's understandable, isn't it?" Mobley stared at Wind Woman. "When half your population lives on government stipends and most don't finish school?"

"But does another handout perpetuate that?" Greaves held up his hands.

Madison knew from her own life something about rationalizing one thing for the good of another. The slippery slope cliché was overused for a reason: one slight loss of traction for love, for money, for power, and before you knew it you're at the bottom in a heap with all the other human trash. She'd lost her traction for what she'd thought was love.

"At least this money will contribute to learning and preserving culture, not destroying it." Mobley crossed her arms.

"We're all in favor of that, Mobley," Madison said.

Mobley didn't answer.

Crystal flecks flashed crimson in the rounded cairn rocks. A sharp wind stirred dust into a tight circle at the end of the ridge. Madison shivered and zipped up her vest. The clouds overhead could in a moment drop whatever moisture they were carrying.

"Little jumpy, Chief?" Greaves smiled.

"Greaves, I understand gallows humor all too well, but please…"

"Sorry Cap, but I can't get that picture of Del out of my head, and this cliff…"

Madison nodded. The afternoon light deepened the minute cracks around Wind Woman's eyes to burgundy. Madison couldn't look at her without wanting to drag what those eyes had seen on Keller's last day from her. Keller had come to this place to gather his thoughts, make a decision, or find peace with whatever had been bothering him. Someone knew he would be here that day, and they made it his last.

She took the letter to President Eliot out of her vest pocket and read aloud.

"'One hundred years. And still no one listens. As Spirit falls from the precipice.' I'd say we're listening now. Tell us why you were killed, Keller." Madison folded the letter.

Greaves lost his smile and kicked a pebble over the side of the cliff. "These rocks aren't talking."

Mobley sighed. "This Dodge, he knew Keller was coming up here?"

"Keller asked him to come along, but he couldn't get away from the job."

"I bet." Mobley lifted her chin.

"You mean something by that?"

"You defending him?"

"I don't think he's who we're looking for."

"Maybe you're sure, but …"

"Look, the FBI is going to pore over everyone's background. I'll ask Parker what he finds out about him."

"You two haven't exactly made friends with Parker," Greaves said.

Madison frowned. Sometimes getting the best of guys bites you later. But she could change that. "I'll remind him again that we're on the same team, and hell, I've never met an FBI agent who didn't respond to a free drink." She knew Parker was smart, had to be to get through Quantico, and even if some in his ranks looked like big dumb jocks, they were sharp jocks, with specialties ranging from accounting to forensic entomology. And they could put you on the ground in a second. For all the turf wars among law enforcement agencies, she could give the respect they were due, if she had to.

Greaves took another picture of Wind Woman. "Did you go any farther up the trail, Cap?"

Madison shook her head. She took her binoculars out of her backpack and had a long look across the empty space between the cliff and the distant mountain peaks. Greaves said something, just as Madison saw a flicker of light on a far-off cliff. Madison squeezed her eyes as the light undulated in the thin air and disappeared.

She lowered the binoculars. Probably just the sun.

Greaves followed the trail east, next to windswept trees and shrubs ripe with fall berries that covered the rock wall above and behind Wind Woman. He neared the edge of the cliff and wasn't that far from Madison.

Small pebbles tumbled down as he leaned over the edge. He stepped back.

Madison laughed. "Better watch it, Greaves, we can't save you from here."

"Assuming we would," Mobley whispered.

Greaves waved and started back along the ridge toward them. He pushed aside some branches in his way. "Hey, here's another glyph." He turned his head sideways. "It might be a hunter, he's got a spear."

"Get a picture," Madison said.

"Let me move these away…." He bent over and picked up a long branch from behind the shrubs. "Mobes, I've got myself a fishing pole." He laughed. He lifted the branch up and let it straddle the empty space between them. Mobley grabbed the other end and pretended to pull, then Madison put her hand over hers and stopped.

They looked at each other, then at Greaves.

"Greaves, stand back from the edge, I want to try

something." Madison grabbed the branch as Mobley loosened her grip. "Hold onto the end, but just stand there."

Madison waited for Greaves to get away from the edge. "Okay, just take the end."

When Greaves took the end in his hand, Madison gave the branch a hard shove.

Greaves' foot slipped on the loose gravel. "Hey!"

"Could this be the murder weapon?" Mobley said.

"Greaves, take a look around," Madison said.

Greaves dropped his end of the branch. He searched the cliff and under the bushes. Madison laid the branch down and she and Mobley walked over to Greaves to help search. They found nothing.

"Let's get back," Madison said. "I have to agree with Greaves, these rocks aren't talking."

CHAPTER 40

MADISON OPENED UP the door to her motel room. Everything in place, except a note slipped under the door.

"Run 5 pm, same place? D." It was past 4:30 now, she'd never make it. And besides, what would she say to him? She had to talk to Parker before she talked with Dodge again. Running would have to wait.

She was so tired, couldn't believe this morning Del was making them coffee and now he was dead.

She pulled the briefing book out from under her bed and took out Roy's list of incidents and the large map in the back of the book. Maybe the other cases could tell her something, but some were so old, she wasn't sure what use they would be. The more recent ones, they were spread all over. She'd have to listen to what the map could tell her.

Presidents and Congress had set aside so much land, the full multicolor range of protected places impressed her. National parks, monuments, wildlife refuges, national forests, a lengthy inventory of places sacred to recent Americans and long before that, Native Americans. So many places, if left to corporations, could have been ruined forever.

Madison pulled out the record of incidents. Roy's lengthy table made Madison sigh. So many. She had looked at the tally before, but only to see if Imelda was on it. She wondered if any of the others listed were children. She didn't want to think about it.

Roy thought every mark on the map related to tribal issues, but the more recent ones? Didn't seem possible.

Each incident had the same information she had seen for Imelda: "#53, Imelda Sampson, 2003, unsolved. Letter delivered October 2003." The letter's date matched the time Denver's mayor had received the letter that blew their case apart and forced her out. She wasn't sure she wanted to see this presidential letter.

Roy's table was two pages long. There were gaps in time. An incident in 1901, then nothing until 1902. Then 1906. Mobley might have an idea if the years corresponded with anything related to tribal history. She'd ask her over dinner.

There were enough government SUVs parked outside the general store to make Madison feel safe enough for uninterrupted steak and potatoes. Parker and one of his cohorts were sitting at the bar. Greaves and Mobley slid into the booth across from Madison.

Madison waited for Betty to take their orders, then pulled Roy's table out of her pocket and slid it over to them. "Take a look at these time gaps. Anything strike you?"

Mobley slid a red nail down the rows. "We have the first victim in 1901, in Yellowstone. Yellowstone was the first national park, but it was created about 30 years before that. McKinley was also killed in 1901; then Roosevelt becomes president."

Greaves looked over Mobley's shoulder. "Then 1902, 1906, then a big break until 1924, then again in 1928."

"You think it's a pattern?"

Greaves grabbed a paper napkin and wrote down the time periods. "The amounts of time differ for each gap."

"Mobley, you know Indian history and case law better than I," Madison said.

Mobley didn't look up. "Important legal milestones start long before 1900...treaties predate that...1924, Indians were granted citizenship..."

Greaves put his pint up to his lips. "There are a few before 1990. That's when it became illegal to dig up Indian graves..."

"The letters imply that a group wanted something and were willing to kill to pressure the government to get it. In national parks, where they thought it would get bad press for the government?"

"Or make a double statement," Greaves said. "Think about it. Correct me if I'm wrong, but remember the photo of Roosevelt and the Indian chief and the Indians greeting tourists. Yeah, it's exploitive and disgraceful, but at least they are in the park. Mobley, wasn't there a time when Indians had access to the parks, other than to sell baskets to eastern tourists?"

"Early on, local tribes could continue their "normal" customs, hunting, fishing, what we call 'vision quests,' etc." Mobley said.

"Was it allowed at Grizzly?" Madison asked.

Greaves pulled out the Grizzly map. "Says local tribes used sacred sites, collected plants and hunted animals in the park from the park's creation in 1903 until the Wilderness

Act in 1964. That's one of the reasons for the new cultural center, to help them preserve their traditions."

"So initially, I'd say the Kowaho and any other tribes who could assert a tradition of using this land *could*, until the wilderness act changed that." Madison leaned forward.

Greaves mirrored Madison. "That might piss a person off, but enough to murder?"

"It's bigger than that. It's murder of tradition, don't you think?" Mobley said.

"So what happens before 1964 and the Wilderness Act on the list?"

"Two incidents in 1963; four incidents in 1964." Mobley ran her finger across the rows.

"What about 1903?" Madison said.

"Early 1902...," Mobley said.

"We need to find out what was happening around each of these years, and the gaps in between."

"I need to access my law library," Mobley said. "There have been such significant legal questions, hunting and fishing rights, sovereignty of recognized tribes, etc."

"Maybe we can narrow the issues," Greaves said.

"Mobley, if you could do that, maybe Greaves, you could go through Keller's stuff one more time, especially the blueprints. And I know you don't want to, but could you two stay together? I'm still a bit concerned about any of us being alone."

"What do you propose to do, Captain?"

"I'm going to invite Parker over for a beer."

Madison asked Betty to get Parker a fresh mug. He turned around and smirked as she waved him over. He said a few words to his partner, then grabbed the beer and joined Madison at the table.

"Peace offering?" he said.

"You could say that." Madison leaned across the table. "Don't know about you, but this whole thing has me damn frustrated. I want to get out of here before we freeze our butts off, or worse."

"I hear you. It was bad enough when the Senator was here, but after today, this guy is really making us look stupid."

"Have anything yet? ID the weapon?"

"The round we dug out of the tree was a 308. The second we couldn't find. Once we get the bullet out of the victim, we'll know if it's the same gun, but nothing specific points to a shooter yet. We've finished background checks. Park Service personnel have been vetted twice since 911, so zero there, but the construction guys, a few have records, bar fights, DUI, typical bonehead stuff." Parker took a long drink.

Madison started to draw a D on the condensation on her beer glass, then stopped. "And Dodge, the one helping me with Del?"

"Clean. But he has quite the background." Parker swallowed. "Went to Dartmouth, tied to a tribal organization called the Hunters that improves wildlife habitat. Speaks five Indian languages."

Madison leaned back and tried to look blank. She put her hands around the cold beer glass and took a long sip.

"And the kicker? He interned for Senator Brumley right out of school. Something the Senator didn't mention..."

Madison kept her hands secured on her glass. "What's he doing working here?"

"Said he was burned out, trained as a carpenter on the

Rez, and loved this place, thought he'd see if he could still work hard. Man, you never know, do you?"

Parker had done what she should have from the beginning. Ordered a full report on Dodge after she talked to him.

What would she do when she saw Dodge next? Say "Why didn't you tell me who you are?" She was acting like a schoolgirl.

"Find out anything else?"

Parker leaned back into his chair. "Only that there are a million places in this park for people to disappear. Give me a crowded city any day. Squirrels don't talk. We suggested to Corrigan that he close the park, and I thought he would have a stroke. He slumped down in his chair and said it had never been closed, not after the fire, not after 911, not since it first opened in 1903. I told him we would have to suggest it up the chain of command and he basically said he might as well retire, because his legacy could only get worse. I feel for the guy."

Madison took a deep breath. So many victims, not all dead. "No good deed goes unpunished, isn't that the saying?"

She thanked Parker, paid the check and asked him to hold on the park closure for a couple of days, until they all could do more work. She told him she thought they were close to figuring their part out. It was a lie, but she was afraid Parker would get a call from his superior, after he got a call from his superior, who'd get a call from the President. If Eliot was true to the picture painted of him in that strange conference room in Virginia, the last thing he would allow would be a closure. He'd have everyone's head before that.

Sporadic clouds obscured the moon as Madison made her

way from the store to the lake. Her beer started to wear off and what she really needed was a hard run through the woods, hard enough to make her heart pound and cut off the thoughts about Dodge. But she couldn't run a trail at night, not now.

What Parker had told her about Dodge, she couldn't believe. Couldn't believe that she hadn't asked him the simplest questions herself. He probably would have told her. She was thankful she'd missed his invitation to run again.

So much whirled in her head. The pattern in the killings, the dates, why didn't Roy give them more from the start. She was tired of coming up short with someone frightened or dead or their career ruined.

She opened her cell phone and dialed Roy's number.

"Roy," he said.

"It's Dana. It's time you leveled with me about the patterns in the killings. You knew this right?"

"We are very busy now," Roy said.

"What, line not secure? Someone around who shouldn't be listening?"

"That's correct." Roy said the words slower than normal.

Madison stopped, she was just kidding.

"My partner and I are at a delicate task," he said.

"Partner?" Madison asked.

"Yes, I'd be happy to call you back, sir."

"You don't trust this partner," she said.

"Yes, about done."

"Call me back, Roy."

"Thanks for your patience, sir."

Madison had heard that tone before, someone in

crisis making light on the 911 call back from the dispatcher. Domestic violence, hostage situation, people in shock. Don't let the other person know. She left her phone on. The moon played in and out of the clouds and lit the whitecaps forming on the water. She hoped Roy's "partner" wasn't listening as closely as she was.

She took a deep breath and pushed thoughts of danger from her mind. The air so clear at this elevation, and the constant drift of wind, the smell of fresh pine rushed her nose. A wave lapped softly against the rocky shore. If she could forget why she was here, and drink in the rawness, she could be happy. If the whole world could spend time in the mountains without phones or TVs or anything to remind them of civilization, the world might be more civilized. Not like that guy who died in the Winnebago, what was his name? He was on the list, and he died just because he couldn't leave everything at home.

Her phone rang. Roy's number.

"You alone?" she said.

Yes," Roy said. "My assistant, though he doesn't appreciate being called that, just left."

"Who is he that he can't be trusted?"

"I can't tell you now. Talk to Dodge." Roy coughed deep.

That familiar uneasy feeling in her stomach. She sat on the nearest boulder.

Roy coughed again.

"Dodge?" she asked.

Roy cleared his throat. "Yes."

She felt another feeling, left out to dry in front of everyone. A fool. "But why?"

"He knows."

CHAPTER 41

MADISON WALKED SLOWLY back to the motel. She bent her head as she felt in her pocket for her room key.

"Hey..." Dodge waited in front of her door, just out of the beam from the porch light.

She almost ran into him as she turned toward her room. "Jesus."

"Seems I'm always surprising you."

Madison didn't say anything.

"You got my note?" he said.

"Too late," she said.

"I figured." Dodge shifted his weight from one foot to the other. "I'm sorry about today."

"It's over with." Madison didn't know what to say, and she didn't like being outside in the open.

"Have you had dinner? We could talk."

"I just finished buying Agent Parker a beer. He shared a lot." Her voice had the short tinge it got when she was angry. Right now she couldn't help it.

He looked behind her. "I was going to tell you..."

"When?"

"After, … after you figured out who killed Keller."

"You don't think it would've made a difference to me?"

"I wasn't sure." Dodge lowered his chin. "You'd have made assumptions…"

He was right. If he had let her know his connections, she would've been wary, not let herself get close.

"That's true, isn't it?" Dodge said.

"I need to get to work." She held her arms loose against her hips, but her fingers tightened against her palms.

"Don't run away," he said.

"I'm not."

"Then what?" he asked.

"I've made enough mistakes."

"I'm not a mistake," he said.

He knew so much about her, and she'd almost been fooled again, except there was no almost about it. She should slap his face, cold cock him, knock his knees out from under him. She didn't respond.

Dodge looked away from her. "You can be cold." He threw his shoulders back.

She took a step toward her door, but he stepped in front of her.

"But you're cruelest to yourself. I'm not letting you leave, so you better listen." He crossed his arms against his chest.

She wanted to shut the door on Dodge, close herself to his face because it reminded her of her own weakness. But she had to talk to him, Roy had implied that he had answers. Why did it have to be him?

She stood in front of him for a moment. The ray from the porch light illuminated half his face. Deep lines crossed his sunburned cheeks. If she didn't move, she feared he'd touch her arm again.

She got her key out of her pocket. She stepped around him and opened the door. "Get away from the light."

She put her cell phone on the night stand next to the bed and left her shoulder holster on.

Dodge closed the door behind him and stood with his back to the door.

"May I stay?"

"Can't stop you."

"Dana."

Of course he used her first name. "For crying out loud, I never wanted to be involved in this. FYI, I just talked to Roy, too. Know what he said? Said I should talk to you!" She bent both arms at the elbow just in case she did have to take him. "Imagine my surprise when I found out he knew you." She looked toward the door and back to him. "How long have you two been best buddies?"

Dodge took a slight step back and bumped into the table next to the window. He bit his bottom lip. "Roy and I, we collaborated on another case years ago, in Denver."

Madison sat hard on the bed. She grabbed the bedspread with her hands and squeezed. What the fuck was he saying? She didn't have to ask. If Dodge knew about Imelda, then he knew her. She blinked over and over as her eyes filled.

He touched her cheek and she dropped the bedspread and pushed her arms out in front of her. "Don't."

"It's all right." He pulled away.

Rage flooded her body, the weariness and sorrow working tears in her eyes. Everything was fucked. Heart pounding, stomach pulled in all directions, bile rising in her throat. She would not cry in front of him.

He looked straight at her. "You were played in Denver."

"Who the hell are you?" She didn't know if what Parker said, what Dodge was saying now made her trust him more or less. If she had been home, working with Henderson, one day leading into another quiet winter at Yosemite, she could have left Denver where it belonged, behind her. She was so sure she had moved on.

"I wanted to tell you, that night here in your room."

His grief that night. Was it real? She folded her arms in front of her chest. She had been ready to tell him everything, and he already knew.

She took a deep breath. She needed to focus on the here and now. "At least tell me you were truly Keller's friend."

Dodge sighed. "Believe me, fast friends. Couple old guys on the job. I just wish…"

He pushed his lips together and looked her in the eyes. "I should have told you." He stepped back. "Can we get out of this room, take a drive…"

Dodge towered above her, a stranger, but one who knew what happened in Denver. And if he knew, did he know who killed Imelda? She stared at his eyes, waiting for him to look away, a sign of deceit. He didn't. He breathed deep and she mirrored his breath. If he was a threat to her, he could break her neck in a second, could have done it out on the trail. She needed to think, she needed his answers. She needed this done.

Madison stood up with her arms at her sides, waited for her legs to steady. She picked up her cell phone. "I'll be checking in with my team in two hours. Understood?"

"Got it."

Dodge's old truck rattled out of the parking lot. The moon lit up the outlines of trees and the mountains beyond. Dodge took the route Madison had driven before, then turned straight east into the prairie. He slowed as a bison turned his head toward the headlights and wandered across the roadway ahead.

The Milky Way's million stars stretched overhead in a long curve to the horizon, the flat prairie below only broken up by grass-lined streams, the long blades capped by seed heads illuminated by moonlight.

Dodge parked along a stream meander, next to a Park Service interpretive sign just visible in the headlights that showed how a river changes over time, the bends and turns, the sudden flood that carves a new course.

Dodge and Madison left the truck and walked along the soft stream bank. A bat dipped and swirled above the water.

Dodge shifted his weight toward her. "Places like this are sacred. My grandfather used to tell the story of *his* grandfather hunting buffalo on the prairie…"

Madison didn't say anything.

"That's the reason…," Dodge breathed deep. "I thought it'd be easier talking out here."

Madison buttoned up her jacket and waited.

"Christ, it wasn't about deceiving you."

"Never is."

"It's not about any of us, it's bigger than that."

Madison shook her head and raised her arms. "Here we go. The grand scheme. We're just frigging pawns. Spare me, I've seen the movie. Who ends up dead next?" Madison walked ahead of Dodge.

"Listen, I don't have all the answers either."

"But you and Roy and everyone else have the most pieces. Why did they need me? Why Greaves, why Mobley?"

"To help find the truth."

"What truth? Seems the only truth is deception."

"Roy thought…it seemed necessary," Dodge said.

"To get what the President wanted? I suppose the President was breathing down Roy's neck for answers. Did the President even want the truth?"

"Yes, of course, the President was feeling pressured…"

"From?"

"From Roy, Roy pressured him, the letter…Roy said more murders were possible…"

"Roy pressured the President? How can you pressure someone who can fire you?"

Dodge shook his head. "It's not like that. Roy has a lifetime appointment, beyond the President's influence. As a way of protecting the truth."

A far-off coyote howled, its call mixed with the sound of the wind through the dried grasses. Stars pierced the darkness.

Madison stopped and faced Dodge. "And *you* know about this special assignment, this lifetime appointment as if he were on the Supreme Court, and what it entails? I should be convinced because you say so?"

"I only know what he's told me. Roy tracks threats to policy about sacred places like Grizzly and other national parks. He maintains specific records as a way of keeping the country's history and decision-making safe."

Madison shook her head and sighed. "And it has to be

a big secret, national security and all that." She paced along the stream bank. She couldn't wait to tell Greaves; it'd play right into all his conspiracy theories. She might join his little cult. "So there are whackos out there, people we won't make public, government officials we won't make public, Roy's in, you're in, but bring in some cannon fodder for a fresh look at things, outsiders who don't mind being shot at or lied to, for the good of the country? It just might work." She imagined the staff in the shadows of the President's basement conference room nodding together, thinking it was a good scheme, laughing to themselves. Maybe the whole room was fake. She should've asked for Roy's ID.

Madison laughed, then scowled at Dodge.

"I didn't think you were expendable, ever. Roy said you were all good. And it wasn't like that for me."

"Then what was it? And how does this have anything to do with Keller?" She wasn't sure she was ready to ask him how it had anything to do with Imelda. She had to stay angry until she got some answers and she knew she might lose her edge if she asked about Imelda.

"Keller was suspicious about the new lodge and what might happen to it. That's how it all got started."

"Suspicious? About what?"

"Not sure yet. Roy was worried, that's what he told the people I work for."

"And they aren't really doing wildlife work…"

"No, we do our share of behind the scenes lobbying, but we also track tribal groups who believe violence is the way to coerce decisions."

"So, the President thinks one of these groups is connected to these killings."

"If they are, we need to stop them."

Madison had a hundred questions. Dodge had gone from being a construction worker to some kind of undercover tribal agent in less than an afternoon. He was saying Keller's death was part of something larger, far beyond what she and Greaves and Mobley might have guessed. As big as the Milky Way above them. And Imelda's death must have been part of it, too.

"It's all a game." She waved a hand at Dodge. "Take out a player rather than let him score, for the good of the people pulling the strings, the ones who'll make the big money in the end. And if you can't play as dirty as everyone else, you're just a loser."

Madison wanted to run and disappear into the tall prairie grass.

Dodge grabbed her shoulders.

Madison breathed faster and faster. "How could I ever tell Imelda's parents that their child was just part of a game?" Madison stepped away from him. "How did murdering her protect anything?"

CHAPTER 42

MADISON'S SHOWER HAD eased some of her fatigue. She'd dressed and was tightening her belt. Someone knocked twice, hard. She opened the door.

"You alone?" Greaves turned his head to the right and left.

Madison stiffened. "Of course."

"You need to come, now." Greaves was as pale as he was moments after Del was shot.

"Take a breath." She put her hand on his shoulder. "Sit down."

"I can't sit." Greaves took a step back and bumped the table. "Mobley and I went through Keller's box, and…"

Madison looked behind Greaves. "Where's Mobley?"

"She's making some phone calls, because we think we're crazy."

"Tell me." Madison sat on the bed.

"Keller's box, you know the one his wife sent, that he never picked up?"

Madison nodded.

“The one with the magazine articles, laundromats, all sorts of construction set-ups?”

Madison bit her lip. “I remember.”

“We found this article with diagrams and system requirements for slot machines, and…” Greaves opened the file he had in his hands.

“Spit it out, Greaves.”

“It had this note from Keller’s wife, ‘is this the one you wanted hon?’ so sweet I thought Mobes was going to cry.” Greaves took a deep breath and gave the article to Madison.

The wrinkled page from a trade magazine had a torn edge as if it had been ripped out.

Madison held it in front of her. “What’s the big deal, Keller was thinking about his next job….”

“Take a closer look at the diagram.”

Madison held the article closer and saw an electrical plan with a chart of power requirements. “You have to help me here, Greaves …”

“Remember Keller made a note about a second set of blueprints…and there were pages missing from the lodge’s blueprints in his box? I asked Ward for the most recent electrical plan…everything is state-of-the-art behind a historically-correct façade. It had the same kind of layout as this article.”

“That’s crazy.”

Greaves nodded. “That’s what we think, it’s crazy.”

Madison threw her head backwards. Her wet hair chilled her neck. This had to be a mistake, an irrational conclusion. No one could possibly think that they could turn the lodge into a casino. “It just couldn’t happen. For one, it would take an act of Congress…” Madison shook her head. But what Dodge had told her last night about

Roy being worried about the park… "They wouldn't dare, the public wouldn't stand for it."

"I'm telling you, boss, Keller might have been on to something. Mobley's checking into it."

Madison stood up. "Let's go help her."

Madison knocked on Mobley's door. Mobley pulled her drapes back, then let them into the room.

She held her cell phone to her ear. "Craig, listen, I can't get into it. Just e-mail me the link, okay? Thanks." She closed her phone. "Damn security."

Madison nodded.

"This is madness." Mobley sat down at her table. "I have access to files in DC I can't get into from this computer. And I'm trying to download the legislation for rebuilding the lodge, but it's taking forever." She tapped her thumb on her computer.

Madison needed to pace, but with three of them in the room, there was nowhere to go. She shifted her weight from one foot to the other. "Crap. If this is true…. Jesus, I need coffee."

"I'll get it." Greaves shot out the door and slammed it behind him before she could stop him.

Madison sighed and sat on the bed. She noticed Mobley's fly-fishing equipment on the top of her dresser, everything neat, delicate fly in mid-making. Ordered.

If the lodge could be transformed into something as commercial as a casino, then the logic of Madison's world could change too. What had happened to Yosemite in the last 20 years, the commercial shops, corporate fast food, shuttles to keep the number of cars down, all that was an assault, but gambling? She took a deep breath. She needed the silence of the wind, the birdsong, the granitic rocks cracking in the freeze and thaw of winter turning into spring. "Mobley, could they do it?"

Mobley tapped the top of her mouse. "A modification that big would take specific legislation."

Madison rose and pulled back the drapes. Greaves stood with his back to her, talking to Parker. He moved his hands back and forth, forgetting about her steaming coffee. He nodded to Parker. Madison let the drapes drop from her hand.

Greaves opened the door and handed the coffee to Madison. He pulled a muffin from a paper bag stuffed in his coat pocket and held it up. "Got to keep up your strength, Chief."

Madison nodded thanks. "While Mobley's getting her files, I've got something to tell you." She sat back down on Mobley's bed. "Last night I met with Dodge."

Greaves' eyebrows almost met his hairline.

"Settle down," Madison said. She knew what Greaves was thinking. She may have wished that the evening had turned out the way he suspected, but after what Dodge had told her, the night couldn't lead to that.

Madison told Mobley and Greaves about her call to Roy and what Dodge had told her about Roy's concerns for the lodge, and that Dodge wasn't there for the construction job. Just as Madison had imagined, Greaves looked ready to call in the conspiracy theorists.

"I knew it, he held that gun like he'd used one before."

Greaves raised his hands over his head, then let them down. "Wish I'd been there, I would have told him what for."

"Don't worry Greaves, I didn't let him off easy. I'm still pissed about all this secrecy."

"And Roy knew more than he told us, *again*." Mobley licked her lips as she shook her head.

"I plan to give it to him too. But we need to focus on what's really going on here and now," Madison said.

"If Roy was concerned about the lodge, then the push for a casino must be it," Greaves said. "That, and there's an alien landing strip somewhere out on the prairie." He smiled at Madison.

"Not going to dignify that," Madison said.

"Got it," Mobley said. She scrolled down the file, the familiar format of a bill flashing by. Madison didn't have time to focus on any words, just the glare from the screen.

Greaves said "Slow down."

Mobley waved him off.

Madison bent her neck in a stretch. "What did Parker say?"

Greaves looked at the screen, then back at Madison.

"I saw you almost spill my coffee on him," Madison said.

"I just asked about the investigation. They can't find any evidence. No spent shells, nothing. They think it's a professional shooter. There's a memorial for Del this afternoon."

"I know, Corrigan left me a message."

"Parker said Brumley's sending a rep. I'd like to go."

Madison nodded.

Mobley shook her head. "Damn it. When bills are written by committee, everything gets so screwed up." She scrolled faster. "Here's something. Last minute amendment. Under an obscure section."

Mobley read from the screen. "In the event park activities occur that the Senate Energy and Resources committee…" Her red fingernail followed the text. "… deem to be a detriment to the sovereign rights of any tribe, then …the committee shall transfer the park's assets to the aforementioned tribes."

"What does that mean?" Greaves said.

Mobley looked up at them. "I could make it mean anything."

"Who put the amendment in?" Madison said.

"Brumley."

"Anything specific to gambling?" Madison said.

Mobley eyes followed the words scrolling over the screen. "No, but if the land was under Indian control, then they could argue that it was allowed under the Indian Gaming Act. Brumley helped write the act."

"And he's chair of the Senate Indian Affairs Committee right?" Madison said.

Mobley nodded. "Indian nations support him every election. You should see his office, lots of gifts from the tribes."

"What'd you mean?" Greaves said.

Mobley turned around in her chair. "The walls were lined with bookcases filled with Indian artifacts. Some should have been in museums. I said something, and his staffer joked that Brumley's house is full of incredibly valuable pieces."

"Damn it." Greaves put his hand to his face and rubbed the side of his cheek as if someone had slapped him.

CHAPTER 43

White House

May 1903

PRESIDENT ROOSEVELT WALKED through the door fitted snugly into the wall of his Cabinet Room. He admired the workmanship, the detail so fine that when the door closed behind him it disappeared seamlessly into the woodwork. Many dreamed of being president, but as he had watched the craftsmen build his house at Sagamore Hill, he wished for a simpler life, of working wood with his hands and continuing his study of the natural world. Politics had intervened.

Sunlight from long windows flooded the men in suits packed in a tight ring around his mahogany desk. He shook hands with some as he made his way to his chair. The stage was set, the bill to establish Grizzly National Park ready for him to sign into law.

Timber and mining interests couldn't stop Roosevelt's bill. He had bargained well. He had garnered support from those who understood his desire for conservation through the creation of a national park. And the tribes got what they wanted, permanent access to and preservation of their sacred sites.

Roosevelt picked up his pen from the official set on the desk and leaned forward. A photographer stood in front of him, camera secure on a wooden tripod. Roosevelt wanted the photograph of the bill signing to be front page news. He lifted the pen, looked directly at the photographer and held the pose as the camera captured the scene with a flash, then signed the bill quickly. He smiled again for the next shot, then turned around and shook hands with the congressmen he'd asked to sponsor it. For now and all future generations, Grizzly National Park would be secure.

Sky Capture stood against the jamb of the double French doors at the back of the room, members of the Kowaho Nation dressed in their native costumes beside him. Roosevelt saw him and he showed all his teeth in a wide grin under his full mustache. His encounters with Sky Capture had tempered his opinion that Indians were only scattered tribes of savages. They were not afraid to threaten the federal government. And though Roosevelt knew he had the advantage over them, if his negotiations were made public, it could weaken his conservation movement. He couldn't let that happen. Too many of the voters did not understand how deals are made and how compromises keep the peace.

Roosevelt wanted to let the Indians think he was now off guard. He looked at the men at the back of the room, waved his hand and pointed to the intricate woven basket that had arrived from them that morning. Sky Capture nodded to the President and his group slipped out the door.

The next morning, Roosevelt asked Cortelyou, his personal secretary, to join him for breakfast. The excitement of yesterday's signing was gone. The press had given him mixed reviews, and as expected, there was backlash from industry. Carnegie the loudest, with greedy remarks about slowing the nation's progress. The industrialists had the audacity to invoke God to suit their purpose. He could deal with them and the press.

But the Indians were unpredictable.

Roosevelt picked up his fork and pointed it at Cortelyou. "I need you to set up a new bureau. Not through regular channels."

CHAPTER 44

MADISON WALKED WITH Greaves and Mobley through the back door of the lodge into the first floor foyer. Corrigan's message last night had said construction would stop for the day so there could be a brief memorial to Del. She took off her ranger's hat and held it in her hands. The area had been straightened up for the memorial. There had been a small outdoor service for Keller, but everyone thought his death was accidental. This was different.

Corrigan stood in front of the crowd, the vast windows showing the lake behind him, the Xs of the construction tape on the windows simulating a sort of stained glass. He walked back and forth in his spotless uniform, carrying notes in his hands. Corrigan had made a statement to the local press, but he caught one break, most of the national press corps were preoccupied with a scandal in Washington.

Ward sat in a chair in front of the windows, his wounds patched up, his eyes wet, his face a map of shock and grief.

Madison shook Corrigan's hand then walked over to Ward. He held out a shaking hand. "I still can't believe it…"

Madison put her hand on his shoulder.

"But it should've been me…" Ward said.

Madison rubbed his shoulder. Wanting to take the place of the one who's lost, everyone wishes for that. "We'll catch who did this, Ward."

She moved away as other people gathered around him. Greaves and Mobley nodded, then headed to the back of the room.

Dodge sat on a chair next to an aisle, his long legs stretched in front of him. He held his baseball cap in his hands. He lifted his head when he saw Madison and nodded toward the seat next to him. She shook her head and motioned for him to follow her.

Dodge got up and trailed behind her.

Madison looked around the room. In Denver, she and Stan staked out funerals for homicide victims, in case one of the grievers turned out to be the killer. For those services she had some distance from the victim, and they were easier to get through. Parker was over in a corner of the room, doing the same thing, looking for anyone suspicious.

If the shooter was a construction worker, it would be easy for him to blend in. Dodge had told her that Del and Ward kept track of who was where when, as best they could, but on a big construction site, it was easy to wander off for a few hours and not be missed.

Corrigan held up his hands for quiet, then introduced a member of Brumley's staff. Brumley's staffer took a step forward and read a letter from Brumley. Madison knew the staffer wrote the sentiments, that's how these things worked. It was thankfully short. Mobley whispered to Madison. "You going to tell Dodge?"

"Yes," Madison said.

"You're the captain," Mobley said.

Greaves bent his head toward the front of the room and shook a finger at Mobley.

Mobley pushed her lips together.

Madison waited, then leaned close to Dodge. "We need to talk."

Dodge tilted his head towards her.

"We found something worth killing for," she whispered.

The general construction manager stood up, his skin pale around the eyes, the rest of his face red. He nodded to Ward, then his voice caught on Del's name.

Dodge leaned toward Madison. "What?"

"A casino."

"What are you talking about?" he whispered.

"Look around you." Madison pointed to the electrical conduit along the wall and the stubs coming through the floor every few feet. "This place isn't wired for a wilderness lodge."

Dodge looked around the room. "No." His jaw dropped.

Corrigan closed the service, and workers rose from their chairs and milled around to the side of the room where coffee and cold cuts filled a conference table.

Madison pulled her jacket around her and put her ranger's hat on. "Let's take a walk," she said to the others.

Dodge followed Madison out, with Greaves and Mobley behind him, not saying anything. Madison passed the giant boulders at the base of the moraine onto the path next to the water. She walked east, away from the picnic table where they were almost shot, towards the cliffs ringing the edge of the lake. The overcast sky dulled the fall reds of the deciduous trees among the pines. She felt grey herself, sick of memorials and death, if it had at least been spring, there would be signs of life continuing.

They reached a small cove behind a peninsula of boulders, out of sight of the lodge. Madison scanned the striated cliffs, the rock gouged deep by glacial ice. Once cut, never the same. Nature had the power, the right to change things forever. She could handle that.

Dodge paced along the lake. "What did you find?"

Madison traced one natural cut in the rock with her hand. "In the legislation for the lodge, Brumley added an amendment. It says the tribes can take over the lodge if warranted."

Greaves jumped in. "The extra cabling, Keller's power flows, what else could it be, we think it's for a casino."

Dodge shook his head. "Casino? The gaming law is clear. Casinos have to be on tribal land, there's a long environmental review, and the public would be outraged."

"If it's after the fact, what could they do?" Madison said.

Mobley spread her hands. "I checked the language, it would be exempt from the usual process."

"Brumley did this?" Dodge stopped.

"He submitted the amendment, there was a quick procedural vote, no time for anyone to read it."

"Roy vaguely mentioned he was worried about the lodge's construction. He didn't say anything about this."

"The guy who was paying attention ended up dead," Mobley said.

Dodge shook his head. "Keller...."

Whitecaps drove aspen leaves into the shallow water, lining the bank with gold.

Madison watched the array of clouds rip over the mountains. "If the money is big enough…"

"Desecrate the sacred," Dodge said. "The tribe gets money, but a heck of a lot of it goes to the management company they hire."

"They don't run things?" Madison said.

"Most tribes aren't equipped to do it." Dodge took his baseball cap off and put it on again. "They hire corporations that run casinos all over the world. These guys access construction contractors, equipment for slots, table games, restaurants…. It's easier for tribes to hire the expertise. The companies even lend them the funds to pay for it. Hard to resist."

"Tribes need the revenue," Mobley said.

"It changes their whole economic structure," Dodge said.

"Can't blame them," Greaves said.

"But the price?" Madison said.

"Gaming's always been a part of Indian culture," Greaves said.

"So was chest piercing for the Sun Dance, but no one encourages that anymore." Mobley crossed her arms.

Madison leaned against the cliff. In the fading light, the yellow leaves of nearby aspens lost their shimmer as they moved in the breeze. The place still beautiful, even in the muted light. She had seen such ugliness in the human heart. But this, the classic sell-out of nature, decency, the law, it stunned her.

"But why kill Del?" Greaves said.

"Maybe they didn't want Del," Dodge said.

"They wanted us, or one of us," Madison said.

They looked at Mobley.

"Why me?" Mobley said.

"That shot almost hit you," Greaves said.

Mobley shook her head. "No, Brumley was here, it has to be him…And they said there were two shots…" She arched her back as she took a breath.

The last thing Madison wanted was a repeat of that photo of her and Stan in Denver. "We have to be sure. We need proof or we'll get laughed off the front page."

No one spoke.

Dodge looked at them. "We can't go public, but I know what we can do."

CHAPTER 45

MADISON CONTINUED WALKING along the lake as the others returned to their motel rooms. Dodge's plan might just work. She wanted to trust him. But she couldn't quite shake a lingering stomach twitch about him.

The trail wove through a dense grove of pines and cedars. The bullet that hit the pine could have been meant for Mobley. In her work for the Department of Justice she had put away some shady figures, maybe a few with connections to Indian gaming. If the new lodge was turned into a casino, big money would follow, and the people set to receive the biggest cut were usually one step ahead of everyone else. They might have wanted Mobley off this case.

Or Greaves, he still gave her pause. His work on the blueprints, the details gleaned from Keller's scratchings in his notebook, she wouldn't have made progress without him. He seemed less likely a target, but his skill at catching artifact smugglers for the Commerce Department would be known. Maybe someone didn't want his skills pointed in their direction.

The scent of decaying needles filled her nose. She took

a deep breath and pulled gloves from her coat pocket. Roy seemed most worried about her, she was the closest link to him and through him the President. If they wanted her, they'd had their chances. She shouldn't be walking alone right now, but she had to think. And no one would know anything more until they made a move in the open.

The afternoon light grayed as clouds smothered the sun. She rounded a bend in the trail. A thump behind her made her turn. Wind in the branches blew smaller twigs onto the ground. The varied cadence of what sounded like a purple finch floated through the trees. She knew it was a little late for a finch to be so high in elevation, and the song was awfully close to the red-eyed vireo's demanding *look-up, see-me.* She searched the high branches for a glimpse of the bird, but couldn't find it. *Look-up, see-me*, over and over it preached. And she tried. Neither bird should be here. Her ear for birdsong must be off.

Madison sat on a large rounded boulder next to the water. Sunlight broke free of the clouds and crossed the blurred greens of the far forest and the multicolored cliffs. Patches of wind shivered across the lake as they had done for millions of years. The far cliffs lifting up snowy peaks took her breath. The old lodge, such a grand masterpiece, still couldn't begin to challenge the scale of nature surrounding it. In this landscape, no person could have any pretense of one's own grandeur. No place seemed more deserving of Henderson's favorite Teddy Roosevelt quote: "Leave it as it is. The ages have been at work on it and man can only mar it." That anyone could even consider changing Grizzly into an adult amusement park with jackpot bells and slot machine alarms and neon lights...*mar* would be an inadequate word for that.

Madison unlocked her motel room door and took off her coat and gloves. She pulled her phone from her pocket and dialed Roy's number.

If Dodge had talked with Roy, he would have told Roy about their conversation last night. Madison had much to say to Roy, but she also wanted the whole thing to be over.

"You heard from Dodge?" she said.

"It's risky." Roy cleared his throat, then coughed.

Madison waited a few seconds for his coughing to stop. "They've been playing us, and now we reciprocate." It was a good thing Roy was on the right side of this, if he was, or she'd be reciprocating on him.

"It wasn't supposed to put you in danger…" Roy took a deep breath.

Madison shuddered as she heard moist air dragging across his throat. "We'll be careful." She pulled back the drapes and looked across the parking lot. "You've let Senator Brumley's name slip in front of your assistant?"

"Yes. He noticed."

"Good." She wouldn't ever admit it to her old police partners, but she did have more than one compassionate bone in her body, and she wanted to tell Roy to take it easy, go get some rest before … well, whatever was coming next. She knew he wouldn't listen. She also knew that his cough was similar to a last cough. She took a deep breath. "We'll be in touch."

If Roy's assistant was the leak, and Roy was sure he was, then things would start happening. Someone would make a move, this time with people watching.

Now she'd have to wait. She hated it. She put her

phone on the table. So far, no one had bothered her room. That would likely change. She'd plant some information for them to find. She sat on the bed and grabbed the motel pen and notepad near the phone on the side table. She wrote "Brumley? Kowaho tribe, vault tunnel?" and her trademark doodle of intersecting boxes underneath the questions.

She ripped off the paper. The impression on the notepad was clear, maybe not too obvious. She left the notepad on the bedside table; then filled a file folder with other notes and a newspaper article about Brumley cutting the ribbon at the start of construction. She stuck the file between the dresser and the wall, next to Keller's real case file. If they looked at Keller's file and believed it was real, they'd believe the other file was real and get that Madison knew about Brumley and the lodge.

She left the room her usual spread-out mess, and slipped her gun into her shoulder holster. Greaves and Mobley would meet her at the general store, where she'd endure Greaves' endless stories while they ate. If someone wanted to get into her room, she'd give them time.

CHAPTER 46

WHEN MADISON OPENED the door to the store she spotted Greaves and Mobley in the first booth next to the window. They weren't alone. Parker's posture gave him away. As Madison slid onto the bench seat next to him, she nodded to Betty, who was taking Mobley's order. "Whatever she's having, that'll be fine."

Mobley raised an eyebrow.

After Betty left for the kitchen, Greaves whispered to Madison, "I think Parker's on a mission; he won't talk though."

Madison frowned at Greaves.

Parker didn't say anything.

Madison put her hand on Parker's arm. "Come on now, we made up didn't we? What gives?"

Parker shifted on the bench and looked past her toward the bar. "DC said to stay close."

Greaves smiled as if he had planned the whole thing.

"Who?" Madison said.

"Top of the food chain," Parker said.

Madison didn't want to let on to Parker that anything

out of ordinary was happening in case someone was nosing around. Not yet. But Roy must be worried. "Really?" She punched his arm. "Relax, we're fine. Like the three musketeers, four with you," she winked at him. She nodded toward the restrooms at the back of the store. "You don't have to follow me in there, do you?" She leaned close to him "I'm packin'."

He frowned at her and straightened as she left the table.

At the back of the store Madison dialed Dodge.

"Dana, you all right?" Dodge sounded winded.

"Fine. Parker's watching over us."

"What?"

"Somebody high up said stay close."

Dodge took a breath. "Roy must have talked to the President."

Madison knew they'd need the President to take care of details if Dodge's plan was to be successful, but she figured Roy would keep it quiet until they were sure the plan would work.

She leaned against the wall. Parker watched her. Madison turned her back to him. "I don't think Parker knows the details so I better get back and act my cheery self. Where are you?"

Dodge cleared his throat. "In the lodge. Full steam ahead, that's what the general contractor says. Some of the guys quit after Del…I'm not sure when I can get off."

"Maybe you should quit too." Madison wasn't half joking. She wanted him near.

"Things are in place. It won't be long." He hung up.

She hoped he was right.

She closed her phone and joined her team. Betty served

Madison and her glare let Madison know she had arrived just in time.

Madison lifted her hamburger bun. "I miss anything?"

Greaves slid the ketchup bottle across the table. "Parker was just getting to his life story, weren't you, Rick?"

Madison raised her eyes. "Rick? Too bad you're not a ranger. The hat would become you."

"More than you I fear, my Captain," Greaves said.

Parker's lips finally broke into a small grin.

"Hazard of the job." Madison bit into her burger and juice ran onto her hands.

Mobley threw her a paper napkin. "Equally attractive."

Madison picked up the napkin and smiled as she wiped her hands. She looked out the window as a young man, baseball cap covering his head, carried cleaning supplies into her room.

CHAPTER 47

"IT'S ON ME," Madison said as Betty set the bill on the table. She handed Betty her credit card, then said loud enough for everyone in the place to hear, "Betty, we'll be leaving soon, like the autumn breeze; we'll miss you."

Betty's expression didn't change, she just took the credit card as if she'd heard the same thing from seasonal visitors since the proverbial dawn of time.

Parker thought it was a bad idea, but Madison talked him into letting her go to her room alone. She whispered to Greaves as they came out of the store to keep Parker occupied as long as he could with blueprints and notebooks, then meet again after a few hours. The bad guys needed some time to react to what they'd found. Parker surveyed the area around them before he followed Greaves and Mobley into Greaves' room.

Madison's room was as she imagined it would be—fresh towels, bed made. She looked over at the bedside table; a fresh note pad lay next to the lamp.

The real case file and the fabricated one were where she

left them, all but for a small piece of flaking paint she had slipped between two pages inside the fake file. The paint chip was on the floor next to the woodwork. Whoever cleaned her room got the fake file and looked at it, she was sure of it.

She sat on the bed and set her gun next to her on the bedspread. She turned the pages in the file folders. Whoever went through the files left them in their original order. Even without dusting she knew there wouldn't be prints, the person was careful.

The dated room wasn't the most comfortable place to wait, but she had to now. She needed to hear from Dodge that he'd connected to tribes who were as averse to the desecration of their sacred places as Dodge was. They'd be watching the Senator. And some would send others inside the park's boundaries, but they wouldn't arrive for a few hours.

At that point, her team would have to make itself more vulnerable, get out in the open again.

She opened the pocket on the back of her coat where she'd stuffed Imelda's file. She didn't want whoever was in the room to touch it, let alone know she had it. She picked up the manila envelope with the crime scene photos and started to unfold the flap, but stopped. She didn't need to look at the photos again.

Roy had made sure she had Imelda's file from almost the beginning. She didn't know his true motives, maybe she never would. What Dodge had told her that night out on the prairie, she hadn't had enough time to absorb. Dodge had known about Imelda, knew at the time that the person Madison had in custody was the real killer. The tag from the Lewis and Clark expedition tipped Dodge off that the murder was unusual, got him involved. His organization had far-reaching ties to the police and knew about the tag. They had to keep it a secret and sent the letter that ruined Madison's career. But they didn't let her know, or say why the killer picked such a young girl.

What had Dodge traded for leaving Imelda's family without the consolation they could have gotten if the killer had been found, tried and jailed? Preserving secrets that would put themselves or their ancestors in a bad light? What price the truth?

The effect on her paled in comparison, but still hurt. What could have been the harm in letting her know? Dodge thought it was someone from a group who had sent threatening letters to the president. But no one had ever killed a child before. But they killed Imelda.

Keller's death was surely a message to back off. Did these people play a sick joke when they placed the First Regiment button in the crevice on the cliff? Was it a murderer's "fuck you," to make Dodge and Roy feel a familiar tic and know Keller's death was no accident? Dodge had said that the animals responsible for Imelda's death were deranged, but when the button appeared after Keller's death, after the artifact tag next to Imelda, Dodge knew they were somehow connected or made to appear so.

Did the centuries-old killings have a clear purpose, to force action, evidenced by the letters Roy kept watch over and the oral histories Dodge said had been passed down? At Grizzly, at least on the surface, tribal leaders were getting what they wanted with the new lodge construction. Why would they want to call attention to Keller's death? Unless it was supposed to look like another random killing. But the letter to the President made it surely political. That's why Roy got involved.

But who sent the recent letter to the President? Roy's assistant could have provided the details of past letters, and knew what would happen if this killing was similar to historic ones. But why put the lodge construction under scrutiny? Unless. Unless Roy sent the letter. He would know what details to include, he would know that having a letter come to the President would get him all the resources he needed to find out what was happening. If Roy sent the letter, then he would get it to study, and he would know about prints and postmarks and anything that he or his assistant would check. It would land right in his hands.

Madison shook her head and closed her eyes tight. Both temples hurt. The general store's famous hamburger wasn't sitting too well either. She put Imelda's file down on the bed and lay back against the pine headboard.

A slight knock at the door startled Madison. She got up from the bed and slid the end of the drape back. Mobley stood in front of the door with her head turned to look behind her. Madison opened the door and Mobley quickly slid into the room. Her forehead twitched, and she leaned her shoulders back. Madison turned to where Mobley was looking and saw the gun on the bed.

Madison picked up the gun and put it into the bedside table drawer. "You all right?"

Mobley took a deep breath.

Madison waited.

"Can I sit?" Mobley said.

Madison nodded.

"I've found… something interesting." Mobley struggled

to get her words out. She looked down at the floor, then up to Madison again.

Madison sat down on the bed. "What is it?"

Mobley looked away.

"What'd you find out?"

Mobley stared at Madison.

Madison waited again.

Mobley shook her head quickly and took a deep breath. "It's Brumley. He's been sending up bills for the benefit of Indian tribes since the beginning of his career. He has a strong record of going to great lengths to get these tribes what they want, especially land and hunting rights."

Madison had heard as much from Dodge. Brumley was so respected in the tribal community, he'd been adopted by a number of tribes. "Sounds right."

"And he's close to one of the primary tribal lobbyist in DC, that's no surprise, but this lobbyist isn't just pushing typical issues such as health care for the tribes, he's involved in their lucrative efforts: casinos, making cigarettes…"

"That doesn't seem uncommon."

"No, not in itself, but he's also a lobbyist for the gaming management corporations who fund these enterprises and take a large percentage of the spoils. Seems a conflict of interest."

"Never seemed to stop anyone in Washington." Madison bit her lip. She paced in front of the bed. Bring money into the equation, and Brumley had to listen to contributors and let them write legislation for what they wanted. "So, who's the lobbyist?

"Harlen Trent," Mobley said.

Madison hadn't heard of him.

"There's more," Mobley said. "If you look at the map

Roy gave us, there's a definite up tic in violent incidents on the map since tribes started asking for approval to build casinos. Maybe…?"

"But the killings predated casinos…there were other issues…" Madison said. "What do we know about this Trent?"

"Penthouse in the Watergate, house in the Hamptons… quite the philanthropist too."

"Unusual for a lobbyist?"

"No, but …" Mobley paused.

"But, he's obviously been delivering for his clients. I'd like to get him in a room for five minutes."

Maybe Madison didn't need to. He would be a master at doing things behind the scenes, maybe a well-placed phone call would be just as good. "If you were Trent," Madison asked Mobley. "Who would scare you most, a park ranger or a Department of Justice lawyer?"

If Trent was involved, he'd know all about Madison and Mobley. Chances were anyone phoning from DOJ would never get by the secretary, not before a quick message to Trent's law firm on retainer to handle such calls. But Madison and Mobley didn't need to talk to him directly. Other lobbyists had been convicted of a whole host of indiscretions, so a simple request for vague background material wouldn't be that unusual. But Mobley's name attached to it would raise suspicions, if indeed her name meant anything to Trent.

Mobley pulled out her cell phone and dialed. "Hello, my name is Karen Mobley, I'm an attorney with the Department of Justice. Would you please connect me to Mr. Trent? Yes, I can hold. Thank you."

Madison leaned back on the bed. They could have scripted this. She had enough experience with criminals who could afford lawyers to know the gatekeeper's drill. Mobley had experience creating sweaty palms, too.

"I see," Mobley said. She nodded at Madison. "Of course, I realize he has a busy schedule. Perhaps you could leave him a message. I'm in the field now working on an investigation, but I'll be back in DC in the next few days and we can set a time for a personal interview. Mobley, yes that's the correct spelling. I'm looking for some background information, for another case. Thank you."

Mobley smiled like she did when Madison had food on her face.

"Well done," Madison said. "You'd be good in a street fight."

The smile drained from Mobley's face.

"What'd I say?" Madison asked.

"You know nothing about me," she said.

Madison shrugged her shoulders. "I'm not following."

Mobley breathed hard through her nose. "Before, when you assumed I came from an upper class family, far as possible from rough streets and guns, you couldn't have been more wrong."

After Mobley's response to the shot exploding the tree behind her, Madison knew there might be more to her reaction than the perfectly normal fear of death. Shock can do almost anything to a person. But Mobley's fly-tying episode made Madison scared for her.

Madison wasn't sure if she should say anything or let a pause draw Mobley out. Madison smiled and finally said "It wouldn't be the first time I misjudged someone."

Mobley took a long breath and leaned hard against the back of the chair. "You couldn't know."

Madison felt she should've known. Mobley had lost no

time checking her out, with Madison's own reaction in the general store confirming Mobley's research. Madison hadn't taken time to check anything but the briefing book Roy had given them. And the information there was only what Roy wanted them to know.

"You want to enlighten me?" Madison said.

Mobley leaned forward. "Did you ever have to shoot someone?'

The images going through Madison's mind made her stomach jump. Looking down the barrel at a body, not the person behind it, just the living body taking a gun out of his pants, not responding to her order to drop the gun. Just the mention brought a jolt of adrenaline. Her lips went dry. She nodded.

Mobley squeezed her eyes closed slowly. "You never forget, do you? I was on a reservation once, until the tribe made me and Mom leave because we didn't have enough Indian blood. When we left, my Poppy, the only relative left of my grandfather's generation, the one who taught me to dance, and ride horses and fish, Poppy gave me a small gun. He had taught me to shoot, so he could take me hunting with him. But the tribe didn't let us stay, and he knew we'd be going back to unsafe city streets. 'You'll need protection,' he said. And he was right. If they'd let us stay, if they hadn't looked at our skin and seen black instead of red, I never would have had to shoot a kid in the face to save my life."

Madison didn't jump right in and start empathizing with Mobley. She knew better. When Madison had to shoot to kill, when afterwards her partner took her gun and sat her down on the curb, anything anyone would have said would have been pointless, an insult almost. She remembered her partner's hand on her shoulder. She knew she wasn't supposed to talk to anyone until she could give a statement. When her mind cleared for a moment, she knew she was in shock. But then the shock would take over her mind again. If she hadn't had training, she would have run over to the boy, yelled, done something physical, tried to help.

But others were already there, someone had called for an ambulance, people were giving aid. She didn't have to do that. She had to look away and sit and wait. The blur of people and other cops, and crime tape and screaming passersby, she remembered the smell of the garbage in the gutter, the dampness of the remnants of a thunderstorm soaking through her uniform. Wondering why she was getting so cold.

Mobley's hand trembled. She looked at Madison, then made a fist.

Madison took a breath. "I'm sorry."

Mobley squeezed her lips together. "People wonder why I'm in this job, why I could be so hard on the people others think are my own. My own people…they did to me what others had done to them. I ended up in law school only through the grace of a prosecutor who took pity on me, but with that boy on my soul forever."

Mobley's perfectly manicured nails trembled. Her Ivy League pedigree not the result of middle-class privilege, gotten a whole different way.

Madison leaned toward her. "I'm not going to say I know how it is, the way you carry yourself, the way you're on guard and always strong. What I say doesn't mean squat. Just hang in there until we get some kind of payback."

CHAPTER 48

MADISON LOOKED AHEAD and back as she jogged through the cold air up the road to the park's temporary office next to the construction site. As she opened the door, a male voice boomed "tried the Hail Mary pass," from the break room, then a laugh. She still rooted for her Denver Broncos, and hadn't quite grasped the mystique of the 49ers.

The row of jackets and hats hanging on a rack along the wall made her homesick for Yosemite. Her park seemed more than a world and a few days away. She'd give a lot to be back there now, growing irritated with the folks who talked too loud in the government-issue cube farm, as if no one could hear them. She'd think about being nicer to them.

Corrigan's staff tried to look busy, shuffled papers, leaned toward their computer screens, but they watched her. A ranger from another park investigating an incident at Yosemite would have gotten the same response. It was like Internal Affairs in the police department, the officers who tried to ferret out the bad apples. She believed in their work, but never wanted to do it herself. The thin blue line and all.

She smiled to those she caught looking her way. She was one of them, as dedicated to protecting the birds and bunnies as they were. They couldn't know that, but still…

"The Superintendent in?" she said as she walked past the receptionist and into Corrigan's office.

Corrigan looked up from his desk. Thin bands of sun streamed through the metal blinds half opened on his windows, forming more creases on Corrigan' face than his time outdoors warranted.

Madison closed the door behind her and sat on the chair in front of his desk.

Corrigan's mouth slipped from a smile into a tight horizontal line as he pressed his lips together. "I heard you might be ready to leave."

"Doesn't take long for news to travel," Madison said. She wondered if his staff had heard her in the store, or if he'd learned they were leaving through another source.

"Your conclusions?" Corrigan leaned forward.

"You have to ask? Keller was murdered."

Corrigan took a deep breath. "Damn it. Are you sure?"

"After the events of the last couple of days…."

"But," he shook his head. "I was hoping it was just you they were after."

Madison watched pain race across his face as muscles twitched.

"I didn't mean that," Corrigan said. "What'd we miss?"

"Your folks did what anyone would've done." She leaned closer to the desk. "They found a guy who they thought slipped on the loose gravel at the end of that ridge. Nothing too remarkable about that. But there were clues…."

She waited for Corrigan to ask about those clues.

"Still…" Corrigan looked away, then back again. He seemed to be ignoring the details. "Why kill him, why Del?"

Madison wanted to let Corrigan know that his world was about to get even more complicated. If all went as planned, the truth would win out, but behind the scenes. The lodge construction plan would change. Corrigan would take the heat for the delay, without any good press to go along with it.

Madison looked at the pile of papers on Corrigan's desk. "How closely did you follow the lodge rebuilding legislation?"

"What?"

"After the fire, how involved were you in the legislation to get the lodge rebuilt?"

"What does that have to do with….?" Corrigan said.

"Can you answer the question?" Madison looked straight at him.

"Not much. I was busy here, trying to keep the park operating," Corrigan said.

"You didn't review it?" Madison said.

"Review it? I got a courtesy call from Brumley's staff about the Wind Woman debacle, but the actual legislation, they didn't ask for my input."

"Brumley's staff didn't run anything by you?" Madison said.

"No. You know how it is. HQ handled it in DC."

"Right," Madison said. She'd have thought they might run a few things by the park superintendent, but in the end Corrigan wasn't a player. "Keller was a bit more curious."

"About the legislation?" Corrigan said.

If Madison knew people, she could almost see Corrigan dismissing Keller as a dumb construction worker. Bad habit of the so-called educated class.

"About the details of construction," Madison said.

Corrigan frowned. "And you found this out how?"

"Just basic police work."

"My staff…"

"Nothing wrong with what your staff did, even the FBI did a cursory overview, did you know that?"

"No," Corrigan said. "Jesus, I was trying to keep the architects from killing the construction contractor and vice versa. And you found what?"

"I really can't tell you any more." Madison leaned back in the chair.

"So, you're saying I have not only one murder, but two on my watch." Corrigan slumped lower onto his desk.

"Sorry," Madison said.

Corrigan took a breath. "At least tell me you know who's responsible."

Madison nodded.

Corrigan started to get up. "Are they in custody? Is the park secure?"

Madison waved him to sit down. She didn't reply for a second. "No need for you to do anything. No one is in harm's way."

"You're sure? Jesus, I couldn't…Can I see your report?"

"You'll get our report." Madison wasn't so sure he'd get anything but a scrubbed account. Roy would see to that.

Madison left Corrigan's office. If Corrigan had been part of the whole thing, he lied well. His body language didn't give him away. Madison mentally checked him off as part of the plan to turn the lodge into a grand casino and Grizzly into nothing more than a roadside attraction.

A cold sun flashed off the vehicles outside the park office. She zipped her jacket and put on her hat.

The gravel road to the motel was empty of cars. Hammering and compressor blasts pierced the air. Every construction day counted now before winter.

The road turned and she walked through the roadcut she and Mobley and Greaves had run to when the shooter fired the shot that hit the pine tree behind them. Those moments seemed an ice age ago.

Wood smoke drifted high, and pushed away from the lake as the wind flowed over and across the glacial moraine. The slanted sunlight caught the tips of browning leaves on the trees next to the store. Her cheeks tightened as cold air rushed by.

Ground squirrels scrambled in and out of the nearby boulders, getting their burrows ready for winter.

Madison took an awkward step and loose gravel on the road rolled under her feet. She regained her footing and saw Greaves and Parker come out of Greaves' motel room. Greaves' hands waved about his head, his long arms seeming out of proportion to the scale of his body. Parker shook his head, then lowered his jaw. Madison could tell by the way he bent his neck he was listening to his radio.

Greaves kept talking. Parker held up a hand in front of Greaves' face and Greaves put his arms down. He shifted his weight from one foot to the other like an anxious kid. Even from a distance Greaves' movements could rub Madison the wrong way. He cocked his head toward Parker.

Parker jerked his head up and said something to Greaves. Parker pointed toward the rooms at the end of the motel. Greaves nodded and Parker gave him a push with his hand.

Madison watched as Greaves headed toward Mobley's room. Madison started running down the road. Parker turned and sprinted toward her. He waved his hands for her to stop and get down. She dropped to the roadbed. Before Parker reached her, the crack of a gunshot reverberated high off a far cliff, then bounced off another and another.

A moment before, at the top of a cliff east of the lodge, the young man had slipped his rifle off his back. He flipped the lens cap off the scope and slid the bolt into place. A fleck of light glinted off the metal as he lifted the rifle up onto a nearby boulder and steadied his aim. His finger bent slightly as he peered through the scope. A small branch snapped behind him, then a bullet pierced his skull behind his right ear. His body fell and his rifle dropped without firing onto the trail.

CHAPTER 49

MADISON CROUCHED. PARKER squatted beside her, his eyes darting, gun in one hand, his other hand resting on her back. The sound of the gunshot had disappeared into the construction noise. If the workers heard it, they hadn't reacted. Madison stayed low but searched the cliffs, then the trees, trying to catch a flash, a movement, any unusual rhythm.

Dodge came from the lodge toward them.

"Get down!" Parker yelled.

"What the …," Before Madison could finish her sentence, Dodge was next to her.

"It's all right." Dodge held out his cell phone and motioned for them to get up. "I got a call. There's no danger."

Parker shook his head. "What the hell is going on here?"

Dodge helped Madison up. "Follow me."

Parker pushed himself up from the dirt.

"Let's get Greaves and Mobley," Dodge said.

Frightened and frustrated they walked in silence with Dodge to the RV park down the road from the motel. One after another they climbed the steps into Dodge's trailer.

"I don't like this," Parker said. He lifted up the window shade slightly to look outside.

Greaves sat down at a small table next to Mobley and Madison.

"I've just about had it." Madison swung her head around and stared at Dodge. "Somebody better start spilling what he knows."

Greaves bent toward her. "Captain, when you're mad, you're so..."

"Damn it, Greaves! Shut the fuck up," Madison said. She turned to Dodge. "What the hell was that? And why the hell are you so calm?"

"Our plan was to let whoever killed Keller and Del know we were on to them. Right?" Dodge looked at Parker. "We had a pretty good idea who was involved, but we had to make sure. We had to force them to make another move. We set the trap, and they took the bait." He paused. "We had someone waiting."

"Who?" Parker said.

Dodge leaned against the counter. "You know the Hunters, the group I work with, well, they aren't really interested in wildlife...we have skilled trackers...."

"Your trackers found this shooter when we couldn't?" Parker scowled and rechecked the window.

"They recognized his pattern, and they know these mountains."

"And?" Mobley said.

Dodge inhaled deeply. "The shot you heard? Our men found him before he could act."

Mobley clapped. "Good."

Madison couldn't have agreed more.

Parker pressed the auto-dial on his cell phone. "A car back-fired. No… don't argue with me. No need to mobilize." He snapped the phone shut.

Parker rubbed his head. "Greaves told me about the plans for the casino. I understand why they might want Keller gone, but a random shot at you three musketeers?"

"Maybe a warning to scare Mobley off," Dodge said.

Madison tipped her head at Dodge. "I remember two other musketeers being in the vicinity of that first shot."

"Mobley's a known quantity in Indian country." Dodge looked at Mobley. "She's successfully prosecuted so many complex cases, they'd want you out of here."

"It almost worked," Mobley said.

"But the construction trailer?" Madison said.

Dodge leaned forward. "They needed to ratchet things up, take your team leader out."

Everyone looked at Madison. With responsibility comes risk, she knew that. Del had taken the shot meant for her. That didn't feel good.

"But Brumley, why would a senator get involved?" Parker asked.

Dodge shook his head. "He's a known quantity too. He'd been accepting museum-quality artifacts from tribes for years. He'd call them gifts, but…."

Madison remembered what Mobley had said about the objects she'd seen in his office.

"His collection was a secret everyone knew about," Dodge said. "He passed some legislation generally beneficial to the tribes so those same folks who could have cried foul, and made a case for bribery, they ignored his indiscretions."

"Then why the hell worry?" Parker said.

Greaves spoke up. "The gaming management company knew they could get him to do what they wanted, turn Grizzly into a neon spectacle, or they'd go public. He had no choice. His reputation, his career would be in trouble unless he cooperated."

"Old-fashioned blackmail," Mobley said. "And the Kowaho tribe, they made a choice too."

"An opportunity for money and getting their land back," Dodge said. "No saints here."

It started to make sense to Madison. So far, Dodge's plan and his and Roy's contacts had paid off. The FBI protected her, while Dodge's friends went after the shooter. She had no problem with that. So why did she still feel so uneasy?

"Why did they write the letter and leave the button?" Madison asked. "Why didn't they let people think Keller's death was an accident? We never would have gotten involved."

"My best guess?" Dodge said. "The gaming company wasn't sure Keller was the only one who suspected, and they didn't want to be exposed." He shrugged. "If we thought it was similar to some previous murders, then the casino would get built and it would be too late to stop it. But the button's authentic, unlike the tag found with your Imelda."

Her Imelda. His words stung. "What do you mean?"

"The exhibit tag left next to Imelda was a good copy," Dodge said. "There've been other murders where copies of artifacts were found. It's their statement, their ego. Really, they're just insane."

Greaves leaned toward Madison. "That's one reason we knew Keller's murder was different from some others. The group who killed Keller knew about the other murders, but they didn't know those other artifacts were fake. That was always classified. This group left the button intending to throw us off. What they didn't know was it would tip us off because it's real."

Madison looked at him. "Us?"

Greaves opened his FBI badge. "Agent Greaves."

Madison swelled with rage. They hadn't been straight with her. "But I thought the FBI… damn it. I knew it." She looked at Greaves. "Damn you."

Greaves leaned closer. "Roy asked for complete secrecy. Would you have treated me the same otherwise?"

Madison thought of how she had wanted to drop kick Greaves if he called her Chief one more time. If she had known he was FBI, she would have trusted him even less and played things differently. He was as bad as Dodge.

"I think I can speak for Mobley too—the way you acted—no," Madison said. "Did you know about Greaves, Parker?"

Parker shook his head. "Not until earlier today. Greaves convinced me you were all worth saving, Chief."

Madison winced and wondered if Greaves' personality was fake too. Or lack thereof. The goofy grin had to be real. Too bad.

"Greaves, you *do* know something about artifacts?" Madison said.

"I'm really an archeologist."

"FBI takes all kinds these days." Mobley shook her head.

Madison turned to Mobley. "I hope at least you are who I think you are."

"Are *you*?" Mobley said.

"Answer a question with a question, you're a lawyer." Madison dropped her shoulders. "I can't claim to be more than what you see."

Mobley took a look around the room. "What's interesting is that we women were the ones telling the truth..."

"Mobes, don't start ..." Greaves pleaded.

Madison could swear he was flirting with her, for real this time.

"I hate to ask what's next..." Madison said.

"There's a helicopter waiting to take Greaves and Parker to pay Senator Brumley and Harlen Trent a visit." Dodge almost smiled.

Greaves and Parker nodded together.

Mobley's phone rang. She answered. "Yes, sir." Her eyes widened. "Certainly sir, right away." She hung up. "It was Roy. He said the President wants me to draft an executive order negating the exceptions to the Indian Gaming Act in the legislation for the lodge. No press release on this one."

"I better let Superintendent Corrigan know what's happened," Madison said. "He's probably sweating bullets."

"Don't say bullets," Mobley and Greaves said together.

Mobley left with Greaves and Parker, and Madison stayed behind. She wanted to talk with Dodge.

The air in his RV was filled with Dodge's smell, the soap he used, the pile of sweaty clothes in the hamper by the bedroom door. On a small cork board on a cabinet an old newspaper clipping showed two Indian elders in full regalia. Maybe his grandparents? A picture of a beautiful young Indian woman rested next to his cell phone on the kitchen counter. She would have been a little younger than

Dodge. Madison's stomach ached for a second. No, she wouldn't go there. Assumptions always got her into trouble. She hoped it was his sister.

In her room he'd seen only what she'd had a chance to drag with her, nothing personal, not like Mobley and her fishing kit, Greaves and his stupid Lost Patrol hat. If he saw her house in Yosemite, he'd find the corner of her desk stacked with old copies of the Denver Post. She used to scan the pages for any mention of Imelda's case. She did that online now, but she kept that stack as a reminder to check once in awhile. That's what she told herself.

She didn't know what Dodge would think of that.

Dodge smiled at her, as if he'd read her mind. He handed her a beer.

She touched his arm. She didn't want to go into any more of her darkness, not with him so close. She wanted to share his calmness, but couldn't. "If your people found Keller's killer, have you found Imelda's too?"

"We're close," Dodge said.

"But her murder was on Roy's map, there was a letter right?" Madison asked. There'd been a notation in her briefing book. A letter was sent.

Dodge took her hand. "We… I don't have all the answers. As Greaves said, the person who killed Imelda left a fake artifact. His group thinks they're sending a political message, but they're wrong. They're violent and insane. Maybe talk to Roy. He knows more than I do."

"Not about Imelda he doesn't." Madison pulled away. "Nobody does. I swear I will track them down myself." Madison couldn't stand how her stomach felt knowing the killer or killers were free. She couldn't stand the guilt.

“We’re on it, Dana,” Dodge said. “We know where they are.”

“But how?” Madison asked.

“A recent murder.”

CHAPTER 50

MADISON ASKED SUPERINTENDENT Corrigan to meet her along the lake, far from his staff. She told Corrigan as much about what had happened as she could.

Corrigan shook his head. “Murders and the lodge was about to become a casino, and I don’t have to worry, that it’s been taken care of? Damn it, this is my park.”

“Sometimes justice is served outside regular channels,” Madison said. Her sense of relief was tempered with sadness that Keller and Del wouldn’t have the formal justice they and their families deserved.

“You’re asking me to believe…” Corrigan stared at her. “I can confirm this with HQ, the FBI?”

Madison lowered her eyebrows.

“You’re saying I shouldn’t ask?” Corrigan paused.

“You’ll be getting a call,” she said. “They’ll obliquely confirm what I’ve told you. Then the public relations folks will spin it for the press. ‘Construction delayed for architect’s modifications. Loss of life unfortunate accidents.’”

Corrigan paced. “I don’t like it, don’t like being a part of it. But murder to build a casino—for God’s sake…

We almost lost what we have here. I should have paid more attention."

Madison nodded. "You and everyone else."

CHAPTER 51

MADISON LEANED AGAINST the door jamb as she watched Dodge slide into the cab of his pickup parked halfway across the parking lot. Work would continue inside the lodge through the winter, but without him. Soon the cliffs and peaks surrounding the lake would be deep in snow, the swells brushing against the shore already creating thin sheets of fractured ice.

They had talked through the night about Imelda. Dodge knew why Madison was set up, why her case had to be ripped apart to protect something his people thought greater. Imelda's killers, once trusted with the knowledge that their ancestors had coerced presidents to protect sacred places, now murdered innocent people, thinking they were somehow saving Indian culture. Even Tibbetts, the guy Madison thought tripped in his RV in Yosemite. Killed by the same insane group.

She and Dodge hadn't talked about what might happen next, not as far as their lives went. Madison had once wanted more than anything to get back to Yosemite, to normalcy, if that was even possible. Greaves might have been right that day in Pete's Cafe when he had said she could write her own ticket after this was over. That day seemed so long ago. Now, she wasn't as sure about what she needed as she had been then.

Dodge put his baseball cap on the dashboard and smiled at her.

Madison took a quick breath. Her face hurt as she grinned back at him. Maybe it was the frost in the air.

She jogged across the empty parking lot to his pickup.

Dodge rolled down his window.

Madison put her hand on the window ledge. "We have some fine running trails in Yosemite."

"Mysterious spirits, too, I hear." Dodge leaned onto the steering wheel.

Madison let her hand drift from the cold metal of the pickup to the worn leather steering wheel. "Not so mystifying, once you get to know them."

"Might require some serious investigation," he said.

"With an experienced detective, of course." She pushed her hair behind her ear.

"I'll ponder that." Dodge turned on the ignition and beamed at her again.

Madison nodded and stepped back from the truck. She wrapped her arms around her chest. As Dodge drove away, aspen leaves twirled out of the bed of his truck and landed in a drift of gold at her feet.

CHAPTER 52

WIND CARRIED THE sweet smell of the White House roses to the side garden where Madison, Mobley and Greaves waited, just steps away from the Oval Office. Though surrounded by metropolitan Washington DC, the manicured landscape was surprisingly serene. Madison pulled down her jacket and straightened her ranger's hat as Roy crossed the portico and joined them.

Greaves rocked on his big shoes. "Here we go, Mobes."

Mobley shot him a frown.

After she received the call, Mobley had come over to Madison's room. Seemed Roy and the President had a new job for Mobley, and for Greaves. If she accepted, Mobley would become the new Roy. Greaves, much to her surprise, would become her second. Roy's assistant, who had leaked information to Trent and Brumley, had been secreted away.

"Greaves will drive you mad," Madison had said.

Mobley shrugged. "He's growing on me."

Roy's slow shuffle showed he had changed in the days they'd

been at Grizzly. His cheeks fell into deep hollows, but his eyes lit up when he saw them.

He held out a large black notebook for Mobley and squeezed her arm. "You had us worried, but well done."

Greaves grinned at Mobley.

"Please, everyone sit." Roy sat in a white rocking chair in the garden and waved them to the long bench across from him. "Ah, I've seen so much, more than you would believe, though young Greaves would believe just about anything." He shook his head at Greaves. "Ms. Mobley, I'm afraid you'll have to keep him on task. But you can handle him, and your most important responsibility, keeping our nation's secret records intact for future presidents. Not all of our history is something we can be proud of. And some want to deny our mistakes and destroy the evidence for their own gain. At least past leaders had the foresight to protect the truth, no matter how objectionable, with a special process, albeit clandestine, that keeps historical assets protected from the winds of politics. This information must remain confidential until we can reveal it, knowing that it will be used wisely. Now, as you know, is not the time." Roy's wet cough racked his shoulders.

Madison leaned forward. Roy's coat hung like a blanket on him. "Do you want to go inside?"

"In a minute, Dana. I like to be outside as much as possible these days. Too much time in basements." He laughed.

He continued. "Mobley and Greaves, your intellect, your thoughtfulness, your humanity, and yes, your stubbornness, will work to our country's advantage. You were threatened and had the courage to continue. We had to test you because you will advise and judge future presidents.

And, if your counsel falls on deaf ears, there is a special course of action that I can only reveal to you." Roy winked.

Roy congratulated Mobley on negotiating plenty of time for fly fishing and then started reviewing her new responsibilities.

Madison heard Roy say "Chapter One and the other chapters" and her mouth went dry. Chapter Seven, that was the reference in their briefing books. What were the other chapters and what else was kept secret? It was supposed to be an open society. People like Roy, and the President, were honorable, but if the wrong people were in office, it could be tragic. Mobley could stand up to anyone, Madison had no fear about that. What might have been a weakness on their investigation together, her attitude, would now be her strength. She'd need it.

Roy stood up. "I have more for you inside. And Dana, the President wants to meet you."

Madison could barely breathe. As Mobley and Greaves followed Roy into the White House, Madison felt a bit the lonely stepchild. Never thought she'd miss them.

President Eliot's secretary showed Madison into the Oval Office. The President and Secretary of State Meyers sat across from each other on couches in the middle of the room. They stood as she entered. Eliot held out his hand. "Nice work, Ranger. Meyers said you'd be good."

"Thank you, Mr. President." Her upper lip felt familiar sweat.

“So, you’re a regular civilian again. Back to the grind, that’s what you want?” Eliot asked.

Madison stood next to him. “Yes, sir. I look forward to it.”

“You realize, of course, all the restrictions about secrecy are even more important now? I don’t have to worry about you do I?”

“No, sir. Case closed.” This was the last thing she wanted to talk about with anyone. But there was still Imelda’s case. “But I have a request, sir, for the parents of the young girl killed in Denver. I’d like to see her killer prosecuted when he’s found.”

Eliot looked at Meyers.

Meyers nodded. “We could, with some precautions. A public arrest, and plea deal, no trial.”

“Thank you.” Madison shifted from one foot to the other. “And if my old partner, if he could be given some credit, it would only be right.” She couldn’t believe she wanted Stan to experience anything but guilt, but this would end it.

Eliot huffed. “That’s generous. Meyers tells me your ex-partner was a royal ass when it came to you.”

“Yes, he was an ass, sir, but he was willing to help me bring these two cases together, at risk to himself. We need to move on.”

“As you like.” Eliot checked his watch. “Now, if there’s nothing else…my staff has a military jet ready to take you home. There will be a *gradual* increase in your pay. Wouldn’t want to alarm the bean counters. Carry on.” For a moment he grinned as if he was channeling Teddy Roosevelt.

Madison shivered.

Eliot took a briefing book off his desk and headed out of the Oval Office without looking back.

Meyers held out his hand. "You finally got what you deserved."

"Thank you, Mr. Secretary."

"Thank you, Ranger, till next time."

CHAPTER 53

THE FADING LATE afternoon sun lit up the high cliffs of Yosemite. New snow whirled above Half Dome, disappearing into the mixed clouds of fall. Cold wind blew across Madison's back. More snow would fall overnight. Flakes would fly into cracks in the faces of the grand granite cliffs and turn into stone-breaking ice. This place, this sacred place crushed by glaciers, stripped of rock layers by wind and water, this place held its own trail of wonders and history.

Outside the front door of the park office, Madison shook light crystals off the brim of her hat. Henderson's reading lamp flushed a simple warm yellow against the pine-framed windows. How and what would she tell him? There wasn't a lot they would let her say.

A hearty laugh. It was a young ranger leaning his shoulders over the front counter, talking to someone in another room. The last five days had aged her five years.

Madison stood straight and took a deep breath. Fresh pine smoke lifted, then dropped from a nearby chimney.

The joy of the season, this smell. Reason enough not to live anywhere else. Reason enough to open that door again.

This was one park she could watch over, like Wind Woman, now that she knew there might be more unnatural powers ready to rise against it.

An owl's familiar cry lingered in the wind as the door opened from the inside.

Henderson leaned out. "I thought I recognized that slouch. Get your butt in here." He put his hand on her shoulder and grinned for the briefest moment.

She might just tell him everything.

ACKNOWLEDGMENTS

THOUGH WRITING IS a solitary act, for most writers it takes a team to write a book. I have many people to thank.

First and foremost, family and dear friends. No friends like old friends, and family, well, it goes without saying, they're always there for you.

Special teachers and writing mentors: Tom Spanbauer, who said he would change my life and did, and Michael Collins, the most generous teacher, who encouraged me to keep writing, while sharing fine beer and an Irish heritage.

Members of my writing group (past and present) who offered tough critiques and brilliant suggestions, but especially Rachel Hoffman, Jonathan Eaton, Patsy Kullberg, Linda Sladek, Deborah Reed, and Joshua Waldman—you helped me get this done. Bless you.

The Centrum Writers' Conference at Port Townsend, for providing a gorgeous place to write and meet such wonderful, fun writers, whose secrets are safe with me.

And of course, Larry Hopkins, for making it all possible in so many ways.

19415293R00186

Printed in Poland
by Amazon Fulfillment
Poland Sp. z o.o., Wrocław